Praise for
Saints in Limbo

"River Jordan's *Saints in Limbo* is a compelling story of the mysteries of existence and, especially, the mysteries of the human heart."
　　—RON RASH, author of *Serena* and *Chemistry and Other Stories*

"River Jordan's artful writing style is utterly captivating. Add to that the heartfelt, intriguing story line of *Saints in Limbo,* and you're hooked."
　　—T. LYNN OCEAN, author of *Sweet Home Carolina* and the
　　　Jersey Barnes Mysteries

"In the quiet of light and shadow, on what portends to be an ordinary day, miracles and magic envelop Velma True, a widow, a mother, and a lonely woman who does not suffer fools. Readers will care deeply about Velma's life: her past, her present, her future, and her good heart. *Saints in Limbo* brims with truth and insists on hope. River Jordan has written a lyrical and relentlessly beautiful book."
　　—CONNIE MAY FOWLER, author of *Before Women Had Wings*
　　　and *The Problem with Murmur Lee*

"*Saints in Limbo* is a lyrical and transcendent novel that will linger with me for years to come. I was entranced from start to finish."
　　—KARIN GILLESPIE, author of the Bottom Dollar Girls series

"Strange as it sounds, River Jordan's fascinating novel *Saints in Limbo* somehow reminded me of Walker Percy and Dean Koontz simultaneously. It's that original. It's that good. It's a wise, funny, joyful, and deadly serious book. *Saints in Limbo* is the kind of story they ought to publish in leather-bound hardcover with gilded pages so you could leave it to your grandchildren."
　　—ATHOL DICKSON, author of *River Rising* and *Winter Haven*

"*Saints in Limbo* is an elixir that combines two doses southern literary tradition and one dose magic realism. Jordan evokes elements of mystery and evil, wisdom and family, to make your heart surge and your skin tingle."
　　—KIM PONDERS, author of *The Last Blue Mile*

"River Jordan's words flat-out sing. Some pages of *Saints in Limbo* will soothe you with lullabies, others will reach inside you for the blues, but they'll all pull you inside and slow your multitasking self down. Her stories court you to pace yourself and give them their due. It's hard to close this novel without wondering why River Jordan isn't a household name."

—SHELLIE RUSHING TOMLINSON, author of *Suck Your Stomach In and Put Some Color On: What Southern Mamas Tell Their Daughters That the Rest of Y'all Should Know Too* and creator and host of *All Things Southern*

"Mystical and magically written, *Saints in Limbo* is a beautiful novel. With its vivid characters and lush language, readers will find themselves thinking of Augusta Trobaugh's *Resting in the Bosom of the Lamb.*"

—MICHAEL MORRIS, author of *A Place Called Wiregrass*

"River Jordan writes about love's triumph over fear, reconciliation, and dissolving ancient hurts in words as lyrical as a poem. Her characters wriggle into your heart from page one and will stay there long after you've regretfully finished the last page. *Saints in Limbo* is not only a tribute to the power of place and community but a rollicking good read as well."

—CHARLOTTE RAINS DIXON, director of The Writing Loft, Middle Tennessee State University

"River Jordan's written words are as poetic and captivating as her name, and her story, *Saints in Limbo,* is as powerful and healing as the River Jordan itself."

—DENISE HILDRETH, author of *The Will of Wisteria*

River Jordan practically sings her characters to life. *Saints in Limbo* is a triumph of the spirit and a reminder that there's much more to life than meets the eye. Read this book to remind yourself that heaven can be found right here, right now."

—NICOLE SEITZ, author of *A Hundred Years of Happiness, Trouble the Water,* and *The Spirit of Sweetgrass*

"*Saints in Limbo* reminds me of the adage 'Life is not about the destination but the journey.' In this case it's not about the ending of the book but the telling of the story! The journey in River Jordan's latest book is to savor every word, every sentence, and every paragraph."

—KATHY L. PATRICK, founder of the Pulpwood Queens Book Clubs and author of *The Pulpwood Queens' Tiara-Wearing, Book-Sharing Guide to Life*

SAINTS
IN
LIMBO

A NOVEL

RIVER JORDAN

WATERBROOK
PRESS

SAINTS IN LIMBO
PUBLISHED BY WATERBROOK PRESS
12265 Oracle Boulevard, Suite 200
Colorado Springs, Colorado 80921

ISBN 978-0-30744-670-1
ISBN 978-0-30745-791-2 (electronic)

Published in the United States by WaterBrook Multnomah, an imprint of The
Doubleday Publishing Group, a division of Random House Inc., New York.

WATERBROOK and its deer colophon are registered trademarks of Random
House Inc.

Library of Congress Cataloging-in-Publication Data
Jordan, River.
   Saints in limbo / River Jordan. — 1st ed.
      p. cm.
   ISBN 978-0-30744-670-1— ISBN 978-0-30745-791-2 (electronic)
   1. Widows—Fiction. I. Title.

PS3610.O6615S25 2009
813'.6—dc22

                                  2008052799

Printed in the United States of America
2009—First Edition

10 9 8 7 6 5 4 3 2 1

For my sons, Nick and Chris.
You make your mama proud in every way.

Prologue

It was the kind of day when even the lost believed. When possibilities were larger than reason, when potential was grander than circumstance, when the long, dark days of doubt were suddenly cast off and laid to rest. Brushed away with a smile and a certainty. And in this moment, from this place, you knew the real magic could happen.

It was exactly this kind of day at the edge of a town in a southern place called Echo, Florida. Lying safely on the state's northern border, Echo was first brethren more to its Alabama cousin than to the Gulf Coast. The land rolled by in rural peace and contentment, not given over to the moods of salt-water tides and open horizons but to the soft singing of wind in the pines, of roosters calling in the early morning light, of small cornfields and freshwater fishing holes.

The firstborn leaves of March had sprouted into the tiniest sea of baby green. The world was breathing in and out, moving everything in its path slightly, and on due course, with a gentle, four-edges-of-the-earth kiss. The birds had filled the trees, rumbling from their winter's sleep, and here they were now, glorious and in full song. Squirrels scampered, quick and unseen, beneath banks of dried loblolly pine needles, then ran up the trees so fast they left nothing but a trail of falling bark.

Down at the edge of the powdery dirt road was Mullet Creek, running quietly, steadily throwing off stars of light from its surface. You could hear the airborne fish breaking the bonds of water, then falling with a plop back into the chilly green of the creek.

Within all the living things—the dirt, the water, the cloudless sky, the pine trees long and whispering—was the expectation of something coming. Something full of light and wonder.

When the expectation had stretched as far as it could, had built a crescendo into a feverish pitch, a peculiar wind appeared. Only a tiny thing at first, but even then something special, something delicious and unique. A whirl began to take shape, collecting dirt from the dry bed of the middle of the road and spreading it upward into a spiraling funnel of substance. For a moment it appeared to be an errant breeze that caught the dirt and gave it a twirl, a bit of a dance, before it would settle itself to the nothing it once was. But the dance didn't settle. Instead, it climbed higher and higher, pulling a stream of sandy soil, twisting it to and fro, as if something was shaping it with a manner of something in mind.

At first, there was only the wind, the dust, the dirt, but then, shifting in and out of visible, were two well-worn and traveled boots.

The dirt traveled higher, faster, revealing two trousered legs and then a waist, a chest, two arms with hands, until finally a head and, on that head, a hat well lived in. The image presented a man who had been around, a traveler or a storyteller.

For a time the man and the whirlwind were one and the same. Man and whirlwind. Whirlwind and man. But after a long moment, but still only a moment, the man stepped straight out of that wind, and without the least bit of tussle, he planted his boots on solid ground. And in this exact manner, on this kind of a day, the man was born feetfirst onto the earth.

He adjusted himself, pulling the clothes about his body, arranging the pants, the shirt, the jacket just so. He was a million miles roamed and completely at home. King to the subjects who might demand, but simple statesman to the orphan clan.

He removed the hat and ran one hand through his thick white hair and surveyed the territory before him. Then, after careful and appropriate consideration, he replaced the hat and pulled a watch from the left pocket of his pants. He opened the cover and music began to play. Music so sweet, so hypnotic, so full, it exuded a scent with each note and left it hanging there in the air. "Right on time," he declared aloud and then launched himself forward in a southern direction on the road that had given him life.

He traveled only a rock's throw toward the creek, and there just before the edge of the trees that made up a plot considered the woods, he paused and contemplated a house. Just a small white house of little consequence. A small shelter from the storms of life. There was an old mailbox by the road on which a yellow vine crawled and encircled its wooden post.

Green bushes bloomed with early white gardenias on both sides of a little porch where there was a swing. In the swing sat a small hen of a woman.

The man drew closer, almost but not quite visible, as he watched her from the north side of the pine tree woods.

The woman stood slowly and went to the porch railing, leaned out as far as she could, and peered down the road. Suddenly she stepped back two steps and wrapped her arms about herself. She pursed her lips, pulled them up to one side, listening to that spring breeze singing through the pine needles and thinking.

Then she spoke to her husband, dead now a year. It was an odd, comforting habit she'd taken up. It kept her lonely voice from rusting.

"Did you feel that? That shift in the air? Well, what can I tell you, Joe? It changed. It was one way, then it was another." She paused, looked out toward the tree line. "And somebody's out there standing just beyond the trees." She called out, "Who goes there?" and waited a moment for a reply. There was no answer, but that didn't move her. She was certain that she was right. That someone was watching, waiting just beyond her line of sight.

The woman called again with a more forceful voice. "'Who goes there?' I said."

With that, the man stepped from the edgy shadow of the trees. A chill ran up her back. Perhaps it was a sense of things being torn out of their place, of the future being snapped up and set on another course. She didn't know, but the chill was there, and her heart beat a little faster. The woman cupped her hand above her eyes, squinting into the distance. She was summing up and deciding. She didn't recognize the man, and she was alone—no husband to offer his quick opinion—so she turned and moved into the house as fast as her old legs could carry her. Then she turned back and looked out to see what the man would do. He was still standing in the road, not thirty feet away.

He walked toward the house, and she saw that there was a rhythm to his walk as if he were riding the earth, as if the earth were a creature that moved and breathed beneath him. She decided then and there that he was something like a man but he wasn't a man. She clutched her arms tighter about her.

He stopped at the mailbox and surveyed the strange web of strings that ran from it to the railing, and at the multiple-colored threads that stretched out from the porch and ended without explanation at various points in the yard, lying next to flowers and bushes and bird feeders. He looked up at the woman and cocked his head to one side as she slowly reached up to latch the screen door. The man walked to the edge of the porch, to the bottom of the steps, and then, without a word or an invitation, he forcefully walked up those steps, one, two, three, four—if you could call it walking—and then he was there, right there, before the door. They stared at each other through the screen, unblinking and unmoving.

"Velma True," the man said matter-of-factly with no uncertainty in his voice, no question in his countenance.

Velma contemplated the man and his hat. She looked at his boots and studied those for a time. Then she looked past him, up and over his shoulder, to the green leaves and thought about the kind of day it was. About how all the dark edges of the world had seemed to bust right off this morning. Then she considered the man differently, as if he were a part of the day and not something separate from it. As if the day itself brought the man to her. It was a strange thought, but it was the one that caused her to reply, "Yes, that's exactly who I am," as she reached out, unlatched the screen, and opened the door.

The man removed his hat with a smile, and for better or worse, he stepped inside.

One

Velma True told the man where her husband had gone, explained that she now lived alone, even though it struck her as not a good thing to confess to a stranger. That maybe she should say he was only around the corner, this absent husband. That he would come through the door any moment. But completely contrary to the good parts of her mind, she told him instead about Joe's death and that they were married during the war but not the last one or the one before that. As they walked down the hall, she prattled on about these things in a nervous chatter as if she were trying to save herself. From what, she didn't know, but she felt forever breathing down her neck. She continued talking as she ushered him into the kitchen, but none of the telling satisfied her, so starting over seemed best. She ran her hand over the apron that covered her from the waist to the hem of her dress.

In the moment that the man had stood on the other side of her screen door and called her name the way he did, like he'd known her all her life, well, there was something in that call that had caused her to unlatch the screen and step back, almost against her will. Something in the tone, the timbre of his voice. But now that he was here in her kitchen, she was nervous about what kind of man he was, about what she had done and how she might get him to go.

The man placed his hat on the table, pulled the chair out, sat down, leaned back, and smiled again at her.

"Would you like some coffee?" she asked, attempting to appear natural.

He said, "Coffee will be fine," like he had known all along what the woman had to offer and what she didn't. Like he had known her heart was beating a mile a minute and she was looking for an excuse to busy herself.

Velma lit the front burner on the stove, reached into the open cupboard, and got her cup. She paused and, after considering, pulled down the old cup next to hers and placed it on the kitchen counter as well.

She sat at the table, waiting, looking at the man and then out the window. The two of them did not say anything until the coffee was ready. They heard an occasional noise that was nothing more than old wood and old times. On occasion the wind would stir just a little, and they could hear the pine trees still whispering through the open kitchen window.

When the coffee was ready, Velma poured and asked, "Cream?" and he said, "Yes," and then they sat some more. In spite of her nerves, in that quiet, coffee-drinking moment, Velma True felt repaired. Sitting at the table with a warm body and looking at her husband's cup coming up from the table and going back down again. What a simple thing a cup can be. What a simple, familiar thing that can cause an ache when someone is gone. And what a simple thing to find comfort in seeing it filled and moving as if a part of that someone had come back to visit.

So Velma looked into his eyes as he watched her while he drank.

And then she said, looking straight at him, deep into his eyes over the cup rim, "I wore a regular Sunday dress when I got married. It wasn't white even though it could've been." She raised her eyebrows at him so he got the point. "It was powder blue, like a robin's egg, and I looked down when Joe first saw me. I guess I was nervous and a little ashamed not to be wearing a true wedding dress, but it was the best I could do. And do you know what Joe did? He tipped my chin up, looked in my eyes, and said, 'That blue will always be my favorite color. You remember I said that, now.' That's just what he said. He sure did." She looked out the window, watched a fat brown bird land on a tree limb. "We buried him last spring in that exact shade of blue."

She got up and went to the window, tried to identify the bird without her glasses on. She was guessing a robin. Female and fat with eggs.

She turned from the robin and surveyed the man at the table. A spark of courage ran up her spine, and she said, "So tell me, mister, what brings you to my kitchen table? I don't remember you or the shape of your face. Don't suppose you are from Joe's people, seeing how he didn't have any. Sure don't recollect you being any of mine. But you called my name. I figured you know me from somewhere, somehow. But now I'm wondering about that too."

What she didn't add was *I don't think you are even what you appear to be.* She might be snappy, but she was still afraid.

"I do so know you, Velma True," the man said for certain, easy in his skin, undaunted and fearless. "You've just forgotten where and when we met." He smiled again, and a snap of light ignited inside his eyes that made Velma's heart jump. "And I've come due to the great occasion." He leaned over the table toward her, the smile and the spark taking their mark. "There is cause for celebration, don't you think?"

"Who told you?" Velma whispered and was more than a little suspicious now. She turned her head slightly to the side and narrowed her eyes. She kept her stare trained on the man.

"Told me?" The man laughed, head back, eyes closed, mouth wide open. When the rumble of the laughter passed, he leaned over the table and laid his large palm on the back of Velma's hand. He turned it palm up and dropped something into it with a motion too quick to see. "Happy birthday," he said as he looked in her eyes.

What Velma saw was an old man, or what she had thought was an old man, but now she wasn't sure at all about his age. She wasn't sure of anything. There was something happening inside her palm. She could feel it. Her heart started beating faster. She tried to act as if it were nothing so the man wouldn't notice. But the stranger's eyes were on her in a different way. She thought it must be the beating of his heart somehow filtering through her skin. When she looked down, Velma saw her hand covered in a light so thin it was nothing more than a mist, as if her fingers were wrapped in a tiny cloud. Beneath them, curved cold against her fingers, lay an ordinary-looking rock. She looked at the man again, a question in her eyes, and he smiled once more.

"Happy birthday, Velma True." He picked up his coffee and took a sip. "I've traveled a long way to see you on the great occasion of your birthday."

Velma looked back at her hand. She clenched her fingers, and they wrapped around the cold, smooth rock. She willed her eyes closed, demanded of herself to look away, to regain her composure and her right mind. She thought she heard the robin call outside the window and the soft response of a mate, and when she opened her eyes, she was in her bed with Joe sleeping beside her. She could feel her husband's breath against her neck, warm and soft, and him fast asleep with his head bent down toward her shoulder. Velma didn't want to wake him, didn't want to shuffle or move an inch but to hold fast to the feel of his sleepy breath running along the corridor of her shoulder blade. She lay there looking out their bedroom window at a piece of the moon that was still visible through the pines and wondering how this could be.

Then she was back at the kitchen table.

She looked at the man to see if he knew that her neck and

shoulder were still warm from a breath long gone cold. She reached up to touch the spot and found the skin beneath her palm was still breath-breathed warm.

"How?" Velma fell silent. She now had no reason for the man to leave—fear or no fear—no reason to hurry her words. "What is this?" She studied the rock's light that covered her shoulders, her chest, and fell across her lap.

Then the man spoke. "Velma,"—his voice didn't sound like that of a man now but instead like that of many men, a kind of rolling thunder—"this is your last good wish and…" He was interrupted by a crashing noise from inside the house. Velma jumped, made to go find the damage, but he said, "No, sit down," in such a way that she obeyed even though she was a stubborn woman.

She tried to protest. "Something has broken." A lamp, a picture maybe, but her eyes returned to the moving light, and the rock had become a splash of color across the table. She sat transfixed. There was the sound of another crash, but Velma sat still, looking at the colors and listening to the man's odd voice.

The man said, "Nothing's broken. Just scouts are out, and more are coming. They want what you have now." He looked out the window for a moment. He narrowed his eyes, then picked up his hat and waved it toward the window as if he were shooing something away.

Velma lifted her eyes and locked them on the man's. "Coming for this? Coming in my house?" she asked. "What's coming?" A worry plucked at the back of her mind, but there was the space of the man and in that space a peace profound. She had thought his eyes were blue, but now as she looked again, they appeared to be an emerald green and then a deep dark brown, until they slowly turned blue again. They caused her to forget about the alarm, about "scouts" and "coming" and just say what was on her mind.

"My purposes are all dried up," Velma said, the words slapping at her. Words she had been feeling but not thinking, not saying. Her hand went to her trembling lips; her eyes filled with tears.

"Who told you such a thing?" His voice came out butter soft, as if he were rubbing balm into her bones.

"My time's almost run out." Maybe the words had been resting in her lap all along. Resting and rocking and waiting for somebody to come by to pick them up.

"This is your time, Velma." He reached across the table and tapped the rock. "*Your* time." He paused. "Look at me."

And she did. She looked into those eyes again. They didn't exactly scare her, but they were different, and they caused her to tremble slightly.

"Remember this." He softly tapped the back of her hand. "If something, or a something that looks like a somebody, shows up to take this"—he motioned at the rock—"to take what's yours, you just tell it to get on." He picked up his hat from the table, held it in his lap, readying to go. "Got it?" He winked at her but didn't stand. Perhaps he waited for her questions.

Velma decided to settle on one. "What is this?" She lifted the rock and held it out to him.

"Velma, I told you. It's your last good wish." He pointed over his shoulder to the porch. "The one you were making before I arrived. I clearly heard you whisper it from your heart straight up. It was that one word—'again'—but you said it a thousand times."

She lifted the rock up to her eyes, peering at it closely. Its presence had begun to displace things, old gray matter and weak sore spots. It began to put warmth in her blood she hadn't felt in a long time. She closed her eyes and thought of the time she and Joe had gone down to the Gulf of Mexico and stood with the sun baking warm on their skin, water washing their feet, the sand shifting beneath them. The undertow, the tide, pulled her, called her out deeper. She could feel this tide pulling her now. Pulling until she felt herself sway like she was in the water. It felt something like water, but not water at all, lapping up against her, wrapping around her. She thought, *Oh no,* and tried to open her eyes, but it was too late, and then she was pulled under. She was moving in a warm liquid of remembering.

Velma opened her eyes to discover she was standing in the barn. Their old barn made new again. She was looking at the tanned, sweating back of a man. He was stripped to the waist and held something metal in his hands—something he was sharpening. Her first funny thought in all of this was that she had legs. This was an old fact and a brand-new fact that rushed into her because she felt them—her legs—standing strong like she hadn't felt in, well… Just how long had it been since her legs could carry her forward without a doubt or a care? She lifted her hands, and they were spotless, just the flesh of her, no evidence of where they'd been or the toil they'd endured.

The man whistled beneath his breath. She stepped behind him, trying not to breathe, trying not to make him fade away, fearing to touch him, but she thought she would die if she didn't try. The man wasn't just any man. It was *her* man. The old hunger was suddenly back, filling the space left in those last few inches between them.

For Velma, there was only this minute. Her legs standing strong, the sun hot and dry outside, her hand as it moved toward her husband's right shoulder. She knew it was the end of the first summer they were married because she remembered a part of this moment. Now she was in that moment again, breathing it in brand-new.

Her fingers were only a half inch away now, reaching, seconds from touching the back she had been robbed of this past year. She closed her eyes, falling into the sensation of his hot, sweaty skin alive beneath her skin. A bead of sweat ran across his back, ran over her fingertips. She pulled them up and placed them against her lips and tasted his salt and made a vow at the same time. She tasted sweat and swore to remember this.

Joe moved, lifted his head like he had heard something

calling from far, far away. Then he turned and looked at her, was looking at her right now, and she was drowning in her man's blue eyes. He studied her, her fingers at her lips, her eyes full of wonder and heat and promises, and he emptied his hands before he stepped forward. *This, right now, is forever,* she thought. *This moment is forever and always. It is everything.*

"Velma?" he questioned, his lips against her ear, his breath hot.

She put her arms around his neck, ran his hair between her fingers. She was smelling man and remembering and living.

"This is it," she told him.

He just said, "Velma?" He lifted her off the ground and took her to the corner, and right there, in the middle of the day, in the corner of the barn, he laid her down.

The sun sliced through the slats of the barn, hit the hay and corn shucks, and fell against the side of Joe's boots as he studied her while he took one off. "I'm here, Velma," he said. "I'm right here."

When she got frightened in the night, woke up from a bad dream, he reminded her of this immediately, as if he lay awake all night watching her. "I'm right here, Velma. Right here."

Velma could see that he didn't know what was upsetting her but that he saw something in her eyes, and he pulled the other boot off and dropped it and said, "I've got you, Velma." He covered her from head to toe with his body like the shelter of rock that he was.

She breathed in flesh and skin and hair and man and held her hand over his heart to feel it beating. "Let this be forever." She locked her fingers into his.

When her eyes opened again, Velma was alone in the dark. She sat in the kitchen chair with her coffee cup before her. She pulled it up and drank the cold coffee down in one swallow as if it were strong whiskey. "Well now," she whispered to the dark kitchen.

Night had fallen, and a rising new moon was shining through the open window.

The man was gone. The only evidence he had been there was Joe's empty coffee cup and the rock in her palm. "Well now," she said again.

The cat wandered in and wound himself in languid circles around her right ankle. "What do you think of that, Tomcat?" She turned from him, looked out the window, studied the moon for a time. "No dream…" She shook her head, then sat there in the dark kitchen with the moon and the cat. There was no wind now. Nothing stirring. No owls or birds calling. And it was peaceful like it hadn't been since Joe had gone away. A whole peace, without the sharp, broken edges of loss.

She got up from the table and walked dreamily through the kitchen door into the small hall that led from the living room to her bedroom. She crossed the room and then sat on the bed. The bedsprings creaked with the round, old weight of her as she took off her shoes and then lay down on top of the quilt, clothes and all, and said, "Good night, Joe," like she had every night for this last lonely year. Only this time she slept with the taste of his salty skin still lingering on her tongue.

Two

awn had passed by the time Velma woke. It was late for an early riser. Velma was always up in the gray dusk hours before the rising sun, but not today. Today she slept like a schoolgirl. Deeply. Peacefully. It took a moment or two when she opened her eyes for her to realize where she was or even who she was and what age she had become. For the first few moments, she was open to the possibility of anything as she remembered last night and all it held. This moved her to hurry as fast as she could from the bed, through the living room, and back to the kitchen, where there on the table she found the two coffee cups as a testimony.

Velma went to the front door, pushed open the screen, and stepped onto the porch. She looked up and down the road, but there was no sign that the man was ever there. Except for a cup on a table. She walked back into the house, looking over her shoulder one last time before she shut the door.

The remaining days of the week passed without significance. Velma did what little chores were left to her. She fed Tomcat True, dusted the pictures on the shelves, and swept off the porch. Then carefully, with a thread in hand, she wandered into the yard to water the rosebushes, the gardenias, and the azaleas. To fill the birdbath with water and the feeders with seed. To put corncobs out for the squirrels to nibble.

With these duties done, she sat in her rocker or in the porch swing and waited for a sign. She patted the rock in her pocket. As the days passed, she began wondering if it was just an ordinary rock after all and if she had been only imagining things. The tired mind of an old woman at the end of her days.

Velma rocked and longed for sight of the man. For his boots to appear before her on the road. For his hat to come into view through the trees. But there was no sign of him the first day, the second, or thereafter for days on end. She hoped for something more. *Instructions might be in order,* she thought, *a bit more of an explanation. Like maybe how to control this gift, this sliding in and out of time. Of memory. Could I go forward too?* she wondered. But there was no man. And so there were no answers.

Velma had stopped going to the mailbox the day after Joe's death certificate had come in the mail. That was the end of it for her. She was standing right out there by the box, had opened the door and pulled that envelope out. Maybe the mistake was opening it there in the road. Maybe if she had saved it for a few days, laid it on the mantel, and worked her way up to it. But no, she opened it right there, right then, as if she might have won the sweepstakes. Or as though there had been a mistake that was about to be cleared up. But there wasn't a mistake. It was cold and final and forever.

Velma's strangest first thought had been to call Joe, to

look up at the porch expecting him to be standing there, looking down slightly and over his glasses at her. "What is it, Velma?" he should have asked. She would have held it up like he could have seen it all the way from the porch.

"Well, honey, bring it on up here. I can't read the dang thing from that far away." But he wasn't there, didn't come through the door at her call, wasn't standing there waiting for her, and would never again be there waiting for her to walk up those steps.

The road had started moving like a river. The next thing Velma knew she was down on her knees and holding on to the mailbox post with both hands, trying to crawl out of the road before it pulled her under and she drowned.

"Wasn't a river there, Velma," Sara told her later. Sara was Velma's oldest friend and would tell her the truth to her face. "It was your breaking heart that was pulling you under, not the road."

They had been sitting on the porch—Velma in the swing, Sara in the closest rocker of the two—when she told her this. Velma stared off the porch through the trees at the fireflies lifting off the ground and moving up into the low branches.

Sara had leaned way over and touched Velma on the knee. "You're gonna have to get back down there—just like getting on a horse again."

"I don't ride horses."

Sara looked out over those glasses she had taken to wearing about twenty years ago and said, "You know exactly what

I mean, Velma True." She used Velma's entire name to remind her of the facts.

"You can be a real horse's butt, Sara Long." Velma had determined that the secret to remaining Sara's friend all these years was not to back down just because Sara was long and smart. "I'm not going back down to the mailbox, and furthermore, I'm not diving back into the road."

Sara had just looked at her and not said a word.

Velma hadn't stepped foot on that road or opened that mailbox since. In her mind it wasn't stubborn pride. It was survival.

Velma wasn't afraid of night or afraid of the woods. Neither one had ever tried to drown her or kill her. Sometimes she would go out her back door and cross through the pine trees to Rufus's store.

People said it made no sense that Velma stayed tied like a crazy dog to her front porch. Or that she wouldn't ride in a car but she would head out her back door, go down to the creek or through the woods to the back door of Rufus's store.

Velma didn't care what they said. She was taking it as it came—one day at a time. She knew what she could and could not do. It was as simple as that.

"Well, would you look. Here comes the mail," Velma said to the cat who sat by the door. She got out of the swing and leaned on the railing. "That Rudy thinks he's the mayor of this town and the mayor of me, but I don't live in town, and nobody's bossin' me around." Velma moved to her top step as Rudy's truck drove up to the mailbox.

Rudy watched her from the road like he knew something. He was a slick one, that Rudy. The rural-route man. Velma thought it was God's way of laughing at her, because Rudy had taken the mail job right after she quit reading it.

"Hey, Rudy, got the time?"

"Springtime, ma'am. Can't you feel it? Birds and the bees and the flowers and the trees." He sang a tune and flashed a smile at her.

"Not too particular, are you?"

Rudy hung out the truck window. "Got a question for you."

Boy, he's extra full of it today, she thought, *like he's the cock of the walk.* "What's that, Rudy?"

"Why don't you come down those steps and get your mail?"

This was an old trick of the trade. This was Rudy's way of trying to get Velma off the porch, into the yard, and to the box.

"I've been there before."

"C'mon"—he rolled those baby browns up her way—"for old times' sake."

She paused, could feel old times pulling as he continued to entice: "Do it one more time." There was a crack in his voice, one where he used the chance to tuck in "for me." He wasn't a baby anymore, full grown now, and he still tried to get his way.

There was an itch in Velma's feet, a stirring like her soles were waking up from a long sleep. Like they possessed a yearning all their own. She wondered how two separate feet way down there on her leg bottoms could yearn so much. *Stop,* she said to them in her mind. *Stop that business.* She closed her eyes, hung on tight to the porch railing. But one hand was not enough to hold 'em back. Her feet moved forward of their own accord. She reached with the other hand and hung on before the current of Rudy's enticement swept her off the porch and into chaos.

A hand rested on her shoulder, and Velma opened her eyes. Rudy's shades were propped on top of his head. From this close, she could see the dark half-moon circles under his eyes. And she knew what was underneath those shadows, what was the cause of them.

"Are you not sleeping well, Son?"

"I'm doin' all right, Mama," he lied and passed her the mail.

Velma took it and looked down at the flat envelope. "Nothing but the light bill. Wasn't worth driving out here for."

"It's my job." He looked like he was about to say something else, but he didn't. "I guess I'd better get going."

"You can sit a minute, can't you?" Velma thought the company might do her good. She wondered if she should tell him about the visit, warn him that something strange had come upon her, but the next minute he jumped the porch steps, bounded through the yard. He turned and looked back at her, full of himself, shades back on his eyes. "Not today, Mama. Too much to see, too much to do. You take care now, ya hear?"

That was a joke between them, and she chuckled under her breath. He got the best of her, Rudy did. And he grinned at her like he should know better. "Keep Sunday open for me." He ducked into the truck, closed the door, and pulled away with one very tan arm hanging out the window. He raised it over the roof, waving until he made the next corner and was out of sight.

Velma looked at the dust still hovering above the road where he had pulled away, watched the truck until it was out of sight, and thought that maybe on Sunday she would tell him about the man and about the coffee and about what went with it. "'Course I might as well of named him Tomcat and named you Rudy," she said to the cat. "That would have suited the situation better, don't you think?"

There were not many women in three counties that Rudy had not charmed into bed. Between those good looks and that twinkle in his eye, women seemed like they were caught under a spell. People cracked jokes about it, but it wasn't funny to Velma. He shamed her, he did. "I raised him right," she said to anyone who would stand still long enough to listen. "Tried to carry him to church. Tried to introduce him to the kind of woman who would make him do right." She would pause as the women would shake their heads in consolation and understanding. Rudy was known far and wide by easy women and easy-to-please women. "The boy is nothing like his daddy and nothing like me. Where'd all that sassiness of his come from?"

Must be from the grave, she thought. From some old, good-for-nothing ancestor. Lying there doing nothing but passing on all that dust and desire.

One time Rudy had brought home the sweetest girl. Three times, matter of fact. Brown hair and big hazel eyes, and Velma had told Joe, "Now this one might just catch him." It seemed they were together a long time. All the way through summer and into the fall. And when winter came and she was still around, Rudy had brought her out for Christmas. That's when Velma had thought it might just take for real. There were presents passed back and forth and all of them laughing late into the night with the lights blinking on that little tree Joe had put up in the corner by the fireplace.

Velma and Joe had looked at each other, thinking the same thing: *Maybe this one. Maybe this time.* That's the way they had known each other, talking without speaking. Then it wasn't too long after that Christmas when they'd heard she wasn't around anymore. Velma had said, "It's a disease, it is, whatever he's got, but Lord knows I don't know the cure." Joe had just shaken his head in disappointed agreement.

They had mourned the possibilities of a son who was settled down, the hopes for more family—for babies being born. The fullness of a baby on their knees, in their laps, moving through their graying lives. They had been full of hope and expectations. Make no mistake about that; they had seen what might be on the other side of Christmas. Then the girl was gone, and so were the possibilities.

One night, right out of the blue, Joe had offered up, "I reckon if he couldn't make it work with her, he won't make it work with nobody." And Velma had said, "I know what you mean." And in that way they had jumped right back into the middle of a conversation they had been having the week before. In their aging they had become an old, sweet, slow dance. Sometimes they forgot their steps, but their feet keep moving.

For a little while things had been strained between them and Rudy. When they had asked about the girl, about where she'd gone or why, he had shaken them off with a joke, a smile, and a laugh, whatever it might take to change the subject. Joe had snapped off words that he shouldn't have said, and Rudy had clenched his jaw tight, and the night had ended like that. A few weeks went by where they didn't see him. Slowly he came back around, and they laid their disappointment down, and things were just the same between them. Velma never brought up a wife or children again. But she thought about it from time to time. About the way things might have been different but were not.

Now here was Rudy, her son and her mailman, one and

the same. With nobody to care for really but her, and when
she was gone from this world, he would have just plain old
nobody. This troubled Velma some. She didn't like the idea of
leaving him alone and empty. She contemplated cooking up
another scheme to get him married off. She thought about
women she could invite to Sunday dinner and ambush him
with their presence. The thing was, Rudy might be a scoundrel,
but he wasn't stupid. He'd smell a scheme of hers a mile away.
Always had.

"Humph." She grunted her disgust. "One nice girl, one
chance in the bunch, and what good did it do?" Tomcat True
left the porch to chase something fast and loose moving in the
grass at the corner of the house. "Well, now that's exactly what
I'm talking about."

Velma gave up on the idea of finding a suitable woman
for an unsuitable man. "It wouldn't be fair," she said as she
carried the light bill inside the house and set it on the mantel
over the fireplace. It was too warm for a fire. However, she
thought that when night came on, she would open the windows and light one anyway just to cozy up the room.

Suppers without Joe had caused her to dread the evening
coming on. An egg in the morning. A biscuit, a piece of
bread, a bite of this or that during the day. But oh, when the
evening came, when the darkness settled in the house, everything changed. His big chair was now a monument to where
a man had once been.

Sometimes Velma played a word game of her own invention to distract herself from the empty place beside her. A way to keep her mind busy so she wouldn't think.

"Tree, leaf, forty-three. Church, perch, bird, word. Nest, bless, mess, forgiveness." She stopped, contemplated the last one, and then moved on. "Sky, try, fly. Blue, shoe, Kalamazoo." Then she stopped to think of Sara because Kalamazoo was a Sara word. It was a place she swore that she'd move to one day. "I'd be better off in Kalamazoo!" she had said. Velma thought that was a prison, and Sara told her she was thinking of Alcatraz and that was a whole lot different. Sara was retired now but had taught school for forty years, which was too long to be teaching anything, in Velma's mind. "I got an early start," Sara had said.

"I reckon," was all that Velma had replied.

Joe had only tolerated Sara. "Too uppity," he'd told Velma one time.

"She don't mean nothing by it." Velma was right. She didn't. She was just being Sara.

"And she's too skinny." He had grabbed Velma and squeezed her behind. "I prefer a woman with some meat on her bones."

"Stop it." When he didn't, she added, "I mean right now," but she was laughing when she said it. Then he had kissed her, and it wasn't very long before they weren't laughing anymore.

Hello, heat, Velma thought but never whispered a word.

It had stayed that same way for the first thirty years of their marriage. Velma figured thirty-odd years was a long time to carry a flame that hot. If it cooled a little with every passing year after that, well, a different kind of fire replaced it. One that still kept them warm and safe in each other's company.

The clock chimed over the mantel, and twilight settled into evening. Velma sat in Joe's chair and closed her eyes. *Heavy, heavy,* she thought and then fell fast asleep. When she woke, she wasn't certain of the waking.

A fire was burning slow and low in the fireplace. Not a raging, crackling new fire, but one with warm red embers underneath. A fire that had been brewing for a long time. A breeze—chilling for late spring—blew in. The night was clear, the temperature dropping lower as she woke. The room was dark except for the fire glowing in the fireplace.

"I should have told Rudy," she said aloud. "I should have told."

She tried to focus on the mantel clock, but the hands were flowing or moving sideways—if that was possible. The wind picked up the light bill perched on the mantel, caught and twirled it in the firelight before a gust lifted it forward, then blew it backward into the fire. Velma watched the envelope resist only for a moment before the fire captured it, and with a small exhale of smoke, it was gone.

"They'll have to replace that." She pulled her gaze from the fireplace to her palm where the rock now rested and seemed to be moving in a liquid gold that was richer than any color she had ever seen. The most peculiar thing to Velma was how the strangeness of this didn't terrify her. She was not afraid of the wind or the fire or the gold color now circling her hands. She was not afraid of the open windows, and for some reason, at this moment she was not afraid to be alone. Not afraid of the past, not afraid of tomorrow. And she saw just how very afraid of everything she had been.

The rock continued to cast a gold shadow. Velma lifted her palm, holding the rock before the fire, and saw that her hand appeared transparent; the rock could be seen right through her skin and bones. She could see the small flames dancing through the gold. She watched, mesmerized, as the gold moved, began to form a circle within a circle within a circle—a tiny whirlpool that pulled on her heart.

Velma tried to say, *I'm dying.* But the words wouldn't form or escape her lips.

Then she was sitting in her other chair, the smaller one closer to the fire. She looked at Joe, who was there now, resting in his chair. He called it resting, but Velma knew he was sleeping by the steady way his chest rose and fell. The fire was burning low in the fireplace. The windows were closed, and the golden mist about her and the rock had disappeared.

Am I dreaming? Velma asked herself, but she didn't move a muscle. She watched Joe, looked at the gray in his hair, at the heaviness of his stomach resting along his belt line, and she smiled. She stretched her hands toward the fire and felt the warmth on her skin. The clock on the mantel chimed the half hour, but she couldn't see from this angle exactly what half hour it was. Joe didn't wake, and she thought it didn't matter. *Dream or no dream, me and my man are together by the fire. This is enough.*

Then Joe raised his head, yawned, and opened his eyes. "Hey, honey."

"Hey."

"Have I been sleeping long?"

She considered his face, the ash color that had replaced the redness in his cheeks. *It won't be too long now before he'll be gone. Maybe one more summer.* She glanced at the fire. *I don't remember this night. But there were a lot of nights like this. Easy, simple nights.*

"It sure feels that way." She got up from the chair, moving at half the speed she'd like. She knelt at Joe's feet and placed her head in his warm lap. "It feels like you've been sleeping for a long, long time, honey."

Joe placed his hand on her head, slowly ran it across her white hair.

A wind gust blew hard against the door, rattled the windowpanes. "It must be winter," Velma said. "And to think it was just spring this morning."

"Sometimes you can be a strange woman."

The fire popped, a log fell, and the others moved, rearranging themselves to accommodate. Outside, low, dark clouds raced beneath the moon, skirted quickly over the tree line as if they were late for something that called them home. The air felt like it just might snow, a rare happening in north Florida.

"I should put another log on the fire," Joe said and lifted his hand.

"Not yet." She reached for his hand, held it and brought it to her lips and kissed the rough, dry skin. "Don't do it just yet."

"Velma,"—Joe's hand moved in slow strokes across her face—"are you crying?"

"Not too much."

Joe didn't say anything for a while. Then his hand resumed its rhythmic stroking of her hair. "My beautiful, strange woman," he whispered.

The wind howled outside the door, declaring the coldest hours of the night were just ahead. And the two of them, safe and warm inside, let this odd winter carry on. They let the oddness of the snow, which would begin within the hour, keep its scheduled visit. Joe would put another log on the fire, then two, and finally three to keep the house warm while they settled down under quilts, layered one on top of the other until they were so heavy she and Joe could barely move. And nestled there in each other's arms as Joe's breath warmed Velma's neck, as his heart beat against her back, Velma would whisper with all the passion in her soul, "This, right now, right here, let this be forever."

Three

Annie closed the door to her bedroom, careful to turn the doorknob quietly until she heard the *click*. She leaned her scrawny back against the door, brushed her long brown hair out of her eyes, and faced the tiny, barren space. One false move and that aunt of hers would wake up and shout orders to fetch her this and fetch her that. Or she would call Annie over and over again, drunk and wailing about the latest boyfriend who had left town and wouldn't be coming around anymore. She'd want a drink and a shoulder to cry on. Annie would be called on to round up both.

She looked at the blank white walls. They looked just the way Annie felt most days. Her one small window faced the tiny window of the house across the Dallas alleyway that always stayed shut with the blinds pulled down, giving her a view of nothing but more cheap red brick. What could she expect? It was the projects, after all. Or that's what her aunt pointed out to her time and time again. "What do you expect?" she'd ask her. "It's not like your mama died and left me anything. I don't have money to be throwing around here, you know?"

Well, she's right about that, Annie thought. *Sure isn't any money being thrown my way.* Her room held one tiny chest of drawers, a ripped beanbag chair, and a single bed. She walked to the closet, opened the door, and pushed aside old clothes, worn shoes, and a worn backpack, until she found her box. She carefully lifted the box out and took it to the bed. After climbing on, she sat cross-legged, her back against the wall, her hands resting on the box lid.

There were scraps of paper, an occasional movie ticket, a flier for a Miser concert, and a few photographs. The photographs were not ancient but old enough to have become worn from being tucked here and there, pulled out and passed around like trading cards in all her shuffling from one place to another. She laid the pictures around her: snapshots of her as a baby, a toddler, a little girl. The photos came to a halt when she was seven.

She arranged and rearranged them on the bedspread. Then rearranged them yet again. Searching for order, for answers to her past. To her beginning. Then she dropped them from her fingers. Let them lie there in a jumble.

Annie leaned over to the foot of the bed where her guitar rested against the wall, waiting for her, offering to take her places. Offering her shelter and escape during the times when she could feel something unseen watching from the shadows. Something that was not a friend. Something more like an enemy.

She pulled the simple wood and strings onto her lap and played a tribute to the face looking back at her from the photographs. It was a soft song, a song full of longing, wishing, dreaming. Then it wasn't soft at all. It was all hard, with a metallic edge. It was Annie's now face, loud and angry, full of demands and explanations for dead dreams that wouldn't rise again. Her face was wet with tears as she rocked back and forth while she played.

Annie saw a different picture inside her heart than the one she was living. As she rocked and played, she wrote a new beginning. She saw an open road rambling before her and leading east. In her mind she followed the road as far as she could see, across the Texas flatland and into the Piney Woods at the eastern border, through Shreveport, down to Biloxi, and across the back roads north of the Gulf of Mexico. East and out, she heard. "East and out," she sang, and her song rose up from the center of her being, a beautiful voice, a shining voice.

Something slapped hard against the door, and a voice shouted, "Keep that down in there so I can get some sleep!"

Never mind it was three in the afternoon. "East and out," Annie whispered, and she opened her eyes, looked down at that smile, that face, seven years gone. "East and out then it is, Mama," she said, and Annie began to make a plan.

Four

The pine trees whispered outside the kitchen window. Velma glanced up at them and at the sky as she wound the telephone cord around her hand. She listened to the rings and waited for someone to answer. On the fourth ring, Sara did.

"Hello."

"Hey." Velma sat down at the kitchen table. The cord stretched from the wall as far as it could reach. "So"—she twisted her head to look out the back-door window at the pecan tree—"green leaves on the pecan tree," she said. "You know what that means." She stood, found herself nervous. "It's official. Winter's over."

Sara made no comment.

"So," she started again, "what are you doing today?" Velma heard the phone being laid down on a hard surface. She could hear Sara talking to herself, but she couldn't tell what she was saying. Lately it seemed Sara had been slipping a little.

Velma hummed to herself until she heard the phone being picked up again.

"Retirement slows my mental faculties until I do believe the blood boiling in my brain has become as arthritic as my hands," Sara said. "My mind is working at a snail's pace. Do you hear me? A snail's pace. And it frustrates me like there is no tomorrow. My mind was all I ever had going for me to begin with, Velma, and now it's fading fast." There was a pause, and Velma knew what Sara was thinking before she said it. "I hate to think that I'll end up without one."

"You're fine, Sara. There's nothing wrong with your mind." Velma didn't call it lying; it was just a little fib. What does an old friend say to another old friend but what she needs to hear? Velma walked to the back door, again stretching the cord to its limit, and rested her other hand on her hip. She stared at the new grass, the baby leaves, and for no reason a shiver ran across her skin.

"You're wrong, Velma. I used to know things, and I can't even remember what they were. It's just that I know that I used to know something…" She paused a minute before she added, "I used to know something *more.*"

Velma pulled the rock from her apron pocket. The redness of it caught all the light the kitchen had to offer and made it begin to move and dance. She dropped it back inside her pocket and kept her hand there with it, her fingers clutched around the edges.

"Well, I think I need some advice." Velma started to twist the cord, winding it about her fingers.

"There's no doubt about your needing it. You've been needing it a long time. The doubt is about your using it." Sara was snippy.

Velma knew Sara was talking about her stubborn determination to stay tied to the house. She was talking about all the strings threaded to the front porch and trailing off into the yard. "I was thinking you might want to come over for a visit."

Sara started to goad her, to pick on her and tell her no, that Velma could come to Sara's if she wanted to. And that's what she would like, for Velma to come sit with her at her very own kitchen table and have a simple cup of coffee in her own house. But she didn't want to be mean. Not anymore. Not with the way things had been going. "What time?"

"Oh, anytime." Velma patted her pocket down. The rock felt like it was getting heavier. "Whenever you get ready."

"I'll see you this afternoon then."

Sara hung up before Velma could answer, but she said, "All right," anyway to the dead air.

Velma went to the back door and stepped outside. She walked freely out here. No strings were needed. Here she had no fear. It was only the front yard, the road that had tried to pull her under and swallow her forever. In the back of the house, where she was able to look across the field and at the old barn, she could wander around threadless. The barn was rotten now. The boards inside had fallen this way and that. It was a miracle that any of it was still standing. It needed to be torn down, but she liked to look at what was left of it. From the outside it was still not too bad. It had mice that even Tomcat True had turned his back on. *Even so,* she thought, *it's like old poetry.*

She smiled. Sara would like that, would like those words,

and she should remember to tell her just that. *My barn looks like old poetry.*

When Velma felt up to it, she'd walk through the back-woods to Rufus's store and come up to his back door, where he'd let her in. They didn't talk about her malady or why it had to be this way.

The first time she came up through the woods and not by the road, Rufus heard a knocking. And when he opened the back door, Velma pushed right past him and said, "I need some eggs and milk and flour." She wasn't in the mood for telling why's and what for's, so he let her be. And now Rufus left the back door unlocked just in case it was the odd day that she'd turn up. Rufus's back door had become a ritual, and it was always unlocked for her whether she trudged the three miles through the scrambled backwoods path or not.

Today Velma didn't plan to walk beyond the broken barn. She was simply stretching her legs, getting some air, and feel-ing the early-morning sun trying to warm up her bones. Lately they felt as if winter had settled in them. She was never warm enough. Never. "Reckon it'll take me till mid-July to thaw at this rate."

She pulled the rock from her pocket. It had gotten to where it was like an itch to her. More and more she wanted to hold it, turn it over, test it, and try it. She thought about boiling it to see if it would melt or freezing it to see if it would crack. She wanted to understand the mystery of it, although she might not use the word *mystery*—that was a Sara word.

And she thought about saying just that to Sara when she came—telling her she had a mystery.

But the morning was still young. She thought she would make a peach cobbler. Something to offer Sara. Something to put a little meat on her and distract her from her troubles. Warm peaches, warm sugar, warm flour—they made a good thing.

Sara was smart. Book smart. She might be able to help her think this thing through. And Sara could keep a secret. Velma had imagined what would happen if word got out about the rock. She guessed that the next thing she'd know, she'd be in the local newspaper, the *Echo Times*. But then there'd be another and another. Maybe even the *Tallahassee Democrat*. Maybe even all the way to the *Atlanta Journal-Constitution*—and then there would be people at the door lined up past the mailbox and down the road wanting to see the rock, wanting to touch it. "No, no—that just won't do, will it, Joe?" Velma said to her man no longer there, shook her head, repeated, "Just won't do." She patted the heaviness in her pocket and began to grow worried around the edges.

There was a fog that hovered just above the old garden. Velma sat on the back doorstep and looked across at the mist, watched it rise a little. It began to slowly disappear as the sun took its course higher in the sky and burned off the low-lying wetness.

She remembered watching Joe through the kitchen window in his last days as he walked out there, cane in hand, and stooped over until she thought he was falling. But he had come up with a handful of dirt and held it to his nose. She could tell, without seeing his face clearly, that he was closing his eyes and breathing in. It had made her cry. Not just warm, wet eyes, but a sob and a fist to her mouth with a quick heart-break and a realization that Joe was saying his good-byes. To the dirt and the barn and the land that he loved.

Then he had looked up toward the kitchen window, and she had dropped her hand from her mouth and waved a little at him, trying to hide her heaving heart. But he hadn't waved back. And he hadn't smiled. Velma knew he was contemplating her, already seeing her older. Already seeing her alone.

She took the rock out, tested the weight of it in her hand, held it up to the sunlight. She could swear that it captured the sun itself, becoming transparent and then turning into a kaleidoscope of colors with blues and greens, ambers and pinks. Velma chuckled like a child who had found something wondrous and secret. And maybe, she thought, just maybe, when Sara pulled up, she would tell her about other things and feed her peach cobbler, but she suddenly had no desire at all to tell her best friend about the rock. Not in the least little bit.

As she continued smiling and holding the colors up to the light, something shadowed her, watching and moving along through the low limbs of the trees.

Five

"Rudy, this is Sara—your mother's friend Sara. Please pick up the telephone."

After some deliberation Sara had looked up Rudy's number and decided to call him. She knew the boy well enough to be honest. And, yes, whether Velma liked it or not, he was a boy. He was a boy years ago, sitting sassy and bold in her class, and he was just about the same today. Not much progress in him, but Velma thought he hung the moon. Sara was not his mother, and he wasn't fooling her. He hadn't hung anything but his hat in all the wrong places. Manhood was not his number.

She continued talking to the machine. "What I want to tell you is, I think you need to go check on your mother." Sara paused, waiting for either Rudy to pick up the phone or the machine to beep and cut her off. "And you forgot her birthday. It was last Tuesday, in case you care. You might think about making it up to her." Sara added "cretin" under her breath and hung up.

Rudy didn't have to get his dictionary down that morning to figure out what a cretin might be. He knew that it wouldn't be something good. "I can't understand it. That woman has never liked me."

For a moment he forgot he was in bed alone, that no one was there to hear him. Only thin air and the scent of a memory hanging on the sheets. Old Miss Sara Long had caught him, for reasons he didn't quite remember, lying alone in bed, which was something he tried to avoid. He rolled out of bed, reached for the jeans flung over a chair, and pulled them on. He picked up a pack of cigarettes and walked out to the porch in his bare feet. He ran a hand through his hair, yawned big, pulled out a smoke. It wasn't that Rudy minded being alone—he didn't. It was just the sleeping alone that got to him. And he really meant *sleeping* alone. People thought he was chasing sex, but what he was looking for was somebody to ward off bad dreams. Or maybe *strange* dreams was a better description. Rudy's bad dreams never came if someone was lying in bed with him. Never. He didn't know why, but it was true. It was something he kept to himself. Oh, his mama knew, but he guessed she thought that by now he'd outgrown them. And if that was the case, she was thinking wrong. Rudy picked up a coffee can filled with sand and old butts and added another one to the collection.

He lived in the "metropolitan" area of Echo, Florida, a city of all of twelve thousand people, give or take a few. When he got antsy, he would drive to Pensacola, go over to the beach side, and try to get into just enough trouble to count it a good time. He lived in a duplex in what might be considered downtown. His neighbor was an older man from the big city of Chicago, and for the life of him, Rudy couldn't figure out why he would choose Echo, Florida, to retire to. Mr. Springer, an ex-schoolteacher, simply took his money and resettled where the winters were easier to manage and the cost of buying a little place was affordable. On occasion Rudy and Mr. Springer would sit on the swing on their shared porch and talk late into the night.

Sometimes they both had a beer, or Rudy might have a few. Lately Rudy had been wondering if his habits were killing him. But strangely enough, that was only when he was half-drunk. Rock-cold sober, he was as full of his own perfection as the sole rooster in the henhouse. Or he had been. But for the last few days something was pulling on him. The old bugs were coming back. And more than that, he had looked up into the trees last night and could have sworn he saw something move. Something not bird and something not right. Not meant to be there. But he didn't want to mention it to Mama. It looked like his daddy's death was still troubling her mind. He didn't need to add to it with tellings of things he thought he saw. He glanced up to the cloudless sky. *Not yet, anyway,* he thought.

Six

It was almost evening, and a sunset glow filled Velma's little kitchen. Her elbows were on the table, and her hands were folded polite as you please beneath her chin. The rock sat in the middle of the table, caught the closing light from the sun, and tossed it across the tabletop in ruby shimmers. Normally Velma would be awed. She would be delighted with the surprise of the swirling light. But she was not. She had been decidedly perplexed all day. First from wonder and then frustration. "What are you exactly? And why have you come to me?"

Sitting at the table, she was a little worn from scrubbing first the dishes, then the counters, and then the floors. That was the way she worked out frustration and unanswered questions. She had become more and more curious as the day wore on.

"Where exactly did you come from?" Velma asked as she unfolded her hands. She reached slowly, hesitantly, toward the rock. "But aren't you something grand?" She barely touched her finger to the rock's side and pushed it slightly forward on the table. Tomcat True jumped up and sat on the table, hoping not to be noticed.

"In all my life I never expected something like you to

come along." She pushed it again, and it seemed to respond, to grow deeper in color, then lighten, then deepen again, like a beating heart. "Why have you come to me now?"

Velma got up and opened the refrigerator. A pork chop, she decided. A leftover sweet potato she would slice and fry.

"You know it's not as if having coffee in your kitchen with someone with eyes like his is flat-out normal. Everybody knows it's not." She put her left hand on her hip while she coated the chop on both sides in a plate of flour. She stopped, stared out the window for a moment as the last few rays of light made their way over the roof of the old barn and spilled into the yard that was now full of shadows.

"But it sure felt normal." She moved the pork chop to the hot fryer as she said, "It sure did." She paused a minute, her fork on the meat in the pan. She sliced the potato lengthwise and laid the pieces next to the meat.

Soon she was sitting at the table with her supper and only the rock and Tomcat True for company. She said grace and lifted her fork and paused in midair because she realized that tonight was the first night she had not felt lonely while eating alone. "What do you know, and just a rock for company." She put the fork down, put her finger on the rock, gently at first, wondering if it would slip her into the past, if she would slide into memory with no control over the landing. She let her fingers circle the rock, and for a little while she forgot about her food—which wasn't her style.

She pulled the rock toward her for a closer look. "How do

you decide where I go?" Velma turned it over, and the color grew deeper and stronger at the same time. For a second she caught a glimpse of a face, a young girl out in the dark, the shape of trees looming behind her. Velma could tell the girl was afraid. Then the image was gone.

Velma closed her eyes, tried to see again, but nothing was there. She looked over her shoulder, thinking that the sun was setting. Instead she saw only night outside the window. Even the barn at the edge of the yard couldn't be seen. Velma realized that all this time during her cooking, during her eating, it was the light of the rock that had lit up her kitchen with a richness that felt like the evening sun, held there in the sky. She picked up the rock, cradled it in the palms of both hands, and lifted them halfway to her face. The light showed the veins beneath her skin, lit up the bones.

"How come I'm not afraid of you?" she asked, but the rock didn't answer. It began to offer up a dance of blues, greens, and a wine the color of ripe plums.

Velma closed her eyes. When she opened them, it was morning. She was in her own bed. Alone. And heavy with child. There was no sign of Joe.

She rolled over to find that rolling was not so easy to do. She slid her feet forward and off the bed. She didn't have room to breathe, and she needed to use the bathroom something fierce. And she realized that a pain reaching around her middle to her back had woken her. "Joe?" she called, but there was no answer. Her swollen bare feet touched the wooden floor. She couldn't see them, but she could tell their condition. They were watery boats.

She walked out on the porch, ran her hands over the thinness of her gown. "There is nothing left of me but baby," she declared and sat down slowly, carefully in the rocker. "Today's the day," she said. She paused and looked across the yard where Joe parked the truck, but it wasn't there.

"And I'm alone." Velma felt another pain tighten her stomach, rolling its grip around her, front to back. She held her breath and placed both hands below the round belly until the pain passed. She rocked, breathing in and out in slow, forceful breaths, pushing higher and harder with her feet. When she had built momentum, she pitched herself from the chair and caught herself with both hands against the railing.

A slight sweat broke out on her forehead and upper lip. She looked down the road as if she was willing someone to step through the trees. The distant drone of a car engine was all she heard. The sound drew nearer until Old Man Thompson pulled into view, driving his wood-paneled station wagon.

She was still clutching the railing when another pain hit her.

He stopped in front of her mailbox.

"Hey," Velma tried to yell, but it came out whispered. "Hey," she said again, but he was looking at envelopes, sliding them one behind the other until he was satisfied. He opened the door, shoved them in the box. He looked up for a moment. Velma took that as her chance. She held her hand up, and he waved. But then he closed the box, took his foot off the brake, and rolled past the yard.

"Wait," Velma said, but now it was only a wish of wait.

The lights faded as Thompson moved down the road. She watched as the wagon pulled farther away from her, and there was nothing she could do.

She was still watching when her water broke, and she realized all the waiting would end soon. Was ending already. And before she could think of the next thing to do, the car came to a stop, and then it began to back up toward the house. Mr. Thompson put the car in Park, opened the door, and got out of the driver's seat. He stood by the car with the engine running, one lanky arm thrown over the car's roof as he studied a much younger Velma True about to give birth on her front porch.

"Well, I'll be," he said. He was a simple man going about the business of a simple job on a simple day. Until now. He reached into the car and turned the keys.

"I think I'm having this baby now," Velma told him as he stepped up onto the porch. She was thirty-three years old, and there was sweat on her face, and a strand of her brown hair had plastered itself to her cheek. In spite of the fact that she was at a ripe age for having children, she knew nothing about having babies. She had no sisters, no brothers, and no mother. This was all brand-new.

"I don't know…," she started to tell him as another pain gripped her. "I don't know nothing about this."

No matter how many women she had asked, nothing had prepared her for the pain now coming in waves. She thought she might faint. Her greatest fear was that she would pass out during the birth and the baby would die. That life would be snuffed out before her baby ever had a chance to draw one deep breath in this world. She had been afraid of this since the moment she knew she was carrying. First there was the elation. Then came the fear, and the fear settled along the corners of her womb and the shadows of her heart and refused to leave.

Thompson closed one eye, looked at her with the other. "Settle down, sister," he told her. "What you don't know, you're fixin' to find out." Then he put one rough hand on her shoulder as he turned her toward the door and into the house. He looked over his shoulder and shook his head. The mail would be late today every which way. Depending on how it went, he might have to just double everybody's mail tomorrow, which wasn't legal, but then he wasn't much of a legal man.

"Don't you have a mama, Velma True?" He knew everybody's name, but it wasn't from friendly. It was from familiar.

"No."

"Everybody has a mama."

"Not me and not my husband either." She was panting,

and he didn't like the looks of things. "Not anymore. That's why…," and the next words were lost as she gritted her teeth.

"I think you might as well go lie down in bed."

He turned on the water at the sink and ran it as hot as it could get. Velma hadn't moved but leaned into the doorframe of the kitchen, where she had followed him, clinging to the edge. She watched him. "I wouldn't think you'd know any-thing about"—she paused, breathed deeply—"about babies."

He thought something about her didn't look natural. "Done it hundreds of times. So much I done lost count." Mr. Thompson tried to smile, which just flattened out his lips into a neutral line. It was the kindest thing he had ever said or ever would say to Velma. Or maybe it was what he didn't say. That all of his experience in delivering babies had been of a different variety. Calves and colts and fillies. But never a human baby. But how much different could it be, really? He dried his hands. "How long you been this way—having the pains, I mean?"

"Woke up this way 'bout an hour ago."

He grunted under his breath. "Well, I can't do much but check you. The rest is up to you and the young un," he said, pointing to her belly.

Another pain hit Velma, and she cried out, doubled over where she was. When it subsided, Old Man Thompson almost carried her to the bed and not with a gentle hand. Velma didn't mind. Right now she wasn't alone, and that meant everything.

"Mama?"

Velma opened her eyes with a start. A large hand rested on her shoulder. It was dark, dark in the kitchen, and she didn't know who was there until she heard Rudy say, "Mama?" and he rocked her shoulder under his hand.

"Whoa," she said. "Whoa." And she meant for the world to stop rocking, to stop shifting from one time to another so fast she couldn't get her bearings. "Whoa," she said again, and Rudy moved his hand away.

"Mama, what are you doing in the dark?" Rudy moved to the light switch and flipped it on, turned around, and looked at the blinking Velma in the bright light. At the uneaten plate pushed to the side, at the something she was holding in her hand. "Are you all right?"

Velma was still trying to put today on its feet. Here was Rudy grown, and yet he was just coming into this world. She looked up at him. "Is it Sunday?"

He put the box he brought her down on the table. "No, Mama, it's Friday."

"Friday?" Velma began to get her mind together. She looked at the rock, saw there was nothing special about it— no ruby red, no changing colors. Nothing she would need to explain. She put it in her pocket and moved her cold plate of food toward her. She was starving. Starving like she had just delivered a baby. She took a bite of cold pork chop while Rudy pulled out the chair across from her and sat down. "Not like you to come out here on a Friday night."

"A man can change his ways." Rudy watched her more closely. When he had first pulled up and seen all the lights off, he'd thought maybe the power had gone out or his mother had forgotten to pay the light bill. Then he had walked into the house and called her with no answer. Had walked through the darkness back to the kitchen, where he had seen her sitting like a rock at the table. He'd thought she was sitting bolt-upright dead.

Velma took a bite of sweet potato, spooned applesauce into her mouth. "Yes, a man can change his ways, but I haven't seen you heading in that direction for some time." She took another bite of pork chop and watched Rudy closely. It was not like him to come sneaking up on her on a Friday night. She wondered if he was up to something. "What's in the box?"

"Your birthday present." He pushed it forward a little with his finger. "Sorry it's late."

"Do you know that you almost killed me when you were born?"

It was not normal talk, not a normal tone for her to have with him, and he found it disconcerting.

"We both almost died, and it wasn't pretty." What he didn't know was that he had walked in on that moment. Walked in on the two of them struggling to produce his life.

It had made Velma a little mad, and she didn't know why. Not at the baby, not at the boy, but the man—now she was irritated with him for not understanding what it cost. The other lives that it claimed.

Rudy thought he caught a glimpse of something flash past the window. He moved to the window, looked out. "I heard stories about that. That's all." He tried to scratch a place that he couldn't reach.

"What stories did you hear?" Velma eyed him, stared him down. He backed up in the doorframe, started rubbing against it like a bear while keeping his eyes on her.

She's got a streak of mean tonight, Rudy was thinking. *She's got a mean tilt to her voice. Sitting in the dark looking dead and waking up like this.* He walked to the table, shoved the box toward her again, hoping it would change her mood, bring her back to her old self. "Look, Mama. See what it is. I think you'll like it." And he meant it. It was something he wished he had brought her on the right day. It struck him that he didn't do much of anything unless it was convenient. He fished for a cigarette and pulled it out.

"Don't you light that thing up in here."

"I'm not, Mama. I'm just thinking I'll step outside a minute and give you a chance to finish dinner." He looked over at the stove, wondered if there might be another pork chop or two in the pan, but there wasn't. His fingers ran over the box's edges. They were a little bent. He hadn't noticed that. And he hadn't wrapped the present, and now the box looked bare and old and dusty. His eyes rolled up to see Velma watching him as she spooned applesauce slowly into her mouth.

"Why all those women, Rudy?" she asked him clear out of the blue.

"What?"

"You heard me." She raised her voice a notch. "I said, 'Why all those women?' What's that ever gonna prove?"

"Mama, I swear you woke up madder than a hornet's nest from that little nap you had. Maybe I should come back another time."

"Suit yourself."

Oh, she was unmovable tonight. And that was a rare sight. Rudy not being able to get his fingers wrapped around her heart. Rudy not being able to get his way. "Mama, I just wanted to tell you 'happy birthday.' I wanted to bring you a present. I thought you'd like it."

"Son, it took heaven and high water to get you into this world. I just don't know why it doesn't matter more to you what you do with that life and who you do it with." She spooned up the last bite of applesauce and swallowed it with her eyes locked on his. Then she laid her spoon on the plate and studied it for a moment before she looked up again to ask, "Why are you so loose with your life, Rudy?"

He could have cracked a joke at her. Added a grin and a wink. That combination had been getting him out of trouble all his life.

"Why, Rudy, why?" she asked again.

"I don't know, Mama. I honestly don't know." He walked down the hall and out the front door.

Velma heard the slow creak of the porch swing and knew he was sitting there, lighting his cigarette. She picked up her dish and placed it in the sink. She followed Rudy to the porch and sat down in her rocker. Rudy smoked, Velma rocked, and neither of them spoke. The two of them sat in the cocoon of night. The dark was singing. The woods were chanting a strange melody. And the sound of the rocking chair on the wood porch floor, the sound of the chain on the porch swing, the sound of the crickets chirping, the smell of his cigarette and the gardenias and the pines all mixed together made for stories. For truths and lies all woven together. For the past and present to collide with each other with a soft force that produced something secret and yet brought it into the light at the same time. Something unusual.

"There's some things you don't know about me," Velma said to Rudy without looking at him. She was staring at the piece of the moon that was coming up low and red on the horizon through the southern pines.

Rudy didn't comment. He'd been watching the moon too. Just smoking and watching the moon and thinking about his present for Velma lying there on the table in its bare box, looking very second-rate, like an afterthought, and he wondered why he wasn't better at the things that mattered most.

"Some things past and some things now." Velma looked

squarely at Rudy. "And lately they've been about one and the same." She leaned forward in the chair and stopped rocking, stared down at her feet. She was wearing flat, cheap tennis shoes that she had bleached white over and over again until the cotton canvas was worn smooth and soft.

"You want to tell me something I don't know, Mama?" Rudy looked at the end of his cigarette as he exhaled. The butt glowed red in the darkness.

"I used to be young." Velma said it like it was a mystery. "I used to be very young."

An owl called out in the darkness.

"That old owl come back?" Rudy asked.

"That's the first time I've heard him in a month of Sundays."

The owl had been a part of the woods next to the house for the last year. A guardian that appeared the week after Joe died. The owl called out again.

"I know you were young, Mama," Rudy said. "We all start out that way."

"I was different is what I mean." She was trying to tell him something, and it wasn't coming out easy. "I got old so fast when you were born." She paused, rocked a minute.

"I'm sorry, Mama." Rudy felt the blame fall around his shoulders.

Velma didn't hear him right away. Then Rudy's words slowly sank in. "Rudy." She leaned way over and put her hand on the edge of his knee, the fingertips barely touching. "It wasn't your fault." She leaned back again and rocked. "It was mine." She slapped her hands on the flat arms of the rocker. "I just didn't know nothing about babies. Nothing about dying." Her hand flew up to swat something buzzing, but she went on. "I mean, lost my family just like…" She snapped her fingers in the open air. "I was only seven. What did I really know?"

Rudy wasn't listening to her very closely. He was listening to the crickets, listening to the owl, watching the moonrise. He was thinking how different it was out here where he grew up compared to where he lived now. Not twenty miles away, but it was night and day.

"But living and dying, it's so close to being one and the same thing. You know, like a thread, Rudy."

He looked up when he heard his name.

"Just like a tiny thread."

He nodded even though he wasn't exactly sure what she was talking about. He was thinking about how old she seemed to him. So much older than Mr. Springer, or Eddie, as he liked to be called now that they were friends. Eddie and his mama were really about the same age, but he was in the new world, and his mama was out here in the country, living in the past. In the time-warped past. Part of him hated it. Hated her for being so old and slow and difficult in a backwoods country way. Part of him hoped to God, cross his heart and hope to die, that she would never change. That the house would never change. That this little pocket would forever stay exactly like it was. Well, minus those threads trailing all over the porch railing. Besides the evidence of his mama having lost a piece or two of her mind, he wished it'd stay just the way it was right now. The way he couldn't stand it.

"Dang," Rudy said and jumped to his feet out of the porch swing as if he'd been bitten. He shook his arms and legs. "Dang, dang," he said again and continued to shake his head. Velma pushed up from the chair. She started beating and brushing at his chest and arms with the flats of her hands, as if she were brushing something quickly away.

"It's all right, Rudy." She kept brushing as he kept shaking. "It's all right, Son. It's all right."

He slowly wound down like a child's toy. He wrapped his arms about his chest and rocked back and forth for a minute, taking slow, deep breaths.

"Just keep on breathing, Rudy." Velma patted him on the chest over his heart twice, three times, repeating in a soothing voice, "Just breathe."

As Rudy collected himself, she sat in the rocking chair. Finally he stopped rocking, began to breathe a little more naturally.

"Sorry, Mama." He pulled his cigarettes out again, lit one, and leaned on the porch railing.

Velma watched his hand shake as he struck the match. She wouldn't say anything else about living and dying tonight. What she had wanted to tell him, what had been on the tip of her tongue, was how his coming into the world had been a battle, but it was a battle they had won. And it was time that he had something to show for the win instead of his life looking like they'd lost that day. Like him and her and Old Man Thompson hadn't struggled together all those hours with him coming out backward and them almost dying. And how she'd been torn up forever from it. About how they kept making the babies, but the babies wouldn't take. She couldn't hang on to them. That's what she wanted to tell him. "Sacrifices were made, but we got you, and you got life. We won that one battle. All the rest of 'em were lost because of it, but we won that one." She didn't want him to make it all seem like such a big joke. To make his life only about bedding down a paper-doll chain of women. Velma wanted him to make it worth something. To make it worth everything that it had cost.

That was what she wanted to tell him. Velma looked at Rudy and thought about what she should say, or not say. "I see the old thing has come back on you," she said, referring to Rudy's shakes.

A school counselor had told her and Joe that Rudy's bug problem was psychosomatic.

"That's a mighty big word full of nothing," Joe had told the counselor at the meeting that they had been called to.

Velma had sat straight up in the hardback chair with her pocketbook on her lap.

"Counseling is what the boy needs," the man had said.

Joe had told him he wasn't gonna have some doctor poking his fingers around in Rudy's brain.

Velma hadn't said much. She'd listened. And ignored Joe. Not that she didn't admire and love and respect him. She did all those things. But he wasn't there when she won the battle. She had territorial privileges. Fight her if he wanted to, she would have the last say on the bug business. "I think that's all we need to talk about today," Velma had told the counselor. She had listened to Joe grumble and groan about mind doctors the whole way home.

It was a few days later before she'd had a chance to talk to Rudy. Alone. At the kitchen table she had asked him about the counselor. "So, bugs been bothering you lately?"

"Not so much, Mama."

"Kids still laugh at you at school?"

"Oh, they don't do that anymore. They know as soon as I stop shaking, I'll whoop some—"

"Watch that mouth at this kitchen table, Son. You're not to be out there talking trash in the schoolyard."

Rudy had looked at her. "They don't give me any trouble. That's all I'm trying to—"

"That counselor says the bugs are in your brain."

"I know. He talked to me about that."

"He says it would do you some good to talk about some things." They had sat in the silence for a minute. "I guess what I want to know is, do you feel like talking?"

"Daddy doesn't want me talking to a counselor."

"Well, what I'm saying is"—Velma had lowered her voice even though the two of them were home alone—"if talking is worth your time, then you should go on ahead and talk all you want." Then she'd tapped her fingers on the tabletop and bit her lip. "If you think it might do you some good." She'd nodded her head in agreement with herself. "Just don't come home saying anything about it. Understand?"

"Daddy's gonna be mad."

"Well, what he don't know won't hurt him."

And that was the way it had happened that Rudy had been allowed to talk to the counselor. The fact of the matter was, Rudy's skin-crawling shakes almost came to a halt. But that had been a long, long time ago.

Now, as Velma studied her son's profile edged against the moonlight, it looked like something had stirred up the bugs. She knew it was worse than Rudy let on. There was something else bothering him. And sooner or later she'd know exactly what it was.

That much was for sure.

Seven

Sara looked out her kitchen window. She had been trying to finish a crossword puzzle, was struggling with it today. Her mind was wandering, and it irritated her. She had always prided herself on her ability to focus. To mentally follow the order of things to their completion.

"Focus," she told herself for the twelfth time that morning. "Four letters. First letter has to be an *f*." But try as hard as she might, she couldn't summon the answer. Then her mind would be up and gone, flitting here and there like a bird scratching the surface of the earth for substance. As if her mind was searching for something significant. Something that had escaped her conscious mind. Something buried.

Sara lived on the edge of Echo. She always had. The Realtor had brought her to this place, apologized for the solitary figure it cut, apologized for the distance to the school where she would begin teaching in the fall. "Echo will grow around you," the Realtor had said. He had pointed to the left and right and declared that someday houses would cover every inch of ground. He had declared with a solemn look in his eyes, "Miss Long, this would be a good investment. A sure thing where you can't lose."

Sara didn't trust the man for a second, but she had made her decision the moment they'd turned into the driveway. It was a bit of a distance, but she wanted her privacy. She had heard how gossipy small towns could be, how curious eyes liked to peer into your windows to see what proper rituals you might lack. She soon discovered, much to her surprise, that the fact was they left her alone. Left her to her own habits without much show of concern. And the town had never grown toward her any more than she had grown toward it. It had moved off in every other direction, had grown away from her. To the south and to the west, even a little to the north. But the east had been left to Sara to tend to. There was no natural border to prevent it from growing that way. No body of water, no swampland, no rocky overlook. Only Sara standing like a lone sentinel and Echo surrendering its eastern border to her command.

But today the border was the only thing left under her charge. There were no classrooms, no children, no order. She was too old for anything good, she thought.

She picked up the phone and dialed Velma's number. She let it ring as she looked out the tiny living room window. The green didn't move her. She felt bitter and irritated. She realized that she'd been holding the phone to her ear so long it was getting hot. "That's peculiar," she said and hung up. "Where could she have gone on those short legs?" Sara scratched her chin absently. "Nowhere a string couldn't reach, I don't imagine."

She picked up her purse, took her car keys from the hook on the wall, and walked out the door.

Driving was Sara's good pleasure. When she was driving, she was Captain Ahab behind the wheel. She was moving through oceans of time and trouble. Her mind, the same one that worked so hard to remember everything, finally relaxed, uncurled its toes, and let the road lift her above her cares. She might be moving at only forty-five miles an hour and be a few inches off the ground, but to Sara, she was a million miles high. To Sara, she was flying.

Over the years Sara had driven just before sunrise to cities beyond Echo, knowing she had to be back to start her classes in a few short hours. She had tested her willpower at the edge of dawn. When she crossed back into the city limits, she knew on the inside that she'd been somewhere that morning. Somewhere new and different. In the back of her mind she'd know she could have kept moving. The freedom was there, and the choice was there. And she had made the choice to turn around, to go back to the life she had established. To go back to the kids, who year after year seemed to care less and less whether she showed up or not. She missed the early days when she had taught students who had wanted to learn. Of course, there were those who had a joke for everything. Rudy's face came to mind when she thought of those. But he wasn't exactly like those other funny guys either. Rudy was in a category by himself. What he possessed was a comprehension she couldn't teach. The boy had a charisma that was electrifying. Yes, in all her years of teaching, Rudy was one of the few she could point to and say, "Yes, he has it all"—that rare combination of brains, looks, and personality. He was also one of the most useless, worthless, burned-his-life-for-no-good-for-nothing causes that she knew.

And he was her best friend's son.

It was enough to make a woman pray, but Sara wasn't the praying kind. She was the doing kind. Not that she didn't believe. She believed what she believed in her own way. And most of what she believed was that an intelligent being had designed the works of the universe and had better things to do now than get involved with the details. Which meant she had to get on with making the universe a good place to live in. To guard what was worth guarding and to change what could be changed. And now, here she was, old and retired, with her memory slipping and her feeling like she hadn't even made a dent on the surface of the planet. Not the tiniest dent. "Where is my opus?" Sara asked herself as she turned down a dirt road.

When she drove up, there was Velma, standing with the hose in one hand, watering a huge red plant at the edge of the yard. In the other hand was the thread that ran to the porch railing. This thread was red and pulled taut as Velma leaned into the plant. She was standing in her old tennis shoes, wearing her cotton housedress with an apron tied around her waist. Sara looked at her and wondered for maybe the thousandth time why the two of them were such good friends. For as long as they had known each other, she had tried to get Velma to dress differently, talk differently, walk differently.

And she knew this was wrong. She knew it was hopeless, but she couldn't seem to control the impulse to try.

Velma looked up at Sara as she got out of the car. She waved a little, raising the hand with the red thread in it. Then she walked to the front corner of the house to the spigot, turned the water off, then slowly wrapped the hose on the hook with one hand.

"Might be easier if you used two hands," Sara offered and then wanted to shove the words back inside her mouth. She had promised herself she wouldn't say anything about her friend's affliction this time. But she wanted to rush her, tackle her. To bring her to the silly ground she was standing on. The impulse was so strong that she had to close the car door and lean back against it to anchor herself to something large, something that could weigh her down, hold her to the ground. She stood eying Velma, thinking. The car keys jangled in her long fingers. *Jangle, jangle, jangle.*

"Velma," Sara called to her carefully, as if the words needed to reel her in, bait her, one tiny word at a time. "Velma, come here."

Sara had something on her mind. It had slipped in secretly and sideways, and she was not likely to let it go. She had decided to take Velma for a ride. To simply get her into the car and, for the first time in a year, away from the house, down the dirt road, and out into the world. *She'll thank me for it later,* thought Sara. "Velma, come here."

Velma stood at the corner of the house, one hand on her

hip, the red thread in her hand. She eyed her friend suspiciously. She was accustomed to Sara showing up unannounced, because Sara liked to drive even though she didn't have anywhere to go. Velma knew this. She knew a lot she didn't share.

"I'm all right," she said, watching the look in Sara's eyes, hearing the false calm in her voice. *Something strange has gotten into Sara,* she thought. Then she tried to figure out which one of them was faster as she eyed the front door. Velma could feel things starting to happen before they began the process, and she knew they were about to tussle.

She had wanted to call Sara this morning to tell her about what happened last night, about everything, but instead she came outside this morning to water her plants and to think. Velma didn't wonder if she was crazy; she didn't worry about her mind slipping. As far as she was concerned, she didn't have time for that nonsense. And she knew what was happening to her was real. It was not psychosomatic like the doctor said Rudy's bugs were.

"Velma, come here," Sara repeated for the third time, "or I'm coming over there to get you."

"I ain't your Moby Dick," Velma said.

The things Velma understood sometimes shocked Sara right down to her nouns and verbs. "What did you say?" Sara asked with a twinge of disbelief. As if a mother heard her child speak her first four-letter word under her breath.

Velma stood defiant, solid and unshakable. "I said I ain't your Moby Dick."

"What do you know about Moby Dick, Velma True?"

"You gave me the book, didn't you?" Velma didn't budge. Her feet hadn't moved an inch. Neither had Sara's. She leaned long and strong against the car door, the keys still going *jangle, jangle, jangle* in her hand. But she had a wild look in her eyes, and even in the squint of her eyes when the sun hit them, Velma could see the wild in those eyes boring down on her.

"I gave you that book over twenty years ago."

"Well, I read it."

"When? Yesterday?"

"Don't be silly." Velma moved like a cat, staying low to the ground, toward the front porch steps.

Sara slowly released her back from the car, put the weight of her feet fully into her shoes. "You never told me you read it." She took one step, then two, toward the front porch steps.

"Why would I need to do that?" Velma stopped when she saw Sara moving.

Sara stopped too, but it was more to center her words, to try to explain. "Because, Velma, we could talk about it. We could have talked about Ahab's obsession and what Moby Dick was to him."

"Why?"

"To share," she said, and there was a lament to her voice. That was what Sara wanted. All she ever wanted. The good company of shared ideas. Of good knowledge. Not just food and water and the weather. Not just the crops and the news of what was happening around the corner. She wanted to talk about what had happened around the world through all of history. About the creation and continuation of mankind. About all the possibilities that were left to discover. About Ahab's obsession and that whale. She wanted to talk to someone who could understand.

So she kept giving Velma books in hopes that she would read them and that they could start from there. But Velma never did. Or so she had thought. But now she knew the truth. "Velma, have you read all the books I gave you?"

"Mostly."

"Which?"

"What does it matter?" Velma inched forward again.

Sara felt crushed. Hopeless. All these years of trying to build up a better friendship, but she realized this was all it was going to be, and it was all she had.

"You gave me the books to read, and I read them. I read the same words you did, I reckon. Talking about them isn't gonna change anything. Not gonna bring Moby back."

The key jangle was back, and so was that look in her eyes. "That wasn't the point." Without notice Sara took off at full speed in the direction of Velma True.

Velma turned, ran for the porch with all her might, reaching her hand out to try to capture the porch stairs railing, to hold on tight. Her only defense against Sara was to lodge herself with every ounce of her weight against the house. But she wasn't fast enough, and Sara's long, long frame hit her full stride. There was a loud *oomph*—a combined noise of the two of them taking the impact. Velma cried out as Sara took her down in the dirt, and they began to roll.

There was the moment when Velma, in the middle of falling, reached for her pocket and tried to grab the rock. But the rock was already free, falling forward into the dirt of its own accord, causing the tiniest cloud to rise up around it.

Velma and Sara lay sprawled on the sandy dirt of the front yard where the grass refused to grow. They tried to recover from the shock of the tackle. Velma sat up first, legs straight out in front of her, her hair coming out of its bun. Sara, with her short bobbed hair, was still lying on her side, looking up at Velma's dusty face. But then Sara's eyes were drawn away. Were caught by a moving light, a flash of red, of green, of blue pulsing through the sandy soil. Then Velma saw what Sara saw—the rock, full of color and the colors moving—and she uttered, "Uh-oh," as she reached to collect her treasure but not before the long fingers on the long arm of Sara Long did the same, and simultaneously they moved back to a time when they were much, much younger.

Sara sat at a desk in the back of her classroom. It was after school, so for the moment there were no children, no noises, no arguments. No chatter or books being dropped. No young voices calling out to one another with all the innocence of not knowing how quickly, quickly their lives would change. She looked out the window, watched the leaves trying to turn. *But they won't*, she thought. *They may try, but they won't turn this far south. I'm destined to a life without autumn. What am I doing here?*

It was the first six weeks of school, a time Sara felt was critical for establishing the right tone, letting the children know who was boss, and meeting as many parents as possible. For sizing them up. She was already a pro at sizing up the children, determining in advance who would become what and predicting those who would become nothing.

The door opened, and the mother of her number-one nothing stood on the threshold. She was, by all appearances, just one more of the townspeople Sara had met. This one fell into the category called rural. In Sara's mind this meant "simple."

The woman carried a plastic pocketbook with a small handle, which she held in two dimpled hands. She wore sensible shoes and had a sensible bun, which made Sara think she might be of the Pentecostal variety. But a faint shade of color on her lips and a loose dusting of powder on the bridge of her nose ruled out that option. *Baptist then,* she thought. She had noticed Echo had every flavor of Christian—even one Catholic family of Irish descent—but nothing else.

The woman stood by the door, looking at Sara but not entering the room. Sara realized she hadn't spoken, hadn't invited her in. There was something about the woman that took her off guard, surprised her completely. She seemed, for a flash of a second, as completely familiar to Sara as the act of breathing. As if she had known her forever. The feeling was so overpowering that Sara lost her words, which was a rare occurrence. The woman cocked her head to one side, looking at Sara out of one eye, like a bird. She turned her head the other way and did the same thing again. As if she was sizing her up, reading her rightly. Then with both eyes, full forward, full force, she began to advance. For a moment Sara believed that she was about to be toppled. That the woman was about to break into a run and fling herself over the desk, bringing them both down. But she stopped when she got to Sara, set her purse down on Sara's desk, and said, "Well, do you know me?"

"No, but I've been expecting you."

The woman smiled. "I'm Velma True," she said, "and I believe you have the good pleasure of my son, Rudy True, being in your class."

Oh, it is a pleasure all right, Sara thought and almost said it, but she bit her tongue. "Yes." She rose to her feet and extended her hand. "I'm Rudy's teacher, Sara Long."

"Well, I reckon so." Velma looked up at the woman towering a solid five inches or more above her head. "Long, that is. I reckon you are Long Sara."

"Sara Long," Sara said to correct her, to place the words in the right order, and then she sat down. The woman remained standing with that strange smile on her face. A sort of odd cockiness that didn't match her appearance.

"Will Mr. True be joining us?"

"He's waiting in the car." Velma sat. "I don't drive a car. Never learned."

"Oh, I see." Sara couldn't imagine who would trust their freedom to someone else's whims. "Will he be joining us?"

"No, he leaves most of the Rudy business to me."

"The *business?*"

Velma didn't answer. She folded her hands in her lap, cocked her head sideways, and looked at Sara with a slight smile. "I got your letter." Velma opened her purse, produced the letter, unfolded it, and turned it around for the teacher to see. "It says we're to have a conference."

"Yes, the letter." She collected herself and tried to get down to business as usual. "All the parents receive them, Mrs. True. I like to communicate right at the beginning of the school year. I like parents to get a true picture of things, to understand what I can see that might be the strong points or weaknesses their children might face in the coming year."

"Well, then I guess by now you know just how smart my Rudy is."

Again there was that turned-up-sideways smile, that challenging look in the eyes that Sara didn't understand. She was trying to form the words that she had prepared for this meeting. She had coached herself ahead of time, told herself to say what had to be said, to do what had to be done. "Your son poses a challenge to me." She waited. There was no response. No disagreement. "I get the feeling that doing what he likes to do is very important to him."

Mrs. True cocked her head to one side, narrowed her eyes into slits. "What makes you think that?"

She suddenly reminded Sara Long of an animal, but Sara couldn't think of which one. Mrs. True folded her arms across her chest, leaned back in her chair. "Experience." Sara leaned forward and took off her glasses, laid them on the desk. "I've been teaching school for ten years now, and I have never—" But she didn't complete her sentence. Never would.

"What were you before?"

"Excuse me?"

"Before you were a teacher. What were you?"

The teacher looked at Velma True, at the round face, the bright blue eyes, the curious look in them.

Her voice floated up as soft and warm and familiar as a summer breeze as she asked again, "Sara, what were you before?"

The question was as comfortable as the sound of Velma's voice. The question wrapped around her like a blanket of blue, and the blue sliced up through the desk so that it opened down the middle. Sara looked into an ocean that she realized was not an ocean at all but the sky itself. The sky filled with particles of sand, and she began to grab at something. Instead, she felt it grabbing her, pulling her forward.

And then she found herself staring into those same blue eyes. Only they were a breath away from hers, and she was prone—on her stomach—in the dirt alongside Velma. Both of them had a hand on something small and hard beneath the sand. Velma's fingers slid under Sara's ever so gently, ever so easy, wrapped around what was resting there, and lifted it up from the dirt into the light. The red glimmered in the sun— translucent and alive.

Sara rolled onto her back, looked up at the blue sky, at the few white puffs of clouds passing overhead, and said, "I was nothing before. I was absolutely nothing."

Velma stood, the red string still firmly grasped between her fingers, her hand holding on to the rock as she blew dirt from its surface, polished it against her apron, and then held it up to the light. She could almost see Sara's face through the rock. It multiplied into a thousand Saras, and all of them were red. She put the rock into her pocket and patted it twice. She extended her free hand to help Sara up. Sara took it but rose only to a sitting position.

"Reckon I owe you an explanation," Velma said. "I started to tell you days ago, but then I didn't. I just kept it to myself."

"Well, I've learned today just how long you can hold on to a secret." Sara looked more than a little dazed. "Did you already know me the first time we met, Velma? The very first time when you came for the conference all those years ago?"

"The first time was the first time." Velma dropped Sara's hand, let her sit there in the dirt, contemplating. "I ain't had this rock thing that long. Got it this week. On my birthday." She made her way to the porch steps. "I don't know what it does exactly, but it's like an echo." Velma brushed dirt from her backside. "On my birthday I'd been wishing I could just do it all over again. Figured I might get it right this time. Well, it's the again. But I still can't change nothing."

Sara rolled herself to her hands and knees, then pushed herself up, and finally got to her feet. She looked at Velma. There was dirt in her hair, and her clothes were covered in sand. "Where'd it come from?"

"A strange man showed up at my door and give it to me." Velma brushed her arms. "That's the short and quick of it."

"Bet there's more to the telling than that."

"Yep," Velma said. "When you're ready, I'll roll it on out." She sat on a porch step and stretched her back. "You reckon you're ready yet?"

"I guess not." Sara began brushing the dirt off but gave up after a minute and sat down next to her friend. She stared at the pocket where the rock was. "That's a peculiar thing there, Velma—if what I think happened just now really happened."

"It is, and it did."

They sat quietly for a while, a little more shaken than they would like to admit—both of them being strong women in different ways. It wasn't every day that they tussled and rolled in the dirt and traveled through time.

"Why didn't you tell me you read *Moby-Dick*? That you read all those books?"

"You didn't ask."

Sara felt a sadness replace the anger that had driven her to run across the yard and tackle her friend. An anger over all the lost words, the lost ideas, the lost sharing. Now it was sadness over the loss of what could have been and what was not and what would never be.

Velma said, "Sara, I appreciate you giving me the books, I really do. And I can't say that I didn't like them, because that's not the case. But they just don't mean to me what they mean to you. They never could."

"Books can take you places, Velma."

"They can't take me where I want to go."

"Where is that?"

Velma was as still as the day. "I don't know exactly how to say it."

"Just try." Sara took off a shoe. It was full of dirt.

"Into the deep, deep end of the oceans of time," Velma said and then looked quickly at Sara, almost blushing. "Now isn't that a silly thing?"

So, Sara thought, *some of the words she read hit their mark. How else to capture the longing in such a way?* Still, the sadness was there for the loss of all the words and hopes and dreams she had for their friendship in the early days. When Sara was so desperate for someone, anyone, to talk to in Echo, to talk to about the things that were important to her. She had tried to give Velma driving lessons that she didn't want. She had given her books she didn't want to read. She had tried to re-create her friend in her own image. And she had failed miserably. Somehow the friendship had thrived in spite of it. And Sara couldn't understand why. She really couldn't.

"You know that boy of yours could have been something," Sara said.

"He still can."

"It's not likely."

"Well, I reckon becoming president this late in the game ain't likely." Velma smiled as she brushed more dirt from her arms, and it rolled off in a shower of sand. "But becoming something still holds a possibility."

"Anything would be an improvement."

"It ain't over yet, now is it?" Velma patted the top of Sara's bony knee. "And my heart is full of hope."

"And your pocket's full of all that deep-ended time you've been longing for, so it looks like you got the world by the tail." Sara looked at the sky's changing colors. "Why don't we go inside and you make us some coffee, and I'll try to ready myself for a long story."

By the time that Sara stepped into the late-night dark to begin her short journey home, Velma's throat was sore from all the telling about the business of the rock, about the trips to the near and distant past, and about the man who was no man at all.

And later, while Velma dreamed and Sara wondered, Annie began her journey out of Texas, heading directly for Echo. And directly for Velma.

Eight

Annie stood on the side of a dark street, trying to judge which was safer: staying on the back roads or taking the interstate across Texas into the Louisiana panhandle, then down and across into Florida. She thought it wouldn't be easy. But then, what ever had been in her life?

Her stomach growled. She rubbed it but didn't pay more attention to it. She had shoved an apple, a jar of peanut butter, and half a loaf of stale bread into her backpack on top of four pairs of underwear, two T-shirts, and one extra pair of jeans. She had Burt's Bees lip balm, a small brush, a notebook journal, a toothbrush, and a pen. That backpack held all Annie's worldly belongings. That and her guitar, which was strapped across her back.

The guitar would make it more difficult to travel unnoticed, but that wasn't what worried her most. What troubled her was that someone might try to steal it. When she thought about this, she wished she had lifted the pocketknife she'd seen in a kitchen drawer.

She pulled her lips up tight to one side to think.

Cars rushed past her, picking up speed as they reached the ramp to Interstate 20. She could see their taillights for just a moment as drivers hit their brakes, then watched as they hit the gas to merge into oncoming traffic. When she had looked at the map, she thought the interstate was the clear choice. But now, being here at the entrance, looking at the ramp leading up to the rush of cars that could so easily take her across the state, she saw it was too fast. Too visible. She reached up and turned one of the earrings in her ear—a nervous habit when she considered something, trying to make a decision.

"Highway or byway?" she asked, then paused a moment. She licked her finger, held it up to the open air as if she were checking the wind. "Byway it is. Let's get a move on, little pony."

She adjusted the guitar on her back and the backpack on her shoulder and began searching for a turnoff to Highway 80. Her stomach growled again, and she looked over her shoulder to see if anyone was following her. Thirty feet farther she stopped, turned slowly, and looked about again. There was that feeling, that creeping-up-the-back-of-her-neck feeling that something was out there somewhere. But look as hard as she might into the setting sun and all around her, the land looked vacant and dry. She turned and moved quickly, disappearing into the night.

Nine

Velma was sound asleep when she heard the music. It filtered into her dreams and stayed there. Lilting and soulful. But then it lifted her ever so gently, one strain at a time, higher and higher into the awakening world. She opened her eyes, lying very still in her bed, trying to decide if the music was real or if it was the echo of a dream. It took her maybe five full minutes before she decided the music was indeed a real thing, was happening right now, and she pushed back her covers, swung her legs over the edge of the bed. She let them hang down and pushed herself a little. After all this time her bed had acquired three full mattresses, and she was used to sleeping up high, used to the softness and the space between her and the ground. She had a little footstool to get into bed and now used it to come down.

Velma put on her robe but left off her house shoes and didn't tie up her long hair. She opened the front door and looked through the screen. The moon was up high, pushing to full. The front yard was lit up almost as bright as day.

The man sat on her front porch steps, wearing the same hat he had worn before. He held a harmonica to his lips. The music he played was sweet and full of a longing that said *yesterday.* It didn't say it in words, but that's what the song was about. Velma knew. She could feel it in her bones.

Uninvited, she sat on the porch, one step above the man, who turned sideways, his back against the railing. He looked up, and those eyes cast off sparks of white light and then simmered down into their blue again. Velma wasn't afraid. Not of the man or of the rock. Or of what might happen right now. She wrapped her arms around her knees and leaned forward, and her hair fell forward with her, eclipsing her face as she closed her eyes and listened.

The moon moved over the house as the man played so that the rooftop cast a night shadow on the ground.

Velma opened her eyes and followed the shadow across the yard as it made its way down to her rosebush and then beyond to the bird feeders. It almost reached the mailbox before he stopped playing. Then the music hung there on the porch as if the tune hesitated to give up the ghost. Finally the melody began to fade a little. It made it as far as the leaves on the trees, where it clung and echoed with the passing wind.

The man put the harmonica in his pocket and smiled at Velma. He lifted his hat slightly as a greeting, then settled it back on his head.

Velma was quiet. She had thought if the man came again, she would ask him questions. She had formulated them and numbered them in her mind. But now she couldn't remember the first one. Now she was more aware of the music of the man and the smell of him. A good smell and a strange perfume, and just the nearness of him gave her a comfort that erased her questions. Finally she put her hand into her pocket and pulled out the rock, held it toward him, flat in her palm.

The man simply said, "Not yet." He reached out and closed her fingers back around the rock.

Velma managed to ask the simplest of her questions. "Why me?"

"You know, it was one of those peculiar days. Did you feel it? The kind of day where, for just a moment, a gift is given to you that you weren't expecting."

He turned and smiled at her in such a way that she said, "You are just a big storyteller." She said it with a giggle that belonged to a little girl.

"You're right. I am, Velma True." He leaned over. With a more serious tone he said, "I am the master storyteller. And that's how we first met. At your beginning." He reached for her hand, opened her fingers, and touched the rock, which immediately began to whirl in colors of amethyst and ruby and emerald. "And this is your story."

Velma looked into the man's eyes, and what she thought she saw was a white light at the core of his pupils. She looked down before she whispered, "My friend Sara says the rock is a time machine, but it's not, and I know it. I don't get to choose where I go. I think that's what a time machine would do—let you choose. That would be better, don't you think? If I got to choose, I mean."

"But you do choose, Velma. The choice is always in the hand of the keeper."

She wanted to say, "No, not true," but she knew he was right. "Why should I go back to a place that hurts?"

The man stood and stretched his arms high above his head. For the slightest whiff of a moment, Velma could swear she saw him touch the sky, brush his fingers through the stars. Then he was smiling at her, his hands in his pockets. "I didn't say you should. I just said the choice is in the hands of the keeper."

"You know that night, the one I'm talking about. Rudy and Joe had started up like they were prone to do when Rudy got older. One of them said something, the other one said something back, and then it would get on up from there, louder and louder. The bigger Rudy got, the more it was like that." She paused, trying to tell him about the last night she had stepped into, the night that she hated to remember. She had hated it then and hated it the moment her feet lit down in her same bedroom but all those years ago. She had felt that power of disagreement in the air, heard their voices rising in the front room, and knew where she was and what night she had stepped into. She felt around for the rock, wanting to hold it and wish that it would take her away, take her anywhere. But there was nothing she could do but keep walking it out.

She listened as the voices rose higher and higher, hoping the events would turn, that history would fold in on itself and change, change, change. And that is what she repeated to her-self: *Change, change, change.* But still the voices rose higher, and there was the sound of the lamp getting knocked over and the kitchen table getting shoved around and then plates breaking and angry bodies moving from room to room.

She walked into the living room to find the two people she loved more than life itself at war with each other. Rudy with blood on his hand. A bad sweat on Joe's forehead and a pain in his eyes that had never been there before.

She did the only thing that came to her in that moment of madness: she kicked up her heels and began to dance.

Rudy and Joe looked at her like she had lost her mind. She'd act the fool a million times, for a million years, if it would cause peace to fall down on her house and the two of them to smile once in a while in each other's direction.

But they didn't laugh.

Instead, Rudy stormed out the front door, headed for his car. The car door slammed as Joe said, "Velma, you act like an old fool"—as if she had been the one to start the whole thing. As if the shards of glass, the broken plates still tinged with Rudy's blood on the edges, and the broken lamp had all been her making.

Joe went out onto the porch to smoke and left her there, old fool that she was, cleaning up things broken by the men who were breaking her heart.

It was a long time after that before she could cotton to Joe. Oh, she didn't have to forgive him for the tussle. Rudy was a smart mouth, and she knew a man and a son could be pushed to the breaking point. Old rooster and bantam rooster scratching on the same scrap of dirt day after day. And she could forgive him for calling her old. Old was what they had become and what they were. Old from old dreams not fulfilled. "We ain't no Sarah and Abraham," she would tell him. And Joe would say, "Well, who would want to be?"

He didn't understand what she was feeling, didn't realize what she couldn't say was, "We aren't the mother and father I expected us to be." Or that she had wanted a multitude. And that was what she said: "Joe, I wanted a multitude."

He didn't say anything. He didn't even bend over and pat her on the knee and say, "I know, I know." And that would have meant the world to her. Just one touch and those two words repeated a few times over the years. But they weren't forthcoming back then.

Later, strangely later, when he died, she felt all Joe's unsaid *I'm sorry's* fall around her shoulders like a blanket. They were there, and they were real, and she knew it. On nights when she was alone and cold and scared, she wrapped the blanket closer and fell asleep almost contented.

The man pushed through her thoughts. "He was a hard one to make do, wasn't he?"

Velma tried to decipher who he was speaking of—Joe or Rudy—but then she knew it was the boy.

Velma looked at him. "He was," she said. "He still is."

The man was still standing. He seemed taller than before,

as if his body had a difficult time containing him. "But a wind is coming in." The man shifted his weight, then did a soft-shoe shuffle. "A wind of change."

Velma closed her eyes, listening to the rumbling of his words fall around her ears like a rush of rain. When she opened them, she was lying in her bed with the rock resting in the palm of her hand. The light from outside the window was bright enough to spill through the curtains and cut a shadow across the bed and down to the wooden floor. Velma listened for the sound of something—a man's footsteps, a cough, a breeze—but there was nothing. She sat up and swung her legs over the side of the bed, with the rock still in her hand, and walked in her bare feet to the closed front door. She opened it and looked through the screen, but there was no man there. She pushed open the screen and stepped out onto the porch that was bathed in moonlight.

Tomcat True walked out from the shadows to greet his unexpected visitor.

"That old moon hasn't passed the house," she told him.

Velma sat on the top porch step, right where she felt she had been moments ago, and leaned her back against the wood. She looked at the moon and the leaves on the trees bathed in light and felt the desire to dance to a music she could still hear. "Wasn't no dream," she said. "Least none like I ever had."

And then surprisingly, without any ado, more asleep than awake, Velma got up, walked down the steps—like a woman wading into a pool of water—and into the moonlit yard.

Velma began to dance barefoot in the sandy yard. She danced soft and slow, waltzing to the strains of a harmonica she could clearly still hear playing and to the sound of the wind in the pine trees. She danced light on her feet, up on her toes, sweeping in small circles beyond the gardenias, around the rosebush, and down by the bird feeders.

Tomcat True padded down the steps and took a seat by the bayberry bush and watched Velma dance.

The moon moved across the night sky as she danced free of disapproving eyes and the mistakes from dark corners of her past. Free of the threads that would bind her tight to this earth. And as her legs twirled, her arms circled higher, her hair flew long and wild behind her. For at least one night, this night, Velma was finally free.

Ten

Annie was coughing dirt and gas fumes and was now trying to walk farther off the side of the road, down by the tree line. The prospect of hitchhiking made her nervous. Very nervous. And she still had the feeling she was being watched. Being followed. She stopped and slowly slid the guitar off her back, slid down to lean against a tree trunk, and rummaged through her bag. She found a stale piece of bread and spread it with a little peanut butter. When she was taking her first bite, she heard it. A rustle that at first she thought had to be a sudden gust of wind. She took another bite, tried to listen closely. A car drove by, and she could feel the hot air it stirred up. The sound of the tires disappeared in the distance. She chewed and listened. The rustle again, then again. She looked up in the trees, and over her head there it was. A gray form that was…what? Not human and not animal. At least not one she could recognize. Something with pale skin. And it was certainly watching her. Then suddenly it was gone. Annie shoved the rest of the bread in her mouth, then grabbed her bag and her guitar and ran for the highway. She put out her thumb as the next car approached, hoping with a fast-beating heart that whoever it was would please, please stop.

Eleven

Rudy was driving his route. Each stop was at least three miles apart. Most were five or more. His customers needed more space to live than most people. Rudy didn't mind. It gave him time to sing to George Jones or Willie Nelson. Rudy had been singing his heart out since he'd been rural-route driving. Now he could sing most anything. Except for Roy Orbison. He liked Roy, but he couldn't sing one of his songs no matter how hard he tried.

Before the rural route opened up, Rudy had taken odd jobs of all kinds. He had swung a hammer, done a little roofing, a little sheetrocking. He even took a three-month job once in Birmingham building a shopping mall, but he didn't like it. He didn't like the traffic, and as much as he would never admit it, he worried about his mama. About not being a little closer, just in case. So he packed his one small bag and came home.

Now Rudy had his dream job. And while it might only pay enough to cover his rent, keep the lights on, buy himself all the beer he wanted to drink, and pay for his cable and his smokes, it was enough. He was a man of little ambition. He figured driving and singing were good medicine because he didn't have to think. Not much. He just kept going one more day, one more hour, and tried not to think about anything serious that would make him look in the mirror long enough to see anything more than his reflection. His reflection he could handle. It looked very fine, thank you. It was what rippled beneath it that gave him cause for worry.

Right now Rudy was singing Alan Jackson's "Like Red on a Rose," which he had been practicing in order to surprise Rose at karaoke one night.

He could always count on Rose. She was as steady as a dog day's rain. He knew at her place the beer would always be cold, the wings would always be hot, and her mood would never change.

Rudy turned right and headed up to Edgar Road, where he would take a left turn at Creek Bend. He would drop off the Hutchinsons' mail: a letter from Mamie's sister living in Tennessee and some catalogs for farming seeds. There was also a new book of the month for the grandchildren.

In this way Rudy got more intimacy in his life than at any other time, more than rolling in the bed with his woman of the week, more than spending a few hours with his mama on Sundays. In the silent walls of his truck, riding with his people's mail, including their bills and their overdue notices. He had their dreams cradled between catalogs and mail-order boxes. He felt intimate with those mailbox doors. They were always open, and they didn't judge what he brought them or what he didn't. He was just delivering the mail. So he sorted the mail and sang and looked at the tired little houses. He smiled and waved at the folks coming out of their doors and down their front steps to collect the news.

The fact was, Rudy's customers loved him. And Rudy counted on that love and adoration. He needed it like a dying man needs just a little more time. And that made his heart heavy, caused him to look even harder for what wasn't there, and to shudder and scratch at things he could never find.

Twelve

Velma rocked on her porch, watching as the early-morning sky of Echo turned from a rainy gray to a light blue, dusted here and there with slices of pink. "The sun rises, Tomcat," she said. "It wasn't rain at all, just the night of the world blowing away."

She had had restless dreams the night before and woke with a restless heart, as if bad news might be coming. She looked at the mailbox but knew it was empty. It would be afternoon before Rudy ran the mail by her place. Good news or bad, if it came by mail, it all depended on Rudy. "Not much of a steady hinge, if you ask me," she said to the cat. But the cat was sleeping, curled up by the door. She supposed that his dreams weren't restless, that he wasn't troubled.

Velma held a mug with the remains of her early-morning coffee, but it had turned cold. She was thinking about the rock, about where it came from, what it did and didn't do. Some days it seemed a precious gift, and there were days it seemed a heavy cross to bear. "Memories I can relive but not remake is a tough row to hoe," she said aloud.

She had thought about getting rid of the rock. After those brief, sweet glimpses of her precious past, she would never think to go without having relived them. But then there were a few of the other kind. The ones where she wanted desperately to turn time around, to change the frame of something. And yet, no matter how hard she tried to make something different, she'd be saying and doing the same things as before, because that's what it had been.

For her birthday she'd had Joe and the heat and the barn, and that wasn't a bad present at all. It made her smile every time she thought about it. But now, after the other "visits," as she had taken to calling them for lack of a better word, she wasn't so sure. Maybe she should put the rock on a shelf or in a drawer. Or bury it in the backyard. Or toss it in the creek for the catfish to consider.

Velma cocked her head to one side, listening, concentrating very hard on a certain sound, something she was sure she'd just heard from the woods, but then again, had she?

Lately she had taken to talking to the rock the way she used to talk to Joe after he was gone. She would say, "Where you gonna take me today?" but the rock didn't answer. Sometimes she could lay her hand on the rock when it was full of colors and hold it, watch them change, but she didn't go anywhere.

Other times she was barely thinking of the past, of memories, and the rock looked as if it were sleeping, and then she was back. Back in Joe's arms or back in the field or back in Rudy's life when it had been a different place for her.

Sometimes it was only for a moment: a flash of light, a breath, a breeze coming in the window. And she had stood there in the kitchen looking out over the field in the back, and she was full of the life now known as Rudy. But then she only knew that there was a new life forming and they were one and the future was full of promise. She had laid her plain palms on her rising stomach and been as happy and content in that one moment as she would ever be in her life. Just a precious second or two, and a gift worth keeping.

Other times it seemed the rock had taken her away for days. Once she thought she had been gone for a full week, thought she might be stuck in the past, living life over again.

When she opened her eyes, she was sitting in Joe's chair in the living room. First she had to get her bearings, then she had to call Sara and ask her what day it was, which Sara didn't like one bit. She had come over to sit with her, to take her pulse—like she knew what she was doing—to see if Velma had had a stroke. Sara had said, "You should know the early signs of stroke, Velma. Especially with all the butter and fat you eat."

Velma and Sara didn't share the same philosophies on eating.

"It still seems to me that you should go to the doctor if you don't recognize what day it is."

"I recognize it, Sara. I'm just verifying it." Velma had been sorry then that she had even called her. But that was before the day in the yard when they tussled and then remembered together.

Now, after the tussle, Sara bothered her with theories.

With wanting to take the rock to a scientist in Washington. She kept saying things like, "It belongs in a museum."

Velma said, "It belongs in my pocket."

An audible *pop* of sorts, a slight crack of wood, hit Velma's ears. She got up and stood at the top of the steps and looked down toward the edge of the trees. She had that old feeling of someone watching, of someone staring at her, and she was starched certain of it. "Who's there?" she said just like she had to the man, but the feeling wasn't the same. She whispered under her breath, "Maybe I should get a dog." And after another rustle in the woods, "A big one."

She moved down the stairs. At the bottom she plucked a single thread without looking for it. She stepped out into the yard while anchored to the house, walked as far as this particular thread would allow. She hadn't forgotten her night in the moonlight. She hadn't forgotten her dancing. But she marked it down as a night of grace, when the power of something good kept her grounded, kept her safe from anything that would rip her off the face of the earth. But now it was daylight, and real, and anything strange could happen.

Velma searched the yard and beyond. Her gaze stopped on a stand of trees so thick it kept her from seeing in between them to know what was waiting just inside the tree line. "I know you're out there," she said now and meant it. "I know."

She wasn't afraid of things unseen. That's what people like Rudy never seemed to understand. The threads were not for the unseen things. They were for the surprises. The things that would snap her up without warning. And in her mind there was a difference.

Velma paced a little with the string in her hand, back and forth, but her eyes remained locked on the tree line. There was such a power emanating from her, such a strange, old courage, that the shape waiting in the woods just out of Velma's eyesight shivered and shrank back. The shape decided to retreat, but there was a noise in that withdrawal. Nothing loud or obvious, mind you. Just a noise that didn't belong in a place of trees and birds and wild things.

Velma narrowed her eyes and for one solid moment considered dropping the thread and running headlong into the trees the way Long Sara had run into her. Instead, she clutched the thread tighter and tighter in her hand and knew that what was on the other side was just waiting to surface. But this wouldn't be the day for it.

The thing watching in the woods was not actually a thing or an animal but a person. That person slunk back into the green leaves, heart beating and mind racing. She didn't want to be discovered. Not yet anyway. There would come a time for that, but this didn't seem the time. This didn't seem right at all. With that decision, she slowly, very slowly, backed away through the green underbrush and the dry dirt. Annie, her hair matted and dirty, stepped out from the other side of the stand of trees where she hoped she wouldn't be seen. She picked up her guitar case from the side of the road where it had been hidden in the trees, slung her backpack over her right shoulder, the guitar over her left, and walked down the road, pausing once to look at the sky. "Sure could use some rain round these parts," she said as she walked off in the direction of the center of Echo, humming a tune that had been playing in her mind since last night.

She had hitched twenty-two rides and eaten a total of fifteen hot dogs purchased from quick-mart gas stations. Her only real meal had been a cheese omelet, toast, and hash browns bought for her by a woman who had given her a ride as far as Baton Rouge, along with a lecture. Annie had listened while smearing strawberry jelly over her buttered white bread. "I'm okay," she had told the woman.

"Have a fight with your mom, did you?"

"Truth is…" She had taken another big bite—being twelve hours east of her last good meal—and after swallowing had said, "We never had much of a chance for a fight." She'd smiled at the woman without feigning anything untruthful.

"Let me guess—you're sixteen and in love for the first time, and he's someplace you can't get to."

"Something like that," Annie had said and had one more bite of eggs and glanced at the counter, wishing greatly for a piece of apple pie. She'd looked away, out the window. "Don't worry. I'm all right." She had turned her head and looked directly at the woman.

"Where'd you sleep last night?"

Annie hadn't flinched. "The side of the highway but off, you know, far enough not to be seen. But I could hear a car once in a while, so I felt okay."

"Tell you what..." The woman had signaled for the waitress.

Annie ate faster, figuring mealtime was over.

"You let me buy you a bus ticket to where you're going, and I'll let you split that last piece of apple pie with me."

The woman had smiled at Annie, and Annie had smiled back. She wasn't yet sixteen, and if she hadn't swallowed three times real fast, she would have cried from just the promise of apple pie and a bus ticket.

And so Annie, not thinking it wise to tell the complete truth, had asked for a bus ticket to Tallahassee, Florida. True to her word, the woman had taken her to the closest bus station and bought her a ticket just as she had promised.

Annie had climbed on the bus, found a seat close to the driver, wrapped her arms around her guitar, placed her backpack between her feet, leaned her head against the window, and fallen fast asleep before the bus pulled out of the station. She opened her eyes just as they were passing a sign that said Echo, Florida, and so she had gotten off at the next stop, in a place called Marianna. Then she had started backtracking her way to Echo.

Now her mind was tired, her legs ached, and her stomach growled so loud she had been afraid it would give her away. She had planned to walk up to the door and knock, to start

out like that, but something about it—about the threads flying everywhere and the woman knowing she was out there
and yelling at the trees—suddenly everything spooked her.

❦

The phone rang, and Velma paused before she picked it up.
"Hello, Sara," she said with a tired voice.

"This could be worth big money," Sara said.

"You don't care much about money," Velma answered
and sat down by the phone. She was seriously thinking of
throwing the rock into the creek.

"You could travel, Velma. You could see the world."

"I don't want to see the world."

Sara breathed deeply on the other end of the phone. She
was exasperated and excited. She hadn't slept much since the
occurrence between them. Since the trip they had either taken
or imagined they had taken. She had become obsessed with
something that didn't belong to her. The obsession could
become a dangerous thing, and she knew it. There was a long
pause while she thought many things, then she said, "I'm
sorry, Velma."

"I know you are," Velma said and then added, "Bye for
now," and hung up the telephone. She sat staring at the phone
and then raised herself from the chair. She took the rock from
her pocket. "You'd be hard to toss away, but I could do it."

She moved into the kitchen, where she put the rock on

the windowsill above the sink. She got Comet from under the sink and sprinkled it on the basin. She pulled a dishrag out of the drawer, ran warm water over it, and began to scrub.

"If it weren't for the times you've given me with Joe, I'd toss you."

But that wasn't the truth. The truth was, Velma had begun to wonder about Rudy. About the way he had turned out, about his womanizing and his not trying to achieve anything with his life, and about those invisible bugs. She wondered if something could be done about that.

She glanced at the rock occasionally as she scrubbed, as if the answer to the mystery lay somewhere inside it. "You gotta be here for a reason."

She ran the water hot, rinsed the rag, began to scrub again with clean water. "You gotta be more than memory candy, more than a warm turn in the hay with my husband—not that I'm complainin'," she said with a grin.

She stopped scrubbing and was serious to the bone. "You gotta be for more than just me. More than for me to be reliving where I been."

The sound of a match striking caused her to jump and turn around, grabbing her heart in the process.

Rudy stood behind her, leaning against the doorway. He took a drag on his cigarette.

"Rudy! Scare me to death." Velma's skin began to crawl like it wanted to slide right off her body and run out the window. She thought quick, thought of what Rudy's cockiness was and what it was not. She clenched her jaw and began to reach slowly for the windowsill, never taking her eyes off the form leaning against the doorframe.

"What you got there, Mama?" His body didn't move, but she could sense intense desire emanating from it.

"Just dropping by to visit, are you?" Velma felt the rock in her hand, covered it with her palm, and pulled it slowly toward her. *No apron on,* she thought. No pockets. How did that happen? She folded her ample arms across her bosom, her hands fisted tight. The red embers of the cigarette burned bright across the kitchen. "Wasn't expecting you today, Rudy."

The figure took a step toward her. She backed against the wall. And the figure, looking very much like Rudy but missing Rudy's soul, moved so close they were almost touching.

"I'm not afraid of you," Velma said through tight lips.

"Yes, Velma True, I believe you are." The figure stretched out an arm toward her closed hand. "I think you know enough to be afraid." The figure grinned, took a great drag on the cigarette, then lowered the butt until the fire almost touched the back of her hand.

With a start and a cry she opened her fist. There was nothing there but thin air. The figure looked surprised, but even the surprise had a cocky air, like one big dangerous joke. "And I think you're trying to determine if I'm real." It waved a hand like a fluid feather through the air. "Or if I'm just one of the tired tricks of an old, old mind."

"Not so old." She closed her hand back into a fist, shoved it inside the crook of her crossed arm.

The man smiled. "Not so young either, are you?"

"We all got our price to pay for living."

"Now ain't that the truth?" He blew his smoke directly in Velma's face, then quickly turned his head to the side, as if listening to something she couldn't hear.

Velma unlocked her arms and pushed hard on the chest in front of her.

The fake Rudy took one step back. There was a ripple in his face, a blank white in his eyes as he said, "No need to be rude." He seemed to listen again, then turned for the back door. "I was just taking my leave." He walked to the door but didn't open it. Instead he turned and said, "Be seeing you, Velma," and walked right through the screen door.

Velma tried to make her heart slow down so she could listen. She heard the front door open and close, then footsteps make their slow way down the hall and come closer to the kitchen. Velma moved farther back against the wall, looked for something, anything, heavy. Or sharp. Another footstep and then another, and Rudy stepped into the kitchen. They stood and looked at each other. Velma expected her heart to jump out of her chest and land on the floor.

"Mama, we need to talk," Rudy said.

Velma exhaled so hard she almost fell forward. She took a deep breath and straightened herself. "Yeah, Son, we sure do."

Thirteen

Some nights Rudy sang karaoke down at Rose's place. It might be a bar, but it was also a family establishment of sorts with a pizza parlor, a small room with two pool tables—no cussing allowed. And karaoke. Sometimes a family wanted to stay late and let their kids sing karaoke. Rose would tell them they could only stay long enough to sing during the first set. "Kids belong in their beds, not bars," she said. She had her standards. And she was deeply in love with Rudy, but he didn't know about that. He had been her heart since the moment she first laid eyes on him. And Rose knew him for all that he was and wasn't. She had watched him corral women for more than four years without ever saying a word. Sometimes even with a wink from Rudy over the shoulder of his latest conquest as if Rose were in on the joke.

Those winks never amounted to anything. And they never broke her heart. Rose was the kind who took life the way it wasn't: simple, plain, and true. She didn't mind the dim and hopeless light Rudy brought to her life, figuring it was better than no light at all. Rose was a woman who could manage the workings of her heart. But tonight there'd been no sign of Rudy, and Rose was left counting the money and finishing her cleaning.

A sudden gust of wind rustled the overgrown weeds in the vacant lot out back. Mernie had gone home hours ago, and Rose had been cleaning and locking up on her own. She glanced up at the door when she heard the noise.

At first Rose thought it was only a shadow. The third time the shadow passed the frosted glass of the back door she knew someone was where he shouldn't be. She carefully stepped away from the door and returned to the office, where she quietly picked up the phone and dialed 911 with her left hand as her right opened the desk drawer and picked up her .45 revolver. She removed the safety as she said, "It's Rose," into the receiver, followed by, "Send a car, Kelly." She placed the phone on the desk with the 911 operator saying, "Hello? Hello? Rose, is that you? Hello?"

Rose wasn't waiting around. If someone thought he was going to get the drop on her and break in while her back was turned, he had another thing coming. She sat in the dark against the wall where she could watch the shadow move.

Her watching was short-lived. There was the sound of running, then a low snarling. The snarling became a guttural growl, and the shadow that had been passing now rose, swung something in front of it, and yelled, "Help, somebody!"

Rose tightened her grip on the gun and rushed to grab the key already hanging in the lock. The growling got closer. A dark shadow pressed against the glass. Rose couldn't see what was happening. But she could hear something being swung violently back and forth.

She unlocked the door and pushed it against the dark shadow to find one small girl desperately swinging a guitar case at an animal that was trying with each snarling step to reach her.

Then Rose fired at the animal to frighten it, to get it to stop, to make it run. But the animal paid no attention to the flying bullets. Instead of fleeing, it rose to its hind feet and leaped toward the girl. That's when Rose fired three shots directly at the animal. The dog snapped at her, pacing back and forth, surveying Rose, seeming to consider its options.

"I've got two more shots, and I'll be aiming for your brain," she said.

With a final snarl the animal turned and in one jump cleared the ditch and bounded off across the empty lot. The police cruiser barely caught the animal's tail in its headlights as it turned down the street. And a scared and shaking teenage girl sat in the dirt and leaned her head against the guitar case jutting out between her knees.

Rudy had been at the kitchen table with his mama for eleven minutes and forty-seven seconds when he said, "Hold on." He held one finger up so Velma would freeze her story right where it hung. She had been talking fast. She'd made it to the recounting of Rudy's birth and the rueful rural-route man backing up and coming to her rescue.

Rudy stood and went to the kitchen cabinet above the refrigerator. He opened it and took out the bottle of Southern Comfort that had been there since his daddy died. He poured himself three fingers in a water glass before he sat back down. He left the bottle on the counter just in case.

"Don't you want to add some water to that?" Velma puckered up her lips and pulled them sideways.

"Reckon if I did, I would have."

"No need to get smart."

"Sorry, Mama." Rudy took a sip but made himself slow down and sip small instead of throwing back the glass like he wanted to. He was mindful of his mama. "Go on with your story, Mama."

Rudy eyed the rock set in front of him as she spoke. One thing was certain: she wasn't lying about the rock being strange. It was glowing like a crystal from outer space, even he could see that, and that wasn't natural. Not something you'd just kick up in the road or pick up and skip across the creek. So he kept his eyes on the rock as Velma recounted his whole birthday in a way he'd never heard before.

"You mean to tell me that I was delivered into this world by another rural-route man?"

"That you were." Velma knocked her knuckles on the wooden table as if it was a superstition they talked about, as if the world could take Rudy back if she told the truth. "Old Man Thompson, God rest his soul."

"Why didn't you ever tell me that?"

"Because it made your daddy mad as blazes, that's why."

"Mama," Rudy chided her, cocked one eye up. His mama didn't cuss.

"Well, it did." She put her hand over her mouth to hide her grin. "He was mad he wasn't here, mad that you come when he wasn't expecting. You know how he was, always getting everything planned down to the final minute, taking charge, running the show."

"Shoot, that's the way you remember it." Rudy took another sip and slowly put the glass down, trying not to draw his mother's attention.

"And you know, I don't think he wanted another man to see me"—Velma hung her head down a little—"like that."

"Oh." Rudy had nothing to say about that. "Mama, I'd like to know who or what that was trying to take this thing from you when I walked in."

Tomcat jumped onto the table, slapped at the glittering rock with his paw. Velma gently picked him up and put him in her lap, where after a couple of strokes he relented to settling down.

"I don't know what to tell you, Rudy."

"Mama." Rudy wanted to poke the rock, wanted to turn it over. "Who else knows you have this thing?" He wanted to try to bust it open to see what was inside. A craving to discover some untold mystery—like the time he broke into the radio when he was seven to see where the voice was coming from.

"Sara, that's all. Just Sara."

"That's good," he said, but there was a strange look in his eye. "So, let me get this straight. A man came right up to the door, and you invited him inside. And then over coffee he gave you this?" Rudy ran his palms over his face and through his hair, leaving half of it sticking up and out. "Do you think that's normal?"

"Of course not, Rudy. We're not talking normal. It's not normal."

The two of them sat and considered the parameters of normal. Caterpillars cocooning. Fish biting on a full moon. Natural order.

"I seen him a time or two since then." Velma dropped her voice, ran her fingers slowly over the rock, and then picked it up and placed it in her apron pocket. "The man that gave it to me, I mean." She folded her arms over her chest.

"He's been back?"

"Kinda."

"Well, Mama, he has or he hasn't. Now which one is it?"

"Kinda both." She paused, thinking. "It's like this: I think I'm awake when I'm seeing him, but then I wake up like I was dreaming, but it's still lingering so close that, well, Rudy, a part of me knows it was real."

Rudy got up, walked to the back door, opened the screen, and looked out.

Velma came and stood behind him. She rose up on her toes a little and looked over his shoulder. "What's out there, Rudy?"

"I don't know." He stepped outside the door and walked down the steps. Velma followed him out and closed the door behind her. Rudy pulled his cigarettes from his pocket, shook one from the pack, and lit it. He looked at where the moon cast shadows beneath the clouds.

"Your daddy was supposed to build me a back porch." Velma stepped out into the yard, sat in her old aluminum chair. The cushions were already damp from the night air. "But he never got around to it."

"We all mean to do a lot of things." Rudy took a deep drag and looked over at Velma. "Mama, why do you think you got that rock? Why you and not somebody else?"

"I been wondering that myself. And I surely don't know." She patted her pocket down, held her hand over the shape of the rock. "That was the question I asked the man, 'Why me?' Seemed to me that Sara would have been a better pick. With all she knows, all that history stuff she likes to keep up with. And she says it's worth some money."

"Does she now?" Rudy let it slip out as sarcastic as he meant it.

"How come you and Sara don't ever give each other your due?"

"Ahh, not much to it, Mama. She sees me the way she does, and I see her for what she is."

"She's my friend."

"You got that wrong, Mama." Rudy took a deep drag and

looked out into the darkness toward the old pond. "You're *her* friend. She needs you a lot more'n you need her."

"Well, I reckon I need her too."

"Difference is, you could do without her, Mama. And don't say you couldn't, because you could." Rudy smoked, looked out across the field, ran his hands up and down his arms. "She can't carry on so good without you."

He was certain that the thing that had been in the kitchen before him was lingering. And watching.

The two of them let their words rest. Velma rocked slightly in the chair, and Rudy smoked.

"I don't hear the owl," Rudy said. He took it as a bad omen, but he didn't want to mention that part.

"No. Me neither. You know when that thing come in tonight, when I heard it, I didn't know what it was. When I looked up, what was standing behind me was you."

"Me?"

"That's what I said. It was you."

"Wasn't me, Mama."

"I know that now, but what I'm telling you is, it was shaped like you. It's a frightening thing that it could look just like you." She paused, considering. "No, not *just like* but almost—almost like you."

Rudy was a lot of things and not a lot of things, but he was at heart a believer in bigger things and in his mama. He knew if she said something, then that's the way it was, so she didn't have to work at convincing him of anything, no matter how outlandish it might seem.

"That *is* a frightening thing. Don't think this town could stand the likes of two of me." Rudy winked at her.

Then, oddly, Rudy thought of Rose, of her closing up, of the possibility of someone at the door looking like him and her unlocking the door, opening it wide. "Mama, I need to use the phone."

"You know where it is." Velma stayed put right in her chair in the yard, satisfied that the real Rudy was there.

"Did you know they make phones now that you can walk around with?" Rudy called over his shoulder as he picked up the phone.

"Yeah, I do know that," Velma said, but she said it so quiet it was a whisper.

It was the seventh ring before Rose answered. "Rose, you all right?" He was both serious and sober.

"Funny you should ask that, Casanova. Jimmy left not twenty minutes ago."

"Patrol Jimmy?"

"The one and only."

Rudy looked out, keeping an eye on Velma, then lowered his voice. "What's going on?"

"We'll have to talk it over a little later. I just had a run-in with a wild animal and an unexpected visitor."

"Lot of that going on around here tonight."

"What's that?" Rose asked him.

"Unexpected visitors," Rudy answered.

"Thanks for checking on me." Rose paused.

Rudy started to add something, wanted to keep Rose on the phone, but smooth talker that he was, he couldn't think of a thing.

"I'll see you around, Rudy," Rose said and hung up the phone.

Rudy returned to the backyard, lit another cigarette. Velma looked up at him and started to say something about wishing he would quit, but she told him instead, "That's how I first knew it wasn't you."

"What?"

"That thing. He lit a cigarette in the kitchen, standing right there, without apology."

"Well, you know I wouldn't do that."

"And when he got closer, there was another thing." She got up from the chair and went to Rudy. She waved the smoke away from her face, then reached up and took his chin, turned his face toward the kitchen light. Risen in the half light was the white line of a scar that ran through his left eyebrow. "It's that old scar." Velma looked at it good. "He, it—whatever it was—didn't have that scar."

"You don't say." Rudy absently ran his finger over the white line while he studied the trees, looked toward the creek where the water was running steady through the darkness.

"Now, why would something go to the trouble of being a copycat, right down to your cigarettes, and not copy that scar? What do you make of that?"

"Guess it hadn't seen the scar, Mama." But he wasn't really ruminating on that old scar. Rudy was thinking about the rock. The fact that it was real. Despite those colored threads floating around the front porch, despite her imaginings, something in Velma was well grounded to the earth. She was never flighty. "Can I hold it, Mama?" He leaned over and ground out his cigarette under his shoe. Velma didn't move. "Mama?"

"I'm thinking about it." She sat back down, and they heard the owl call. It took awhile, but there was an answer, down the hill, a mile away and a wood over. Another owl called back. Rudy breathed a sigh of relief so loud Velma heard it.

After a minute Rudy asked, "Are you gonna be thinking much longer?"

"Well, Son, it's like this." Velma turned to him, slid her hand into her pocket, and pulled out the glowing red rock. "It might take you somewhere, and I don't know that I could follow. If it was a bad place you didn't want to be, I don't know that I could pull you out, that I could bring you back." She ran her fingers over the surface, turned it over in her rough hands. "The truth is, I don't understand a thing about it."

"Didn't come with instructions, huh?" Rudy looked over at the rock again.

Velma sat up straighter. "Well, as a matter of fact, it did.

Only instructions were that it was mine and not to let any-body take it from me. 'Scouts are out,' the man said. Told me they'd try to take it."

"I'm not trying to take it from you, Mama."

"I'm not thinking of you, silly." She turned it over again. "I reckon that thing that was just here was what he called a scout. The man said they'd be comin'—be lookin' for this." She weighed the rock in her hand, tossing it up in the air slightly and palming it again, then said, "But he didn't say why they'd be wantin' it so bad." Then she added, "Here," and tossed it as casually as you please.

Rudy threw up his left hand, caught it in midair. "Care-ful, Mama." He closed his fingers over it, his hand covering the rock completely. He brought it to chest level and opened his palm. "For all you know this thing might be explosive."

"Well"—she stared at him—"doesn't look like you're going nowhere."

"I didn't think I would."

"Sara took a little trip when she touched it, so I wouldn't be so sure," Velma said to remind him that he didn't know everything.

"Is that a fact?" Rudy held the rock up as if it were a kalei-doscope. As if he would be able to see right through it and straight into tomorrow.

"Technically."

"What is it you're not telling me?" Rudy brought the rock back down, looked at her.

"That I was touching it too." She screwed her lips up, as she was apt to do. "We were kinda tussling around in the dirt, and her fingers hit it 'bout the same time mine did, I reckon."

"I didn't know you and Sara had a habit of tussling." Rudy suppressed a laugh.

"We don't. She had gotten it in her mind to get me into the car."

Rudy did laugh then. "I think I've had that same tussle with you a few times myself."

"Didn't win now, did you?"

"No ma'am." He passed the rock back to her. "I don't know, Mama. I believe you and everything, but I just don't know. It's the darnedest thing." He stood up and kicked at the dirt with his shoe. "Man shows up, gives you a rock, and you start taking trips—on the sly, I might add—without telling me anything."

"Oh, you're always so busy with yourself you don't have much time left for me."

Rudy ignored her comment and continued. "And then some strange smoking thing shows up, changes shapes on you, trying to trick you, trying to take it." He paused, looked at the stars awhile. "Maybe I should move back in for a few days."

Velma was surprised. Then suspicious. "Rudy, now you know I'm not gonna tolerate your drinking and them other things."

He cracked a grin in the darkness. "You mean those other things called women?"

"There are women, and there are those kinda women."

"Not true, Mama." Rudy laid his hand on her head. "There are just women—they're all different, Mama, but they are all women." He bounced backward a time or two in front of her and said, "And I likes 'em all, Mama. I do!"

"That's what I'm talking about right there." Velma got out of her chair and started shaking her finger at him as she walked toward the kitchen door. "I'm not gonna put up with that foolishness." She said it, and she meant it. She thought about the thing that had been threatening her, about how having Rudy in the house would be a comfort, but she wouldn't pay for it with the smell of cheap perfume and stale whiskey hanging in her house.

She left Rudy standing in the backyard. But she didn't see the look on his face or the way he cast a glance off into the distance, over the field, toward the creek. In the dark she didn't see the set to his jaw or the way he put both hands in his pockets and looked down at the ground for what seemed like the longest time before he turned and headed through the back door and into the house.

That night Rudy slept in his old bedroom by the front porch, the one closest to the door. He listened for anything that sounded like it might be hungrily searching for something that now belonged to his mama.

Fourteen

Rose looked across the table at the girl eating a ham sandwich and drinking a cup of coffee. "I'm not a baby," she had said, the way half-grown babies usually do, when Rose had offered her milk. Then she had requested coffee to "steady my nerves." Rose watched the girl take one last huge bite. "You don't have to rush, you know."

"I've kept you way too late already," Annie said, "and I need to be getting on down the road anyway." She cut her eyes toward the back door, where the trouble had been.

"Oh, really?" Rose sat down facing the girl. "You got plans this time of night?" Rose looked up at the clock. "Got business you need to attend to out on those dark roads, tough girl?"

Rose gave Annie a look that told her to cut the nonsense, and Annie dropped her voice down a notch, softened it around the edges. "No." She dropped her eyes down a notch too. "Not really."

"Pretty obvious you're running from something other than the big bad wolf. Somebody looking for you?"

"I left a note."

"A note?" Rose hooked her thumbs in the loops on the

front of her jeans. "Well now, you got the kind of somebody that a note is good enough for? I mean, good enough not to make somebody not worry? 'Cause the way I see it, with what I just got through witnessing, somebody might just have plenty to worry about."

Annie looked at her, sizing her up. Kinda like the woman in the diner but different. Kinda tough, but the kind of tough that looked like it could be trusted. "I came here for a reason." The steel in her eyes matched Rose's, blade for blade.

"Something personal?"

"Very." Annie lifted the coffee cup and drank the rest of it down in one defiant swallow.

"Well, business or not, my guess is you could use a safe bed to sleep in for the night."

"Couch would do just fine," Annie said without smiling. It wasn't an offer she wanted to accept. It was one she had to. There were dark circles under her eyes from sleepless days and nights, and she was at end of her rope. She wrapped her arms around her guitar case and against her will dropped her head forward.

Rose didn't need any more clues or answers. Something stray falls at your back door, you feed it, let it rest, and ask questions later. "I'm locking up, kid, and then we'll take it home."

"I'm not a kid."

"Yeah, I got that, but you know what? You're not full

grown either. Right now if I ask your name, are you going tell me the truth?"

Annie shook her head, still leaning against the guitar case.

"I didn't think so. So for the lack of a better, more star-studded name, *kid* it is."

Rose turned off all the lights. She let Annie step into the windy weather ahead of her, turned, and locked the door.

Rose drove out of the parking lot and turned left onto the empty street. She started to tell the girl that she might as well close her eyes, but when Rose looked, she was already asleep, her head falling sideways until it almost rested on Rose's shoulder. *Like a little bird come through a bad storm,* Rose thought and let her be.

Rose told Annie, "We're here," softly shaking her shoulder.

The small pink stucco house was warm looking, with two palm trees in the front, like twins guarding the walkway. They were the exact same size and width, reaching up to the height of the roof, and were lit from underneath with spotlights. Rose unlocked the door and waited for Annie as she retrieved her guitar and backpack and followed her into the house.

The house was tidy, everything in its place. A smell of scrubbed clean hung in the air. There was a little-known secret that Rose had kept to herself: she was a homemaker. She could make a place cozy at the drop of a hat, and the evidence was everywhere. If the bar was her nest egg, her home was her nest. She mopped her floors every Saturday morning, watered her garden late at night when she came home, washed her dishes by hand in warm soapy water while she looked out into her backyard. These tasks reminded her that dirty things could be cleaned, that messy things could be made straight, that it was all just a matter of focus and hard work. And that when she came home from a long night of work, she had a safe, sweet retreat waiting for her.

Rose turned down the covers in the spare room, and Annie kicked off both shoes before Rose had time to offer a shower or to ask if she had clean clothes. The girl lay down across the sheets, her head on the pillow, and was asleep again just that fast. Rose pulled the covers up over her and rested a hand on the tangled hair before she turned out the light and closed the door.

Then Rose took a beer out of the fridge, lit a cigarette, and sat in her chair, listening to the palms outside the front door rustle in the wind. This was her after-work ritual: one cold beer, one cigarette, and the quiet. She opened the beer and took a long drink. "Lord, have mercy," she said then to no one but the wind and the dark as she thought about the animal that had lunged at her, about the fact that she had first aimed to scare and then had aimed to kill. Rose was a lot of things, and one of those things was an expert shot. And she had not missed. She had aimed for the heart, and she knew that she had hit the heart not once but at least three times.

But the animal had not even flinched. "That wasn't no ordinary puppy dog."

Her hand shook as she raised the beer to her lips. "Sure wasn't." She was seized with the strange desire to call Rudy, to explain to him—what? That she was attacked by a dog the size of a small bear? No, maybe all she wanted was to hear his voice. Maybe, as tough as she was, as used to taking care of herself as she was, she just wanted to hear a voice, a man's voice, on the other end of the line say, "It's gonna be all right." With shaking hands she looked up his phone number and dialed. A number she had never called. But Rudy had called her, from dozens of different phones on nights he was in trouble. Rudy broken down. Rudy stranded. Rudy drunk. Rudy lonely. And once, without his mother's knowledge, Rudy needing to get out of jail for a bar fight with somebody's old boyfriend. Now she was the one making the middle-of-the-night call.

She dialed the seven digits and listened to the phone ring, expecting him to pick up right away. Expecting him to answer at least by the third ring. On the seventh ring she hung up. *How perfect,* she thought. The one time she needed him, he was nowhere around. "Probably lying in the arms of some woman across town."

She started to take another drink of her beer but stopped before the bottle touched her lips. She began to cry. Long, slow streams of silent tears falling on the front of her shirt. She wiped them with the back of her hand, took one more drag on the cigarette, and ground the butt out in the ashtray. Rose hated to cry. Hated to be afraid. Hated to show weakness. Even in private.

She made certain the doors were locked, front and back, and went to the bathroom and washed her face hard with hot water, as if scrubbing the tear-stained streaks would wash away the hurt that ran beneath them.

She undressed and climbed into bed and felt somehow validated. She had told herself that she was better on her own, stronger on her own, and she needed only to listen to her own good sense. And *that*, she thought as she turned out her light, was exactly what she was going to do. She locked down her heart, pushed it safely away from Rudy, and went to sleep. But sometime during the night, in her dreams there was the presence of a strange, dark animal and an ensuing battle as she tried to survive. Then a vision of Rudy's brown eyes surfaced in the dream, and she felt rescued before falling into a peaceful sleep where only the image of Rudy's eyes watching over her remained.

Morning came earlier than Rose expected. She stirred and felt sore and bruised. She was a strong woman. She moved beer cases, scrubbed floors, and washed dishes. But this morning she felt sore like she'd been fighting. Then she remembered the girl, the dog, the empty sound of the unanswered ringing phone.

Rose got out of bed with a groan and stumbled her way

to the coffeepot. While the coffee was brewing, she cracked the other bedroom door to check on the sleeping shape. The girl looked younger in her sleep, Rose thought. Still a baby, really, when it came right down to it.

At half past nine, Rose, in jeans and her favorite Pumas, decided to leave a note and go down to check on the bar and wait for deliveries. She wrote in big letters "DON'T LEAVE," then scratched that out, turned the paper over. "Great, just what I needed. A runaway to feed and worry about." She looked over her shoulder, hoping the runaway wasn't awake and listening. At least she figured her for a runaway.

She tried the note again: "Here's my number at work. Call me, and I'll come pick you up later. Help yourself to anything in the fridge." She stared at the note and wrote "REALLY" in large letters and underlined it twice.

She was in the car and already had it in Reverse when the front door opened. Annie appeared, fuzzy headed and red eyed, with the note in her hand. Rose sighed, put the car in Drive, and moved forward. She shifted into Park but left the car running. She opened her door, got out, stood with her arm on the warm roof, and motioned for the girl.

Annie stepped outside and blinked in the bright sunlight, then shaded her eyes, squinting. She didn't offer any words but stood looking at Rose, waiting for her to do all the talking.

"Sleep all right?" Rose slid her sunglasses down her nose, looked at her over the rims.

The girl nodded.

"Got my note, I see."

The girl looked at the paper in her hand. "I didn't read it," she said.

Rose pushed her shades back up, reached for a cigarette from her case on the dash, lit one, and stared at the girl who had nowhere to go and not much to say. "I'm going to work, kid." She exhaled. "You wanna come with me?"

Annie nodded, seemed to recapture her voice, her momentum. She looked at the running car. "Can you give me just a second? To clean up? No shower or nothing, just a quick cleanup."

Rose looked at the circles under her eyes, the dirty-all-over look of her. It looked like a shower, one full of hot water and soap, would be in order. "You're killing me. You've only been here a few hours, and you're already killing me."

Annie smiled. The first smile Rose had seen, and it took her by surprise. There was something shocking about that smiling, dirty face. It was strangely familiar.

"You won't be sorry." She started to run back in the house but stopped, stood still and serious. "I'll help you work," she said, and then she was gone, disappearing like greased lightning through the open door.

Rose turned off the car, closed the door, and took her coffee back into the house where she'd hand out a towel, point to the shampoo and cream rinse, and search for a clean T-shirt for a young girl who had suddenly found her words.

The found words were like a shotgun loaded full of

questions aimed at Rose. Was she married? Did she have any kids? Did she have a dog or cat? Was she from Echo? Did she know everybody in town? The questions continued to pour out as Rose pushed the girl into the bathroom and closed the door.

Rose stood against the wall, trying to capture the silence. She didn't fully relax until she heard the water turn on. Even then she was half expecting the door to open and the girl to come running out, full of more questions Rose did not want to answer. Not that they didn't have simple answers. Married? Not now. Children? No hope of that. Dog? Only one, but he's dead and buried in the backyard. Cat? No. Don't like their slinky, sneaky ways. All the questions she refused to answer came tumbling through her brain.

It wasn't until she heard a melody coming from the bathroom that her rabbit thinking slowed down. Rose listened as the girl busted out with "Me and Bobby McGee." *An old tune for a young girl,* she thought. "Nothing timid about her singing, that's for sure."

The last strains of "Me and Bobby McGee" were rounding the corner when Rose left the stance she had taken against the wall and went to the kitchen, where she would make cheese omelets and raisin toast and prepare herself to listen to whatever version of the story the girl was going to tell.

Fifteen

Velma was sleeping when Joe came to visit. She was not expecting him. Not expecting anything but the night and then the morning. She had gone to sleep clutching the rock to her chest, both hands wrapped over it and resting on her heart. Now she woke up, and the rock was still right there but beating red. And Joe was sitting on the side of the bed.

"Hey, Velma," he said and smiled. She saw that he was young, younger than the last time, younger than the time before that. He was the just-married age.

"Hey, Joe," she said and released the rock with her left hand to reach toward his face. The hand was not the hand of her past but the hand of her now. And she thought, *How did this happen? How did we get trapped in different times?* "You're not my old Joe," she said and felt foolish saying it, but it was what was on her sleepy mind.

"It's all right." He smiled again and looked down at Velma, pushed back a strand of the white hair laid out across the pillow. "You haven't changed much." He took her hand, and Velma felt the warmth of his flesh and felt the tears well up in her eyes. Joe reached down and brushed them away, but they were quickly, quietly replaced with more. "It's all right," he said again.

"Oh, Joe." Velma completely let go of the rock clasped in her palm, brought her fingers to her lips. "I missed you so much," she said, but it was a whisper. "Can you stay, Joe? Even for a little while?"

"Well…" He slipped off his shoes, and they hit the wood floor. "Why don't we find out?" Joe lay down on top of the covers, his head above hers, his shoulder near her face.

He smelled like Joe. She had almost forgotten that smell, forgotten how she had buried her face in his clothes after he died, held them to her, slept with his shirt until finally the smell had lightened, lessened, and traveled somewhere beyond her reach.

Eventually she had folded the shirts, put them away. But now, here was the smell of Joe, all salt and man and tanned skin. God, she had forgotten how much she loved him. How could that be possible? How could that happen? "Missed you," she whispered, brought his hand to her lips, and held it there. And so old Velma and young Joe traveled together through the night, wrapped in a cocoon that kept them safely separated from the logic of time.

Sixteen

When Rudy entered the kitchen, Velma was sitting at the table with her arms crossed, fiercely contemplating the object before her.

"Morning, Mama," Rudy said and headed for the coffeepot. Velma didn't answer.

He poured himself a cup, added two spoonfuls of sugar, and stirred. He waited until he took a few sips to say anything else. His mama was in a peculiar state of mind—that much he could tell. "What're you thinking?"

"Thinking about burying this rock out in the yard," she replied without looking up.

"What are you going to do, grow a crop of rocks?" Rudy laughed. Velma didn't. He walked past her and stuck his finger in her side to try to get her to laugh. Nothing happened. He dropped himself full force into his old chair at the table and looked at his mother's face. "Mama, have you been crying?"

Velma looked up at him with fresh tears in her eyes. "I don't think I can take the blessing of this thing."

Rudy got serious then. Took a sip of his coffee and looked away. "What happened?"

Velma put her hands over her face, brushed away new tears, and looked up. "Son, even remembering the good hurts when the good is gone. So what do I want with a memory rock?"

Rudy reached out to pick up the rock and then hesitated. Velma just shrugged her shoulders. "Seems like nobody rides without me. I reckon it doesn't matter." She put her hands into her apron pockets. "Of course, it's a tricky thing. I guess it could change the rules at any moment."

He turned it over and over in his palm. There was no light, no pulsing, just a flat, cold, smooth rock. Like a skipping rock, one of the hundreds he had found and skipped across the flat surface of the creek. "Mama, I don't think it was supposed to hurt you." He flicked his wrist as if he were going to skip the rock across the surface of the kitchen table. "It's a weird and wondrous thing, but I don't think it was supposed to make you sad." He looked at her tired face. "Or make you cry." He placed the rock back on the table, reached out, and patted the back of her hand. "Maybe you're supposed to do something, change something."

"Can't change nothing." Velma knew that. Didn't remember if the man told her that or not, but it was something she knew. "What's planted is planted."

"Then something else, Mama. Maybe to remember something. Something important. Something special." Rudy finished his coffee. "Hey, I've got to get to work," he said, even though it wasn't work that was on his mind. He stood up from the table.

"Rudy,"—Velma paused a moment—"thanks for staying last night."

"No problem." Rudy walked to the sink, looked out over the open field. "Thought I'd pick up a few things and come stay a few days."

"So you really are?"

"Yep. I told you last night. I meant it."

"I meant what I said too." Velma smiled. "No strange women."

Rudy walked around the table toward the door. "Mama, you and me know about strange things, now don't we?"

Velma didn't comment.

"Seems to me you got a strange thing going on." He thought about the shape-shifting thing from the night before. "And I do mean mighty strange. Seems you might like to have an extra pair of eyes and ears around."

"I can bury it, Son, and stop this mess."

"Can't bury the past, Mama. It'll just keep pushing its way to the surface. You know that. And whatever those things are—scouts, you call 'em—well, they'll just come around trying to dig it up. I'll see you later. But you stay inside today. I don't like leaving you out here alone." And then he was gone.

Velma listened to him walk down the hallway, open the front door, and push the screen door open and then walk out and across the porch. Listened to his truck start up, listened to the tires crunch the sand as he backed away from the house. Listened as the truck disappeared down the road, getting farther and farther away from the house. Then she began to make her plan.

Rudy drove up to the front of Rose's bar. He surveyed the building for a moment as if seeing it for the first time. Unlike a neon night—when the place was filled with people pressing in to get a beer, sing a song, share a laugh—it looked cold. He got out of the truck and walked to the front door, then put his hands in his pockets, surprised by his hesitation, by his timidity. He had been walking into Rose's bar for seven years, but not once had he approached it in broad daylight. Even the door handle felt alien in his hand, cold even in the sun. He knocked a few times, looked over at Rose's car, and assured himself that she was there. He knocked again and backed up, leaned on the hood of his truck, lit a cigarette, and waited. It seemed a long time passed before he heard the bolt turn and saw the door open. Rose stepped out looking less friendly than he had expected.

Rose studied Rudy hard to determine if he was sober, showing up at this hour of the day, but he didn't look drunk or hung over. Then she thought of the unanswered phone last night, and her true feelings slid across her face.

"What's going on?" Rose stepped back into the shadow of the door. She remembered dreaming last night of Rudy's eyes watching out for her. She put her hand to her forehead and waited for the dream to pass.

"Last night"—Rudy pushed off the front of the truck with the heel of his shoe and stepped forward—"you said there was something strange going on. I came to check on you."

Rose didn't reply.

"On the phone. When we spoke."

"Oh, that." Rose turned and walked back inside. Rudy followed her. She walked behind the bar, picked up a pair of glasses, put them back on her face, and looked over a distributor's invoice. "It was nothing."

"Sounded like a something." Rudy leaned on the bar. Cocked his head to the side, smiling. "Didn't know you wore glasses, Rose."

Rose slid the glasses down on her nose, looking over the rims at Rudy. "There's a lot you don't know about me, cowboy."

"Your mean streak's showing." Rudy tapped the bar. "Listen, I just wanted to check on you. That's all." He wanted to wink at her, but she didn't look up. Just said, "Mmm."

"Seriously, I was out at Mama's last night, and something really weird happened. I'm talking four-star strange. And then when I called you, well, you said the police had just left."

Rose finally looked up. "Your mama's?"

"Yeah."

"What kind of strange?"

Rudy didn't want to tell her everything. People thought his mama was crazy as it was with her threads flying around the porch, with her refusing to walk to the mailbox or across the road or to leave home by car. "Strange enough that I spent the night. Strange enough that I'm going to stay with her for a few days."

Rose took off her glasses, laid them on the bar. She was trying to deal with the fact that she was happy, much too happy, to hear that the only woman Rudy spent time with the night before was his mama. "Care for some coffee and conversation?"

Rudy smiled. "That's what I was hoping for." Then the place inside of Rudy that had been jumpy and nervous settled down, and he could breathe a little easier.

Velma had been thinking about knots. Then she had practiced tying knots. Now she held the rock, tested the weight of it in her hand. She first wrapped the rock in a towel, then added another towel, then wrapped a bedsheet around her toweled bundle. She took her time.

The sky had been sunny when she started, but now a wind had come up from the east, bringing with it dark clouds that whipped her clothes on the line to a frenzy. She quickened her work as drops of rain caught the back of her neck.

She spoke to the rock as she worked. "Weren't your fault, you know. I'm not blamin' you."

Thunder rolled in the distance, mighty and strong like August thunder. Velma finished wrapping the bedsheet tightly around the towels. She pulled out the rope she had brought with her and began to tie the rope around and around and around the bundle.

"I'm sorry about this, but some things aren't natural, and you're one of those unnatural things."

The red beating heart of the rock flickered through the fabric.

The pine trees caught the wind in their tops, shook and shimmered, dropping pine needles that had gotten trapped in the branches. "There!" she said as she stood with the bundle at her feet.

She headed toward the creek, wandering the back way, across the field, past the barn, and down to the water's edge. She slipped off her white tennis shoes and stepped in. The wet sandy muck sucked at her feet, slid up between her toes—a feeling Velma was not fond of, but she ignored it and continued moving ahead.

The current began to pull and swirl around her knees, tugging harder at her legs. Farther, deeper she went. She got waist deep in the cold water before she took her package and began to lower it below the surface. It caught air, tried to surface, tried to fight its way back into the space of earth and sky. Velma held fast. Then, one inch at a time, the rock and its wrappings took on the weight of water and began receding to the murky depths of the creek's bottom.

The trees bent by the wind gusts caught Velma's attention. Strokes of lightning ripped across the sky. She turned and measured the distance between her, the creek bank, and the safety of the house. Then she felt something tug at her ankle. She lifted her foot, pulled as hard as she could, but she could feel the rope that had tied the bundle wrapping around her leg, cinching tighter.

Her first thought was a simple awareness, the way a child might recognize trouble. Her second was of Joe. Of him holding her last night. Of waking alone and thinking, *I'll just go on now. I'll just go on.*

A lightning bolt hit the pine tree only four feet away from the creek's edge, blowing a limb clean off and leaving a fire sizzling. Smoke filled the air.

Velma considered Joe and became very calm, calmer than the raging storm. She figured being with Joe on the other side was better than being without him on this one.

But then she thought of Rudy and how he wasn't finished. How he still held promise, but the promise wasn't fulfilled. She hadn't given up on him, and she so much wanted to be able to look Sara square in the face and say, "I told you so."

Velma took a deep breath and dove under the water. She felt for the rope, the fabric, and tried to untie it. Tried to pull it off her ankle.

She came up for air, and that's when she saw that the storm wasn't normal either. Clouds circled the creek where she was treading water. They hovered there, lightning bolts shooting out from them, striking in a closing circle around the creek.

She tried to pull herself toward the edge of the creek, but while her right leg could move freely, the left was anchored solidly by the rock's wrapping and would not budge.

Another bolt of lightning hit the pond just beyond the water line. Velma whispered, "Don't kill me," and went under for the second time.

Seventeen

Sara had been content with being herself today. She had reveled in her house like she used to do before Velma and her rock business. Before she was aware of the possibilities the rock held and was frustrated, realizing the possibilities didn't belong to her. She had wondered during the hours when she had paced in her home, questioned a universe that would toss such a gem of chance into the lap of someone who couldn't care less. "Only world she cares about is the one right around her knees," she had complained to the walls. Sara wouldn't be limited to the time and space of her own lifetime but would have traveled through history. She imagined holding the rock firmly in one hand and placing her other on a volume about the Renaissance period and then finding herself standing below Michelangelo as he painted the Sistine Chapel. There were many possibilities in her mind. *But Velma takes a trip back in time to her own barn, still sitting thirty feet from her own back door.* When Sara had questioned her, had asked her about the places she had gone, Velma had said, "The barn," as simple as you please and smiled like it had been someplace hot and exotic.

Sara had decided that the day she and Velma had wrestled in the yard was nothing special. Just another day. A slice that had been filled with passion and regret as she determined to haul Velma out of that yard. With Velma being her ornery, stubborn, half-crazy self, somehow Sara now believed she had stepped out of the reason of her own life and down into the rural, twisty-turny life of Velma True. She had been caught at the edge of madness. "A shared delusion is all it was," Sara said. "A moment of memory."

And so, at ease with the lack of possibility, with the limited scope of the way things were and could be, Sara had come to terms with the fact that Velma was a little more scattered than she had originally thought, was losing her mind a little more with time. Sara would continue to be retired, to love her books and her music, to live in the peaceful, comfortable world that she had created, and to take long drives in the countryside. To feel the rubber beneath her, gliding her along like a magic carpet.

Sara sat with a cup of tea while she read a collection of Mary Oliver's poems. She was lost in "The Journey," the one about stepping wildly into the night, when she heard thunder. She glanced out the window. The sky was clear—nothing but bright blue. She readjusted her glasses, began again at the first line, but there was another clap, louder, closer. A plane breaking the sound barrier perhaps? She laid the book next to the cup on the table, went to her window, and scanned the sky. No sign of a jet or contrail streaming behind. Sara stood for a moment looking up. And then in one sudden motion, Sara picked up her phone with her right hand and dialed

Velma's number. She used her left hand to reach for her purse and grab her keys off the hook by the door. She walked out the front door, holding the phone to her ear with her chin as she turned and locked it. Velma's phone was still ringing as she got into her car, turned the ignition, and drove toward Velma's place. When she had driven beyond its reach, the connection went dead.

Velma was almost in the middle of the creek now; the wet bundle below had caught the current and pulled her farther and farther into the deeper water. The rope around her ankle was getting tighter and tighter as the bundle dragged across the muddy bottom. Velma could see the creek bed, imagined the shelf bottom curving ever so slightly from shore until finally it dropped into the deepest holes filled with dark tree stumps and old wood. She was treading water now as hard as she could, her dress rising and floating on the surface around her. The lightning bolts drew closer to the edge, and one struck the crushed rock on the creek bank. The pop was so alive, so frightening, that Velma placed both hands over her ears and sank before she realized she'd made a mistake. She sputtered and flailed, rose to the surface again. She began to scream at the rock over and over, "Let me go! Let me go! Let me go!" But her voice was lost in the wind and the beginning of an icy rain that was turning to hail.

Well, this ain't getting any better, she thought. Her one free leg was cramping, and her arms were getting heavier and heavier from fighting to keep her head above the swirling brown water. "All right, I'm sorry. Is that what you want?" but the cold ice pelted the water, slapped against her head and arms. "Okay. That's a lie and you know it. I'm not sorry," she said in nothing more than a whisper, "but I don't want to die, not yet. I've done decided." And she took a deep breath and sank under the water. She reached her hands around the rope and lowered herself farther down where the water was much darker and colder. She could see the blurry white bundle still moving with the current, still being pulled and pulling her farther and farther from the shore. She tugged on the rope, tried to raise the bundle toward her, but instead it towed her farther down to the bottom until she was hovering over the white cotton, studying it through watery eyes. Her hands clutched furiously at the wrapped blanket, tried to untie it, tried to untangle the rope from her leg, but it was no use. Her arms were too tired, her hands were too weak, and she had run out of air.

Velma let go of the rope and with all her might swam upward. Her head broke the water's surface, and she gasped for air, her lungs and nose burning. Now the storm was a downpour—the rain and the creek were one. Her eyes could barely make out the shape of the creek bank, but there on the edge of the water, blending with the rain and sky, was the front grill of a 1963 Oldsmobile convertible.

A fully clothed Sara Long waded furiously into the water and began to swim in long, confident strokes toward Velma. When she reached her friend, who was now sinking by degrees, she tried to wrap her arm around her to pull her to shore.

"Rope," Velma said.

Sara wasn't listening. She concentrated on swimming with one arm, to no avail against the weight.

"I'm tied down, Sara," Velma tried again.

"What?" Sara yelled, still stroking with all her might but getting nowhere.

"I'm tied down!"

Sara kept stroking. There was no response.

"It's got me!" Velma screamed with all her might. "The rock's got me!"

Then the stroking of Sara's right arm slowed. The words not heard so much as finally felt, she loosened her grip on Velma and turned to face her, their heads just above the water but obscured by rain and pelts of hail. "It's got me," Velma said again.

Sara took a deep breath and dove under the water and saw the wet anchor dragging across the bottom with the current. She tugged at the rope around Velma's ankle, but it was wrapped like a snake, binding her flesh. She swam to the bottom and tugged at the rope around the white blanket. At first it resisted. Then suddenly it pulled free, and Sara shot up to the surface with the rope in her hand.

She wrapped an arm around Velma's chest and said, "Float, Velma. Just lie back." Once she felt Velma relax, Sara began to swim in smooth, strong strokes toward the shiny grill of that parked Olds.

The struggle continued, and they were chest deep, waist deep, until breathlessly and finally they were ankle deep. Then crawling on hands and knees, they flopped down face first. Finally they rolled over, lying in the mud at the edge of the creek, their feet and part of their legs still disappearing into the water. When it was over and they had begun to breathe normally again, it was Velma who spoke first. "Reckon I am your Moby Dick after all," she said.

Long Sara would have laughed, but her heart hurt, and her head felt dizzy. And now that Velma was free and still alive and they were sitting at the water's edge in the middle of a storm, she was frightened. She realized that the peace she felt this morning was something she made up and that Velma was not crazy at all. The rock was a very real thing.

She wondered where a person might find the dividing line, the real dividing line, between what was true and what was on the edge of madness.

Sara considered all these things as she sat in the middle of a spring hailstorm, watching the trees flail wildly while a white bundle surfaced in the center of the creek. *Good riddance,* she thought, expecting the bundle to begin its path southward, caught in the middle of that current.

But the bundle didn't budge. It held its place. Then it began to move toward them, slowly but certainly. As if a giant wave were carrying it forward. But this was no ocean, and there were no waves. Just a swampy creek with a current that could pull a man under and twist him around in minutes, carrying him secretly away and out of sight.

They watched in silence until the bundle reached them, crossed over their toes, and rested there on the sandy bed between them.

Velma screwed her mouth up sideways as she looked down at the package. It was Sara who reached out, picked up the soggy mess, and placed it in Velma's lap, saying, "I believe this belongs to you."

The rain and the hail, the lightning and thunder, all rolled away. The wild wind died like a quick intake of breath. The sky opened up to a color more gold than blue, more pure sunshine than anything. And if someone had stood on the bridge and looked down, Velma and Sara would have appeared to be just two ordinary old women on a bright spring day with their feet playing at the edge of the cool water like children.

Eighteen

When Rudy drove up under the oak tree, Sara's car was parked in front of the house. The sun had just set, and the red stretched across the western edge of the tree line as far as Rudy could see. He leaned against his truck and took in the sky, thought about his visit with Rose, and looked at the roofline of his mother's old house—etched against the coming night—to prepare himself to see Sara. But no amount of red sky would prepare him for what he found when he walked inside.

The lights were on in the living room, but it was empty. He heard voices coming from the kitchen, low, so low he couldn't make out the words. When he crossed the threshold of the kitchen door, his mother was sitting at the table with Sara. It was his mother's face that shocked him. She was old. Not as if she had been growing old in stages, bit by bit over the years, but as if she had suddenly, unexpectedly grown very, very old.

"Mama?" Rudy knelt at her side. He took her hand and felt her tremble slightly. Her hair streamed out wildly around her shoulders. She wore the housecoat he had given her for Christmas. He looked from his mother to Sara and saw the concern in her eyes.

"Your mother has had a tough day."

Rudy waited for Sara to explain, but she didn't. "What happened, Mama?" he said, but Velma wouldn't look at him.

"I tried to get her to let me take her to the doctor, but you know what that means."

Rudy knew what she meant. Taking her to the doctor meant Velma would need to leave the house, the yard, and travel past the reach of the threads. He nodded but didn't leave Velma's side.

Sara leaned back with her arms crossed over her chest. "I guess if she's not gonna tell you now, she'll tell you later, but I suppose you should know a few things in the meanwhile. Just in case…" Sara let her voice drop because she wasn't sure what the "just in case" meant. She did know that after that day, anything could happen. *You know, just in case the moon turns blue,* she wanted to say.

"I guess the most important thing is your mother almost drowned today. Isn't that right, Velma?" Sara was still irritated with her for not going to the doctor like she told her she needed to do. She was old, for goodness' sake. She needed to be checked out by a professional.

"Drowned?" Rudy put his hand on Velma's cheek. "Mama, you almost drowned? What were you doing in the creek?"

"It was the rock, Rudy," Velma said, but it came out all whisper.

"The rock?"

"That's right. I tried to drown the rock." Velma looked

at him, full of old and sorrow and sorry. "Instead, it 'bout drowned me."

"What happened?"

"Sara saved me," she said jumping straight to the end. "She saved me, Rudy, or I would have drowned for certain."

The light outside was evening blue, but inside, on that table, there in the center sat the rock softly glowing in its red center. Rudy, Velma, and Sara sat in silence watching it, trying to peer into the mystery they did not understand.

"I'm tired now, and I'm going to bed." Velma gathered her legs beneath her to stand, got up from the table slowly, willed herself to walk.

As she turned away, Rudy picked up the rock, rolled it between his fingers, and called after her, "Mama, do you want to take this with you?" He held it toward her.

Velma turned, considered the offering, then turned back around as she answered, "No, Son, I do not." She shuffled down the hall and into her bedroom and left her door open. The bedsprings creaked as she climbed onto the bed.

"Now that you're here, I think I'll finally be going home." Sara rose from the table. "It has been a very long day." She looked around the kitchen, gathered up a roll of wet clothes that had been bundled and left by the sink.

For the first time Rudy noticed that Sara wore his jeans and shirt.

Sara followed his eyes, looked down at the jeans. "Velma's just wouldn't do."

"No, I guess not."

Rudy walked Sara to the front porch. "Can you tell me the rest of it?" he asked as he leaned against the porch railing. He took a pack of cigarettes from his pocket and lit one.

Sara had one foot on the first step when she turned to him. She wanted to say so many things to Rudy that had built up inside of her. But what she saw was the wrinkle between his brows, the worry in his eyes, and she relented a little.

"Tell you what," she said. "You offer me one of those cigarettes, and we'll strike a bargain."

And so a bargain was struck, and Sara took her place in the rocking chair beside Rudy. She moved it forward so that she could prop her feet on the railing of the porch as she smoked not one but what would amount to three of Rudy's cigarettes before the evening was over.

Sara rocked her way through the next two hours of unfolding the day's events. Occasionally the owl would call out, but Rudy and Sara ignored him. Sometimes Rudy would interrupt her with a question like, "But how did you know?" or simply, "Then what?" but for the most part he just listened to the telling. About the thunder she couldn't explain and about her desire to get to Velma as quickly as she could. She told about coming down that dirt road with the storm, the rain, and the hail and knowing she needed to drive right past the house to the edge of the creek.

"You knew she was there then? In the water?"

"I knew nothing."

She continued her story up to the sun bursting out and the new heaven coming down. That's the words she used, but they weren't her words. They were Velma's.

"A new heaven has come down," Velma had said when she had finally caught her breath.

Sara thought Velma was in so much shock that she turned to tell her to hush, but the light had been so bright that when she looked at her friend, she wasn't there at all, only an outline of light so bright that Sara had to shut her eyes and wait until the brightness faded into something easier to navigate.

"It was a day filled with fear and wonder," Sara said. "That's what it was. A day of fear and wonder."

Rudy looked at Long Sara leaning back in the rocker, her legs crossed and planted sturdily over the railing, wearing his jeans and shirt and smoking one of his last cigarettes. He wondered so many things, but he asked only one. "How come you never liked me?"

Sara glanced over at him briefly, had to remember for a moment that they had a history, one that was tattered at the edges. She had forgotten in the darkness of the porch, in the rocking, and with the low rhythm of their voices just who she was speaking to.

"It's not that I never liked you. I liked you just fine—better than most." Sara paused. "I expected more because you had more in you." She looked at Rudy again, at the shape of him outlined against the moonlit sky. "All that promise you had as boy just melted away."

She finished her cigarette, took her feet off the railing, and rocked forward to put it out in the can. "You just didn't make much of a man."

Rudy swallowed hard. Then finally offered, "I guess not."

For just a second Sara felt sorry for her words. Thought she might take them back or apologize, but she couldn't. They were simple, hard, and true. "I don't mean to sound cruel, Rudy."

"Cruelty not taken."

She reminded herself that he was here at Velma's now. That he moved in to help Velma in the middle of the crazy rock business. That he came to stay. "It's a good thing that you're here…you know…with her." She nodded toward the house. "I wouldn't leave otherwise."

That was the best she could do. She rose and walked down the steps.

Rudy followed her out to her car. He opened the door for her, and Sara turned, paused for the slightest moment, and looked into his eyes. "Rudy, you are not a bad man." She surveyed the threads barely visible in the moonlight. "And your mother is far, far from crazy." With that she got into the car and turned the ignition, and Rudy closed the door. He stood in the yard, watching her taillights disappear down the dirt road into the night.

He took the cigarette pack from his pocket and counted—one, two, three—and put it back, shoved his hands inside his pockets, and began whistling ever so slightly under his breath.

In the moonlight he could see the surface of the creek water moving ever so slowly, so deceptively, on its way toward the larger river downstream and then on out to brackish water where it would eventually join the Gulf of Mexico. He thought about where his mother might have been, how far she might have washed downstream before they found her. About the way things might have ended instead of the way they did.

"Long Sara to the rescue," he said quietly.

He wandered down to the water, crouched at the water's edge, and ran his fingers through the creek he was raised on. He knew this water better than he knew any woman. Knew all the curves upstream, the currents downstream, where the bream liked to nest, and where the clear spring waters bubbled up from the muddy depths. He knew three places where a man could place a cup over the edge of the boat and come up with something clear and cool and good to drink, not just dirty mud.

Yes, he knew all the secrets the creek had to hold, but he didn't understand today's secret. He didn't understand how it tried to take his mama from him. And he didn't understand the rock business. Or his feelings for Rose that had surfaced.

He remembered her fingers wrapped around that coffee cup, her holding it to her lips, and those green eyes glittering at him from above the rim. He didn't know what to do with that.

A mullet jumped once, twice, three times, making *plop, plop, plop* sounds and then disappearing into the creek again.

Rudy pulled his pack from his pocket, lit a cigarette, and subconsciously counted—one, two—as he replaced it. He turned away from the water and walked back toward the house. Tonight he wouldn't sleep soundly but would wake every few hours, listening intently for something unknown. Then in the ensuing silence, he'd think of first one thing, like Rose, and then another, like Long Sara and her final words. And finally, when fatigue and the sounds of the warm summer night, the window fan, and the crickets would overtake him, he'd dream of kneeling by his mother's bed, her white hair spread out across her pillow, and him saying, "Don't die, Mama," over and over again until she turned, looked at him, and replied, "Rudy, I done decided."

Nineteen

Rose had barely opened her eyes, had just poured her first cup of coffee, when Annie came stumbling from the bedroom. She sat with her hair in her eyes, looking at Rose through the strands. She wore pajamas Rose had loaned her. The sleeves covered her hands, the pants covered her feet, and amazingly she didn't seem to notice. She propped her elbows on the table, her chin in her upturned, pajama-clad hands, and asked, "Can we talk?"

Rose considered the request and wondered how only one day of working her tail off—cleaning the bar, washing the glasses, sweeping, and dusting—how just one day of hard work had set her up for what she suspected would come next: the request for a favor. Something larger than a new bike for Christmas. Something that would require Rose sticking her neck out. Far enough to get it chopped off.

"First," Rose said, holding up her finger, "I need some coffee and the paper. Second"—she held up another finger—"I need a shower." She dropped her hand, took a sip of coffee, and eyed the girl. "After that, you can ask me what you want, and I'll think about it."

"I didn't say anything about asking for—"

"You might as well go back to bed and get another hour

of sleep." Rose walked to the front door, opened it, and picked up the morning paper. She turned and waved it in the girl's direction. "Right now, kid, I have an appointment with waking up my way, and I intend to keep it."

Annie shrugged. It was a simple "have your way; I don't really care" movement, but it didn't move Rose, who sat in her favorite chair in the living room, propped her feet on the ottoman, and unwrapped the paper. She heard the girl push the chair back, slowly pad her way back to the bedroom, and softly close the door. "Smart kid," she said.

Rose was on her third cup of coffee, her second cigarette, and the classifieds when Annie cracked the door open again. This time she padded to the living room and curled up on the corner of the couch across from Rose.

Rose bent the paper and looked at the figure in a ball at the end of the sofa. Catlike. Annie's head was resting on the sofa arm. She watched Rose, unblinking.

"You know what I think?" Annie said without any invitation from Rose, who was amazed at how comfortable this strange little tattooed, pierced girl was in her home.

"What?" Rose asked and laid the paper across her lap.

"I was thinking that the thing that was after me the night we first met…" The girl waited a moment as if she was still thinking, but she never took her eyes off Rose. "I was thinking it wasn't a dog at all."

Rose shivered a little but managed to keep it hidden. She had put the incident out of her mind. Even after she and

Rudy had talked about it. Even after she had first hesitated and then told him the same thing, that she felt like it wasn't a dog, or at least not like any dog she had ever known. Rudy hadn't laughed or made fun of her in the least way. As a matter of fact, he had been more serious about it than she had ever seen him. And as he left, he kept telling her to be careful, to keep her doors locked when she was there alone. And she had felt like there were other things he wasn't saying. Things he wanted to tell her but somehow couldn't bring himself to say. He had mentioned that his mother had run into some peculiar business, that she'd had a strange occurrence as well, a threatening one at that. That was all the information he'd offered. There had been no further details. They had talked with Annie sweeping around them, cleaning bathrooms, stacking glasses left drying the night before.

"New help?" Rudy had asked with a wink, and Rose had just said, "Looks that way." Later she had told him the true sequence of events. About the shadow at the door, about the sounds, the girl, and the animal. She had gone on to tell him about her gun, the rounds she had fired, and how she had aimed dead-on.

Now the girl was bringing it up again.

"What do you think we should do?" Rose asked.

"I think"—the girl finally released her gaze on Rose, rolled over on her back, put her hands under her head, and stared at the ceiling—"we should set a trap."

She looked all of twelve in those pajamas. Other than the

tiny clover tattoo on her wrist, a tiny heart on the side of her neck, a tiny little nose stud, and the row of earrings glimmering in the light—other than all that, she looked like she should be watching cartoons and eating Lucky Charms, not have one tattooed on her.

"A trap?" Rose took the last drag on her cigarette and stubbed it out in the ashtray.

"You know, put out something it wants. Trick it to come, then trap it." She snapped her arms from behind her head and slammed her right fist in her palm. "Then get to the truth!"

"Sounds like a plan. Only problem is, why would you want it to come back? What would the trap be?"

The girl sat up, a cat in motion, quick to spring into action. "Oh, it'll be back. Whatever it was, I don't think it was just passing through." She stretched her arms into the air, her index fingers pointing as if she was full of Holy Ghost fire, preaching behind a pulpit.

"The difference is, it's either gonna come when it wants to, or it's gonna come when you call it." She leaned, elbow on the sofa arm, her head resting on her upturned palm. "And that's a big difference." Her voice dropped to almost a hush, lullaby soft. "And if it comes looking for me, I'd rather not be alone when it shows up."

Rose held her coffee mug up to her mouth with both hands, as was her habit. She held the mug there for a long time, only her green eyes visible above the rim. "Interesting," she said, but she wasn't referring to the plan. She was thinking of the creature on her couch and wondering at the fact that while sweeping floors and scrubbing dishes, the girl had obviously, silently, been deliberating other things in her mind. And Rose also wondered what big, bad things she had been running from. The kind that would make her think so strategically as to form a battle plan before a battle began.

"Is that the favor you wanted to ask me this morning?"

"Oh, no." She looked toward the kitchen, and Rose could hear her stomach growl from across the room. "That was something else."

"Grab yourself some cereal while I get dressed." Rose laid the paper on the table, put her mug down, and disappeared into her bedroom.

Annie uncoiled from the sofa cushion, walked to the kitchen, and began opening cabinets until she found the bowls. She took one and then began to open cabinets next to the stove, searching for cereal boxes. Nothing good, she noted, only Rice Chex and raisin bran. She opted for the raisins and poured out a bowl, happy to see that big sugary raisins fell with the flakes. She doused it with too much milk and then stood at the window eating and trying to talk to Rose in the other room at the same time. "I still need to talk to you. I need to ask you that favor." Milk dribbled from her mouth and spilled onto the pajama top, where she swiped at it with the back of her hand.

Rose yelled something from the bedroom that sounded like *wait* or *late*. Annie wasn't sure.

Annie had felt good all morning. For the first time in a very long time, she felt on the verge of what might be called a very simple, for-no-reason, uncomplicated happy. A happy born out of a sense of hope, out of standing free and safe in a sunny kitchen watching one little white cloud slowly making its way across the blue sky. But the happy was quickly replaced when Annie looked into the backyard. She moved closer to the window and then stood on her tiptoes, looking out.

"Rose," she called and then raised her voice to a near scream. "Rose?" Annie forgot about her hunger and even about the cereal bowl in her hands as Rose walked up behind her and said, "Move away from the window."

Twenty

Rudy heard Velma humming the low refrains from "Amazing Grace," her favorite working-something-out song. She and his daddy had been on opposite ends of the singing pole. Velma sang hymns; Joe sang country. Sometimes they tried to outsing each other, and it had been a funny thing in their little family—"Amazing Grace" dueling with Roger Miller's "King of the Road." Velma and Joe had laughingly played tug of war to get him to choose sides and help outsing the other. It was the only place in life that Rudy had always sided with his daddy. Boxcars were much more fun for a boy to sing about than being blind, no matter how it turned out in the end.

Rudy smelled bacon frying and coffee brewing and thought that it was a good way to start the day. He also thought there was no good reason to put his feet on the floor. That he would just lie there and soak it in. When he finally opened his eyes, he realized he was completely wrong. There was no humming, no bacon, and no coffee. He had been dreaming. He tossed back the sheet, and his feet hit the floor with quickness. His voice called out, "Mama?" with a lament but received no reply.

At Velma's bedroom door he pulled up short and stopped.

Velma was lying pale and unmoving, her white hair streamed out across the pillow. He approached slowly, knelt at the edge of the bed, and gingerly took her hand that rested on the sheet. "Mama," he said softly, willing her eyes open. "Mama," he said louder. "Wake up, Mama."

Velma opened her eyes and looked at Rudy with a slack face, a glazed look about her. "It's me, Mama," he said, thinking she had somehow forgotten him.

"I know who you are, Son." She closed her eyes. "I'm tired, but I'm not stupid."

Rudy smiled. Surely ornery was a good sign. "You've slept late, that's all." He released her hand, stood over her for a second.

"Well, when a person near 'bout drowns, they tend to sleep in just a little bit." Velma looked up at him again for a second. "Now, I think you need to go get some pants on, don't you?"

"Sorry." Rudy took his Jockeyed butt back to the other bedroom to get dressed. "I'll cook you breakfast, Mama," he yelled. He pulled on his faded jeans and a gray T-shirt. He slid his feet into sneakers without his socks and then headed to the kitchen. He stopped at the bedroom doorway where Velma was still lying in bed, studying the ceiling. "Well, are you getting up?"

"I reckon if you're making breakfast, I'll have to get up to be God's witness." She waved a hand in his direction, ushering him out the door. "Go on now; leave me be. I'll get ready."

Rudy walked to the kitchen and began to load the basket for the coffee percolator, counting scoops of coffee aloud as he did it. He looked at the clock over the stove, thought about his mail route and that maybe, just for today, he should call in sick. Maybe ask James Earl to find a substitute.

He opened the refrigerator and took measure of what his mother had and was shocked to see that it was nearly empty, like his. It had a stick of butter, a carton of eggs, a small package of sausage, and some milk. He closed the door and surveyed the kitchen counter. He opened the cupboards and found little there. There were canisters of flour and sugar, along with salt and pepper. Half a bottle of vegetable oil. Baking powder, baking soda, a small bottle of vanilla extract, a little can of cinnamon. There were two jars of preserves—one peach and one fig. And that was it.

It struck him how infrequently he had taken it upon himself to get his mother's groceries. He had brought her milk, a loaf of bread, a bottle of bleach, whatever she might have asked for at the time, but that was all. Now, in his mind's eye, he could see Velma making her way through the woods every week to the back door of Rufus's store. He could see her having to choose between bleach and flour because the walking home meant the groceries got heavy and the way long.

Rudy was so weighted with the image that he had to sit down. "Where have I been?" he whispered to himself. And he sat and ruminated awhile about that question. The words of

Long Sara from the night before echoed in his mind: *You just didn't make much of a man.*

Velma walked slowly into the kitchen with her face still too grayish white to suit Rudy.

She looked at Rudy slumped there. "Well, I see you didn't get too far in the breakfast making."

"Coffee's ready," Rudy said, thumbing at the coffeepot.

"Well"—she pulled out a chair and sat—"that's some progress."

Rudy got up from the table and reached for his mother's regular cup and a mug for himself. He poured them coffee, added cream and sugar to Velma's and just a spoon of sugar to his, and returned to the table with them.

Velma sat, silently contemplating the rock in the middle of the table, which she hadn't touched since she had put it there.

"Here, Mama." Rudy put the cup before her. "Just the way you like it."

Velma picked up the cup, slowly brought it to her lips, and closed her eyes as she sipped.

Rudy hated to see her this way. Wan. Lifeless. One thing his mother had always been was full of giggle and grin. Now she sat ashen, defeated.

"I'm sorry, Mama."

"What for?"

"For not being here yesterday when you needed me." Rudy looked at the closed fridge and back to the black coffee in his cup. "And for other things." He started to take a sip but put the mug down. "I guess I haven't been much of a son in a lot of ways."

Velma looked at him, squinted her eyes, thought, *Well, now.* Then she offered up, "You could've been worse, I reckon." She saw that didn't help any and added, "A lot worse."

"What were you doing yesterday down at the creek, Mama?" Rudy had been wondering if his mother had meant to drown herself. If it wasn't the rock at all but Velma deciding she was taking a quick ticket to the other side.

"I was trying to get rid of this." She pointed toward the rock. "I was trying to lose something." Velma looked down at her hands and folded her fingers together. "I can't seem to keep what I want or lose what I need to." Then she added, "I had four babies after you, Rudy."

Rudy's head snapped up and cocked to one side, the confusion on his face apparent.

"They all died. Every one of 'em." Velma began to cry softly, turned her face away, and looked out the window.

"Mama," Rudy began, but then he didn't know what to say.

"None of 'em even got a chance to grow good. It was like there was nothing left for them to hang on to."

There was an itch at the back of Rudy's neck. He twisted his head, shook it a little back and forth, and tried not to touch the spot.

"How come you never said anything?" He could feel the

bugs crawling, creeping up his legs, shifting from the inside of his skin to the outside and back again, leaving invisible traces. He shuffled his legs as quietly as he could under the table, tried not to jump up and toss his chair over in the process.

"What could I say to you?" Velma rubbed her nose, got up from the table for a napkin from the counter, and blew her nose hard. "You were a child, Rudy."

Rudy tried to will his legs to stop, twisted his shoulder up where the creeping crawled higher. "But later, Mama, when I grew up."

Velma sat back down, took a deep breath in and let it out. She took a sip of her coffee that had lost its heat. "I guess I was waiting for that to happen, for you to grow up, but it never did. Not really. So I just kept it to myself. And, you know, there's not much point now anyway." Her eyes watered again. "It's not that I'm not over it, 'cause, goodness, it's been thirty years or more. But it's amazing what holes little souls can make."

She sipped her coffee, tried to smile Rudy's way. "I just wanted some noise in the house, you know? Lots of feet and voices. Many children and grandbabies and more grandbabies. That had been my wish back then, that I would be an old, old woman with a multitude of kids about me." She stared over his shoulder and out the kitchen window. "But it didn't happen that way, except that I am an old, old woman."

Rudy and Velma sat quietly, circled by stillborn babies and unsung lullabies. It was Velma who finally broke the spell by pushing at the rock in the middle of the table while declaring, "What's done is done." With that she rose to make breakfast.

Rudy protested. "I said I would do it."

Velma made a *humph* noise as she sat a griddle fryer on the stove, poured a little grease on it, and turned on the gas flame. She got down a bowl and poured two handfuls of flour in it, grabbed the baking soda, pitched in a pinch while she talked over her shoulder, poured a little sweet milk in, and began to stir. "You don't know how to cook. Now, I don't mean that you couldn't make me a sandwich or something, but you don't know nothing about cooking breakfast. Not really." She laid another fryer on the other eye of the stove with one hand while she reached for the bowl with the other, then spooned the batter onto the hot grease. "Do you?"

Rudy looked at her, smelling the flour already sizzling, turning into something that would soon be slathered in butter, covered in figs, and melting in his mouth. "Not like you, Mama. That's for sure." He took a sip of his coffee. "I can make a great grilled cheese sandwich though."

Velma smiled. "Well, that should come in handy. Grilled cheese would work for just about anything. Breakfast or dinner."

"I know it works real well about two o'clock in the morning when a person has had too much to drink."

Velma cocked an eye at him and twisted up her lip. "Like I really needed to know that, Son."

"Well," Rudy said, watching her, looking to see if there

was a hint of color coming back in her face, but there wasn't. "Just in case you get a wild hair." He winked at her and watched her flip the hoecake after it had turned golden brown on one side. Then he got up, stepped out the back door with his coffee, and lit a cigarette. He stared off into the field. Then he leaned against the screen door, calling through the wire. "Mama, did you bury them babies?"

She raised her spatula and pointed toward the window and out to the open field where the barn stood at the southern edge. Then she resumed cooking without ever turning around.

Rudy looked out to the morning light gracing the field, the barn, the path down to the creek. Everything looked so peaceful. It was easy at this moment for him to forget about why he came out here to stay this week and about Long Sara's late-night story. It was easy to look over the dirt and the unplowed ground and try to imagine what was buried out there somewhere beyond the rising sun. The small remains of lives unfinished before they had begun. A brother or a sister or two. Maybe they would have changed him. Surely they would have made him a different kind of a man.

"Breakfast's ready."

Rudy stubbed his cigarette out in the dirt and carried the butt inside where he placed it carefully in the trash. He sat quietly at the table. His mother began to eat without asking grace. A tired oversight, and they ate in silence.

The strong drink of truth had been poured. Velma's words, all of them, still hung thick in the air.

"It's good, Mama," Rudy said as he watched her ashen face.

Then he decided too. His done things had certainly made their record known. He'd left a string of his life's mistakes just as easy to follow as his mama's threads. But the undone, those things that were waiting out there in his future for better or worse, well, he still had some say-so over them. And say so he would.

"Your daddy come to me the other night," Velma said in a flat voice between bites. "Not really like the other rock business 'cause we were in different times. I was now, and he was young, like when we first married."

"Were you dreaming?" Rudy took a sip of coffee.

"Nope, wasn't a dream. He was there. In the bedroom. That's the real reason I wanted to drown that rock." She looked up at him, wanted him to understand. "I couldn't take it anymore. Having a piece of him here and there and then not at all." She shook her head, and part of her hair fell out of its bun. "It's all been a little crazy. But this time I didn't go anywhere, you understand? He came to me. Now, Rudy, I ask you, how could that be?"

"Well, I don't know, Mama. I don't understand any of it. But maybe, I don't know, but just maybe sometimes love breaks through."

Mr. Eddie Springer stepped out onto the porch, wondering about things. More precisely and mostly he was wondering about Rudy. About where he'd gotten off to and what he'd done with himself.

Eddie was tired. He had been tossing and turning a little. He wasn't sleeping too well. As much as he hated to admit it, Rudy's presence, drunk or sober, had been a comfort. Just knowing that a person could be close enough to hear him call for help. Then he got irritated with himself for wondering what would happen to him if he fell or hurt himself without somebody being within shouting distance.

How could a man considering traveling to Machu Picchu be so worried about a neighbor being nearby? Strange what age does to a person. Sets him free of every regular demand and then turns right around and ties him down again—in fear.

Eddie got up and tapped on Rudy's door with a half-hearted knock. Rudy's truck wasn't in the driveway. He sat down on the porch swing, wondering what to do with himself. He didn't want to surf the Net, didn't want to read, and didn't want to watch TV. Not even the Travel Channel. Today he wanted to live the life he was in. The problem was, as he sat swinging and looking out to the road, searching for a sign of Rudy in the distance, he wasn't sure what type of life he had. Mr. Springer was wondering who he was now that he was no longer a teacher. What was left of him that identified him as something, as somebody, besides just that old man next door?

Then in the midst of his ruminating, Rudy drove up, and Eddie was so glad to see him that he stood up.

"Hey, Eddie," Rudy said as he took the stairs two at a time. He started to unlock his front door.

Eddie waited for Rudy to bust into one of his jovial recountings of the great adventure he'd had for the last few nights. Instead he seemed serious. And sober.

"What's new with you?" Eddie asked him.

Rudy stopped and turned. "Mind doing me a favor?"

At this point any favor that got him off the porch was a good thing, but he still said, "Maybe." He knew Rudy well enough to recognize there could be a sudden turn of events.

"I want you to meet my mama," Rudy said, then he considered the rest. Decided it was best to tell the whole truth. "Actually, I want you to spend the day with my mama. I've got to get to work, and she's out there alone and not looking so good."

"What's wrong with her?"

Rudy looked at him through squinted eyes. "She near 'bout drowned yesterday."

"Oh my."

"Well, yes, that's reason enough for concern, but I don't think that's the whole problem."

"What then?"

"If I knew, it would be so much easier to fix. Look, I have to get to work, and I'm already running late." He put his hands in his pockets and stared off in the direction of where he had come from. "Something tells me she doesn't need to be alone. Not right now."

❧

When Rudy drove up again in front of the house, Velma was in the living room. She wasn't expecting company and didn't want any. She had been pacing the floor, back and forth, demanding that the rock take her where she wanted to go. But the rock remained cold to her touch. And Velma went nowhere but back and forth on the path made in the hollowed grooves of that timeworn floor.

She heard a truck and went to the screen door. Rudy was slowly walking toward her with a man she didn't recognize. The man stopped, looked at her threads tied to the front porch. Rudy had his head down and spoke to the man. She knew what he was saying. *My mama's peculiar in her own way.*

She knew what he told people in public.

But Rudy wasn't saying that at all. He told Eddie, "Don't ask her about the threads, Eddie. Don't say a word."

"Well, that's two favors in one day." Eddie looked at Rudy and smiled. Rudy saw him then in the light of his mother's front yard. He didn't see his lonely neighbor. He saw the man, the retired teacher from Chicago. Rudy saw that he held his back up straight when he walked and that he had a gentle-man's grace that Rudy didn't possess and never would. Not like that. Mr. Eddie Springer had his own magic, but Rudy had been too self-absorbed to see it.

Velma watched them through the screen door.

"Good morning again, Mama," he began. "I'd like for you to meet my neighbor, Mr. Springer." He turned to Eddie, making introductions through the screen. "Mr. Springer, this here is my mama."

"Pleasure to meet you," Eddie said and bowed slightly.

"I wasn't expecting you." Velma stayed put where she was, not opening the door or inviting them in.

"Well, Mama, I didn't really have time to call, and look, here's the thing." Rudy reached for the door and opened it as Velma took two steps back. Eddie Springer remained stand-ing on the porch. Rudy kept talking. "Mr. Springer is on medication."

Velma narrowed her eyes; she could hear a story com-ing on.

"It's new medication, and the doctors don't want him alone. They want him to, you know, be watched for precau-tion because"—Rudy turned around, motioned to Eddie, and nodded—"because he has fits, and if he should have any allergic reaction to the medicine, then…" Eddie remained on the porch, caught between Velma's knowing stare and the lie coming out of Rudy's mouth. "Then he would have a heart attack and die." And with that, Rudy reached back, grabbed

Eddie by the elbow, and pulled him inside the house. "Matter of fact, Eddie, I think you should sit down right now." And he pushed Eddie into his father's old chair.

Velma watched all of this, put her hands firmly on her hips. "Son," she began, but Rudy interrupted her, talked over her.

"I gotta get to work, Mama. You know how you love me to work." He opened the screen, prepared to take flight. "Better not lose my job because you know I won't get another that lets me sing so loud to the radio."

With the grin that normally would melt his mama's heart, he jumped off the porch, clearing the bushes with one leap. He had started the truck and pulled out on the dirt road, honking the horn, before Velma could close the door.

Velma turned, crossed her arms, and cocked her head to one side, thinking, *Well now, what has Rudy dragged up in the house this time?*

Twenty-One

Rudy stepped into the dark, cool bar. When his eyes adjusted to the light, his heart took a little side step.

Rose was standing behind the bar, wrapped in the big arms of Dave, the beer deliveryman. And she seemed to be enjoying it. Her head leaned on Dave's shoulder as he softly whispered something in her ear. Rudy saw her head nod slightly. It took him a minute or two to register that Tom Scott, the pride of Echo's police department, sat at a table with the tattooed girl, who jabbered on and on about something. Rudy could hear her talking, could see them both out of the corner of his eye, but he couldn't seem to peel his eyes away from Rose. Strangest of all was the fact that she didn't even notice he was there.

"And I just kinda froze, like it was hard to breathe or to move away or anything," the girl said. "Then I called Rose to come over."

"And what did the man do when you called her? Did he have a reaction?" Tom took a sip from the cup in front of him.

"Oh, he had a reaction all right," the girl said, twisting a lock of her hair around and around her finger. "He smiled."

"He smiled?" Tom stopped writing.

"Smiled. But it wasn't like a 'Hey there, nice to meet you'

smile. It was more like an 'I'm gonna eat you now' smile, if you know what I mean."

The pale-faced ghoul out the window had definitely reminded her of something hungry and horrible. Like an old, scary movie some of her aunt's boyfriends loved to watch. Something bad and evil and, yes, hungry.

"I'm a little creeped out. After what happened the other night when I got here..." Annie stopped. Realized that maybe she was in dangerous territory with the police around and asking questions. She wished she had worn the ball cap that she'd shoved to the bottom of her backpack. Wished she had her hair in a ponytail or something, anything to make her look a little different. Not like her school picture that they might use for a runaway report.

"Creeped out?"

"Well, it was a very creepy smile."

"Where exactly were you coming from the night you showed up here?"

"Birmingham," she lied. "Bus station in Birmingham. Busted my butt just to come down and help my aunt for the summer." She spoke loudly so Rose could hear her.

Tom caught sight of Rudy standing still and silent near the door. "Hey, Rudy," he said in a loud and friendly way.

"Hey, Tom. What's new?" Rudy said but stayed frozen by the door.

Rose moved away from Dave, sliding out of his arms way

too slow to suit Rudy and too fast to suit Dave. Dave didn't bother to greet him.

"More trouble?" Rudy asked as Rose came out from behind the bar.

"Yeah." She stood in front of him, her green eyes locked with his brown ones. "Is your mother all right?"

Rudy's heart slipped back into his chest. "I think so. For today anyway."

"Come back later, will you?" Rose tossed her hair over her shoulder. "Maybe I can get Mernie to watch things for a bit, and we can take a drive."

Rudy wanted to say something, but instead he just nodded, looked once at Dave, who was leaning on the bar with his big, muscled-up, beer-toting arms. He was watching Rudy too, like he owned the place.

Rudy said his good-byes and stepped out into the morning sunshine. It was hot out, but it wasn't the reason Rudy was sweating. And it wasn't the reason his hand shook a little as he reached for the door. He started the truck and backed out of the parking lot. He wasn't the least bit moved by the threat of man or beast, but his heart bounced around over a woman. Now that gave him great cause for concern.

"Hey, Tom," Rose said from behind the bar, "you need anything else from me?"

"Just the truth about where this kid comes from," he said without taking his eyes off the girl.

Rose and Annie were both wearing poker faces. "That brat?" Rose said. "She's from Birmingham. Sister sent her to help me out a little, but she's more trouble than she's worth. You need someone to push a broom down at the station?"

Tom stood and picked up the hat that he seemed to carry around but never wear. "Nope, not this week." He walked by the bar and eyed Rose as he said, "Been knowing you for about four years, Rose, but I never heard you mention you had a sister."

"Yeah." Rose lit a cigarette. "We're not that close anymore."

"That's a shame," Tom said, brushing his hand through his short black hair. He moved his lips around as if there was a toothpick dangling there, but there wasn't. "It happens," Tom said. "Family trouble happens." He shifted his weight to the other foot and changed subjects at the same time. "We're gonna go over to your house. Take a look around. Look for signs of any attempted breaking and entering." He looked down at the hat. "Really wish you had called us right away, Rose. You know, from your house. Guy could be anywhere now."

"I know, I know. It was just instinct, Tom. To get out as fast as we could. I'm sorry, really I am. Believe me, if he's wandering around out there, you'll notice. He sticks out like…" She tapped the ashes and thought. "Well, just trust me. He sticks out."

"I'll give you a call if we find anything." He pointed his hat toward Annie. "Try to stay out of trouble. I got a feeling you've got enough of that on your side already."

"Yes sir," Annie said.

After Tom walked out the door, she looked at Rose. "Thanks for covering for me," she whispered.

Rose leaned close to her and said, "Lucky for you I picked up that big, bold-faced lie of yours. If I hadn't been eavesdropping over here, you would have been up the creek."

Rose signed Dave's invoice and put it on the counter. She refilled her coffee cup from the pot and went to sit with Annie at the table by the window. She dropped her voice as she spoke. "I guess you and I need to get caught up on some things," she said.

Annie nodded, looked over her shoulder toward the whistling.

"He's in the cooler and can't hear us." Rose took a sip, stuck her fingers between the blinds, and looked out at the road. All looked normal with the world. She dropped the blinds and turned her attention to the young face before her. "That was pretty spooky this morning." Annie nodded but didn't say anything. "The man looked like a menace, didn't he?" Rose lit another cigarette and blew the smoke away from Annie.

"Have you thought about giving those up?" Annie pointed at the pack on the table.

"Hmm," Rose said, ignoring her question. "Annie, have you ever seen that man before?"

"No, not exactly. Not him."

"What do you mean 'not exactly'?"

Annie toyed with the paper place mat on the table. "I mean I saw something. I'm not sure what it was, but it could have been him. Well, not to get all Hollywood on you or something, but I mean a number-one freaky-like movie freak. Like, unholy."

"Where'd you see this?"

"Something followed me. Must have been in Louisiana then. I was off the side of the road, heard something in the trees, and looked up, and there it was—something hanging there and watching me."

Rose tried to hide the shiver that ran up her spine. "Then what?"

"Well." Annie thought for a minute. "I ran for the road. Hitched a ride with the next car coming down the highway. But funny thing was, I never felt like I really got away." Annie tapped the table, then looked at Rose. "Maybe I do need you to make a call. To let someone know that I'm all right. That at least I'm alive."

Rose softened at the request, at the concern on Annie's face. "I imagine your mama would love to hear your voice. Why don't you call her yourself?"

Annie folded her fingers together on the table as if she were making a business deal. "My mother might love to hear from me all right, but my mother is dead."

Rose watched her and searched for signs of the big lie.

They weren't hiding in the circles under Annie's eyes, in the mass of curly, dark strands of hair, in the fingernails bitten to the quick. "I'm sorry," she said.

"It was a long time ago. She died when I was seven." Annie looked away, ran her fingers across the slats. She pulled one slat down and looked out. A blue Olds convertible drove by slowly. The woman driving was wearing sunglasses and a long scarf.

Dave rolled the dolly forward from the back and stopped whistling and said, "If you need me, you call me, you hear? Day or night, Rose, and I mean it."

"I know you do, Dave." Rose waved at him and waited for him to leave, then locked the door behind him. She returned to the table and sat down. She crossed her arms, leaned back to listen, and said, "Go on."

The light at the corner turned green, and the lady in the convertible drove forward and turned left, and then Annie couldn't see her anymore. She dropped the blind and returned to her story. "It was like this. My mother died suddenly, unexpectedly, from a brain aneurysm."

Annie didn't know what the word meant when she was seven. She heard it spoken high over her head by doctors, by her teachers in whispered voices to other teachers, to the principal, to the guidance counselor. Little by little she learned exactly what an aneurysm was. How to pronounce it, how to spell it, and how heavy it felt on her tongue. She knew everything about aneurysms a young girl could discover from the

Internet and library books. What she didn't know was how to take one back.

"My aunt took me in," she continued, "only she was much younger, not ready for kids or something." She looked at Rose. "She's not like my mother. Nothing like her at all. I don't think she's gonna be worried really, but just in case, you know." Annie threw her arms out in exasperation. "Like, I really don't want my face on a milk carton or something." Her voice filled with such frustration. "Maybe a phone call would help."

Annie brought her nail to her lips, started to put it in her mouth, but didn't. She locked her hands in place on the table. Back to business. "Maybe you could just let her know that, maybe, sorta, that I'm kinda working for you…" The sales-pitch plan trailed off weaker than she had imagined it when she first bounded out of bed so comfortable and so certain Rose would say yes. But that was before the man, before the police.

"Where'd you come from, kid?"

"Oklahoma. Tulsa, Oklahoma."

"It's a long way from Oklahoma to Echo. How'd you manage that? You hitchhike?"

"Just a little bit." She smiled. "I had some unexpected help though," she added, thinking of the woman from the truck stop. "Was able to ride the bus the rest of the way."

Rose leaned forward, put her elbows on the table, and locked her hands together under her chin. "Now, the million-dollar question is, why here? Why Echo?"

Annie flinched, unprepared. She started to get up from the

table, to not answer Rose at all. Rose pointed an unpainted fingernail at her. "Sit." Annie sat. "What brings you to Echo with dirty clothes, no money, and dragging that precious guitar of yours?"

There was no ready lie waiting for her. "I told you last night. I have business." She nervously lifted the blinds again, hoping to see a fire truck or a parade. "Personal business."

Annie figured if she couldn't escape the whole truth, she'd offer up a slice of it. Maybe a little truth was better than none at all. "Okay, okay. Here's the truth. I'm not from Tulsa. I've never been to Tulsa. I was raised…if you want to call moving from one dive to another being raised…just outside Dallas. That's where my mother's people were, but they're not there now. And trust me, you don't want to hear the long version of the story. I don't hate my aunt, and that's the truth too." Annie paused and felt too tired to go on. "I never did finish breakfast."

"I'll make you a pizza. Keep talking."

"She just didn't… I don't know. Look, I was one step away from being a ward of the state. She's always threatening to turn me over to them. She has just enough guilt to keep her from going through with it. Well, so far. She wasn't meant to be a mother. Never wanted kids. Ever. She still doesn't. She has other things."

"What kind of things?"

"Boyfriends." Annie twisted the strand of hair hanging next to her face. "She has lots and lots of boyfriends." She looked at the Coca-Cola sign hanging over the bar. "And you know, she's pretty, like my mom was, and she's smart in her own way. She's a nurse, I mean. It's not like she's a bartender or something, so there's no reason for her to be dragging up these stray men like she does. I mean, she'll have one in her bed and one on the couch, and…" The girl looked up at Rose, whose expression had tightened. Annie remembered who she was talking to. She tried not to look at the bar again, but she glanced that way in spite of it. "I'm sorry. I didn't mean anything."

Rose's expression relaxed. "Do you think this smart aunt of yours has reported you missing?"

"It's possible. To be honest, it kinda depends on what she's taking and who she's hanging out with. If she's suddenly alone and not high, she'll remember me and maybe make a call." She ran her fingers over the surface of the table. "She might feel like it's, you know, her responsibility."

"Was she alone when you left?" Rose lit another cigarette, letting Annie's bartender comment run off her back like water. Rose figured Annie didn't know how much smarts it took to survive and carve out a piece of this world from nothing.

"No, she wasn't," the girl replied. "She hasn't been alone for more than three nights since New Year's Eve…"

"That wasn't so long ago," Rose said, inhaling.

"In 2002."

Rose coughed as a cloud of blue smoke disappeared down her throat and couldn't seem to find a place to exit.

Twenty-Two

Mr. Springer sat upright in Joe's old chair. The chair didn't suit him. Mr. Springer was clean and lean. There was no wideness to him, no bulk or girth. He wanted to look at his watch, to see how long Rudy had been gone, and to try to anticipate his return, but that would be rude. He thought that Rudy's mother didn't look well, not well at all. "I think I'll step outside for some fresh air."

"Suit yourself," Velma said, not feeling the least bit gracious. She felt waterlogged and hopeless. And she didn't know what she was hopeless about, but it was there.

She watched the man get up and move to the screen door, push it open, and step onto the porch. He put his hands in his pockets and simply stood there.

This is just hopeless. She had gone to bed hopeless, had waked up hopeless. Then, before she could stop herself, she had told Rudy about the babies she had lost.

The man talked to her through the screen door. "You have some lovely flowers."

"Thank you," Velma said from her chair.

"I particularly like the roses. You don't see many of those around here." He paused a moment, watching her through the screen. "I used to grow roses, but I understand they don't do very well down here."

When she didn't respond, he turned to survey the yard and plants again. Finally, with nothing left to do, he sat in one of the rocking chairs. This time he looked at his watch. Rudy had been gone for only thirty-four minutes. It was going to be a very long day.

Annie placed a phone number scribbled on a cocktail napkin in front of Rose.

"This is it?" Rose asked.

Annie nodded but didn't answer.

"You think maybe I should know your real name so when I call, I can mention that you're here in the flesh?"

"Annabel."

"That's a little old-fashioned."

"Everyone just calls me Annie."

"After Annie Oakley, I presume."

"No." She sat on Rose's office floor with her legs crossed. "Annie, after the orphan."

"Oh." Rose fingered the piece of paper, tried to fashion a few words worth something. Then it occurred to her. "You never mentioned a dad."

"There was never a dad to mention."

Rose figured that was enough for her to rely on. *Orphan it is, then,* she thought and picked up the telephone. She dialed the number. On the fifth ring a recording picked up. It was the voice of a woman who sounded young, in a desperate, perky kind of way. "Hi, sorry I missed your call, but if you leave a short little message, I'll call you back just as soon as I can." Then there was a pause, and in a different tone of voice she added, "And if this is you, Annie, I've had enough of your crap, and you can pick up your stuff anytime. I really mean it this time. Or I'm calling the state. Suit yourself." And then there was a beep.

Rose opened her mouth, but what she had thought she would say wouldn't surface. Instead she said, "This is Rose McClarney. Annie's with me. She's working for me in my pizza place, and she's fine." And hung up the phone. She looked at Annie's big eyes. "I didn't say a lot."

"You said enough." Annie uncoiled and stood in one fluid motion. "That'll keep her from thinking she was skipping out on her duty." She put imaginary quotes around *duty.* "She just guilts out sometimes, you know, on how she hasn't done the right thing, made the right home, blah, blah, blah. Then she'll get drunk when a guy's not around and start crying and saying, 'My poor, poor dead sister's baby.'" Annie made a whining, crying sound as she spit out the words. She looked at Rose for a minute. "Her dead sister's baby. That's all I'll ever be to her."

"Why don't you get some glass cleaner and those big paper towels and lift the blinds up to the ceiling and wash those windows."

"All right." Annie walked out of the tiny office space that could barely hold the two of them.

Rose knew the girl needed some basic things. She needed a safe place to sleep, clean clothes, decent food, and someone who cared an inch. What she didn't need was pity.

Velma rose from her chair, walked to the screen door, and stood there looking at Mr. Springer. She finally opened the door and walked out to the far end of the porch and looked at her azalea bushes and the empty bird feeders. She didn't want to look silly to the man, reaching for her threads, kiting her way out into the yard. The birds would have to wait on her. She sat in the rocker next to Eddie Springer's.

They rocked back and forth for a while. Mr. Springer felt no need to force conversation with her. He had no nervous qualities that would make him try. They listened to the katy-dids humming, unseen but heard all around them. The hum was so strong Eddie thought his skin was vibrating. After a while their rockers took on the same pace and rhythm. And still they didn't speak. They rocked and listened to the earth, glanced over at the shimmer of the water's movement in the distance, catching reflected light through the leaves of the trees.

"I've read a lot of books," Velma said, offering up the words like sugar on a spoon.

"Is that a fact?" Eddie tried to hide the smile that tugged at his upper lip.

"It is." Velma realized she was still wearing her housecoat. It was a strange revelation, and she didn't know what to do now but to plow on with her story, sitting there undressed. "I've read *Moby-Dick* and that book about the old man and the fish."

"*The Old Man and the Sea,*" Eddie offered.

"Yes. That was it," Velma said. "But I always thought they should call it *The Old Man and the Fish* because it wasn't about the sea. It was about the man and the fish."

Eddie considered this for a moment, then nodded in agreement. "So it was." Then he asked, "What was your favorite book?"

Velma stopped rocking for a moment. That was the first time anyone had asked her such a thing in her life. Joe would see her reading, and he would ask, "What's that about?" and she would tell him, but he didn't really care. He knew they were from Long Sara, and he would tell Velma that Sara was just trying to change her, to make her more like herself. "I know," Velma would say, because it was true. But Sara had never asked her about them, so she never offered her anything. The truth was, talking about the books with Sara would have been work, and Velma knew that. Sara would want to rip them apart and study them, to have conversations about if they were good or not and why. And then the story wouldn't have been a story at all. It would have been homework. And Velma didn't like homework any more than Rudy did. Sara would have picked, picked, picked at her brain until there was nothing left for Velma to use.

"Well, it wasn't the fish stories and all that water." Velma began rocking again. "And there were some that were all about love." She glanced sideways at Eddie. "The romantic kind, I do mean."

"I understand." Eddie leaned forward a little in order to see around her and watch the water through the trees. *Mama almost drowned,* he heard Rudy say in his mind, and he turned slightly to look at Velma, to look at the color in her face. *That was only yesterday,* he thought.

"Favorite books, hmm? I'll have to think about that awhile." Velma ran her hands over her lap. "I don't remember all of 'em. Just some."

"I'm the same way."

"Really?" This sparked Velma's interest. She thought everyone who read remembered them all.

"Oh yes. I read a lot of books and newspapers. And now with the Internet…" Eddie threw his hands up in the air and smiled at Velma as if to say, "You know what I mean," but when he saw her blank expression, he dropped his arms back down and continued. "Well, you can't remember it all. You just can't."

Velma's rocking got slower and slower until it stopped completely. Eddie did the same until his stopped too.

"Did Rudy tell you about my rock?" Velma screwed her lips up sideways.

"What rock?"

Velma looked at him. "Nothing much." But then she told him, "I got a rock that helps me remember."

"Oh, I've heard of such things. A memory starter. It's a trick of sorts. Not like a magic trick but a trick of the brain. Short-circuiting your brain's wiring so the impediments to memory are bypassed and…"

Velma touched his arm. He stopped talking and looked at her. She had her brows furrowed, looking at him like he had lost his mind. "No no," she said as if speaking to a child. Without another word she reached inside the pocket of her robe and brought out her rock. The center of it glowed red as she held it out, perched on her palm. With her left hand she reached for Eddie's hand that rested on the arm of the rocker. His hand was old, like hers, covered in blue veins, sprinkled with age spots.

Before he could protest, she turned his palm over and laid the rock in it. "My memory rock. It'll take you places."

She moved her hand away. He looked at it, noticing it seemed to beat slightly, like a heart, on the inside.

"Well, that is, it'll take me places. Don't guess it can take you anywhere without me, and since I've got no memory of you, I don't imagine we'll be traveling together anytime soon."

Eddie leaned over, observed the rock, and ran his fingers over the surface. It was smooth, like a river rock, like something worn from the weight of water, and it was cool to the touch in spite of the glow beneath the surface. "How peculiar."

"Oh, you don't know the half of it." Velma began rocking again. "It was a birthday present from"—she stopped rocking for a moment and then continued, her toes pushing off the porch planks—"from a man."

"And it helps you remember?" Eddie never took his eyes off the rock.

"Something like that." Velma looked at him. "Why don't you just sit right here and hold it. I need to get some clothes on."

Eddie nodded. He was mesmerized by the color of the rock. And for reasons he couldn't explain, he expected to hear music emanating from the center. He realized he was waiting for it to play something harmonic. Something universal that would answer the questions he carried around in his heart but never asked. But there was no music. Only the slow, lazy sound of the creek in the distance, so low it was almost imperceptible, the low hum of katydids in the warm, high grass, and the occasional sound of Velma's wind chimes hanging in the trees.

He sat back in the rocker and pushed off with the heels of his feet, back and forth, back and forth, the rock resting in his hand. With every movement his eyelids got a little lower, a little heavier. In only moments the chair was still, and he napped deeply.

From a distance Mr. Eddie Springer didn't look at all like a retired teacher from Chicago but simply an old man who had nodded off on the front porch, waiting for someone to gently wake him or to call him home.

With a heavy sigh Velma sat in the kitchen chair. She was still tired. Just water weary, she thought. She had gotten herself dressed, tidied up her hair, and gone back out to the porch where she'd found Mr. Springer sound asleep—leaning back in his chair, mouth closed, the rock still resting in the palm of his hand.

While watching him sleep, she could study him a bit without feeling self-conscious about it. She had to admit he was a looker. Even at his age. Something striking about the narrowness of his nose, the cut of his chin. *He must have been a dandy in his day,* she thought and turned to tiptoe on those short, round legs back inside.

She had considered making herself a snack. But after sitting down, she decided to call Sara to check on her. If nearly drowning wore a person out this much, surely rescuing one couldn't be far behind.

"Hello," Sara answered.

"It's me," Velma said. "I'm calling to see if you're all right."

"I guess." Sara waited for Velma to say something more, but she didn't. "Are you all right?"

"I reckon."

"Well," Sara said, "I guess that means we're about the same and not sure we're all right at all."

"Something like that."

"I've got company here," Velma said.

Sara paid closer attention. "Company?"

"It's Rudy's neighbor. He brought him out here to baby-sit."

"Who's baby-sitting who?" Sara asked.

Sara's clock chimed the half hour. Velma could hear it through the phone. It was a deep bass of a clock, a grandfather clock that stood in Sara's hallway. Velma remembered it from back when she went places for no good reason other than to visit. "I'm not sure." Velma felt tired. And hungry. "Maybe we're watching each other."

Then Sara had a strange idea. It was a vision of sorts. She saw herself driving in her car with the top down, Velma in the passenger seat beside her, and her unexpected company in the backseat, with all of them laughing like they were eighteen and the world was laid out before them like a long, winding, never-ending highway.

"You know, Velma,"—Sara tried to figure out how to softly guide Velma her way—"I could come get you, and we could all take a ride. We could go out for lunch, maybe downtown to the diner. You wouldn't have to cook anything." She waited, but there was no response. "It would be so easy, Velma, really. Just once is all it would take to shake this thing."

Velma thought about her empty cabinets but shook her head no even though Sara couldn't see her. "I can't, honey. I know you mean what's best, but I just can't."

Then the line went dead. She looked at the phone,

shocked, then saddened. Not at Sara but at herself. She knew she had pushed her friend to the limit. And that the limits for Sara were changing. That Sara had been losing little pieces of herself. She got up and took the jar of peach preserves out of the cupboard, opened it, and then stood there with spoon in hand, eating out of the jar.

Sara looked at her phone, the line gone dead. "That was certainly a knee-jerk reaction," she said aloud. "I guess it evens the score for tackling her in the dirt." Sara sat in the chair next to the phone, waiting for Velma to call back. The window was open, and she looked out over the empty spaces of Echo on its eastern border. "We're too old for such nonsense as not speaking." She decided that something must be done about the situation, so she got up quickly, picked up her keys by the door.

She just didn't know what that *something* was.

Rudy was tired in a way he hadn't been in a long time. Normally he could outrun worry, and he could sing his way down the road. But today that wasn't working. The image of Rose wrapped in Dave's arms kept coming back to haunt him. That, and his mother's face when she talked about dead babies. Then there was that weird rock of hers. Most of this weird stuff seemed to have started happening when it showed up. Maybe he should think about busting it open to see what it was made of. Maybe there was a simple explanation for the color, something scientific they didn't know about. For all they knew, it could be a piece of a meteorite.

He drove from mailbox to mailbox, wondering about these things. He tried to practice "My Love Is like a Red, Red Rose," but even that didn't come out right. He usually had the voice for it.

Tonight he would take Rose for a drive, and maybe the two of them could talk about it. Could put some pieces of the puzzle together. Then he'd take Mr. Springer home and then…and then he didn't know what. Stay home alone? Go back to the bar? Or, maybe, just do the right thing and stay with his mother? Maybe keep an eye on that rock and the things that seemed to show up after dark.

Maybe they were all going just a little bit crazy.

Rudy turned the radio on, waved at a passing truck, and then pulled up next to the Johnsons' mailbox. He opened it and dropped off a power bill, a circular from Piggly Wiggly, another from Walgreens, and what looked like a real letter from someone named Pearl in Macon, Georgia.

Mrs. Johnson was coming down the steps of her front porch, but Rudy didn't wait. Not today. He gave her a wave as he pulled away from the mailbox. George Jones was singing about living and dying with the choices he's made, and Rudy thought about the same thing. Rudy began to sing along, and in just a little while, it was as if he and George were good buddies.

❧

It was 12:35 when Sara drove into Velma's driveway. She drove over two small groups of daylilies, narrowly missed a creeping wisteria, and just about ran into the bottom of the porch steps before she came to a complete stop. She got out of the car, closed the door, and walked up the stairs.

Velma approached the front door and looked out the screen where she could see the front bumper almost touching the porch railing. "Why, Sara?" she asked her and then again, "Why?"

Sara stood with her hands on her hips, her feet shoulders' width apart. Velma could swear she was wearing some kind of a uniform from World War II. But that couldn't be. Could it? A Wac's uniform. A Wac's flying uniform. "Sara, were you in the war?"

"Don't be silly, Velma." As she talked, she walked away from Velma and went over to stand in front of Mr. Springer, who hadn't moved a muscle. "Is he dead?" she asked.

"I don't think so." Velma pushed the screen door open and stepped outside. "Not yet anyway."

"He's got your rock."

"I know, Sara. I gave it to him to hold."

"Well, maybe it killed him."

"Now, don't you be silly." Velma gently lifted Mr. Springer's hand, but he still didn't move. She gingerly took the rock away. "The rock doesn't kill people." Then she screwed up her lips, thinking hard about yesterday. "Anyway, I don't think it wants to kill him."

Sara turned to her, losing interest in the man and the rock, and focused on why she came. "Look, Velma." She showed her the car keys, holding them out in front of her. "They're for you." Sara took Velma's other hand and placed the keys there.

"Now you *are* being silly." Velma began to chuckle. "You know I don't drive. And I'm not going anywhere." Then she looked at the car parked at the bottom of the steps and taking up almost all the small front yard. "Why would you park like that? Good Lord, you could've driven right through the house."

"Because we're going to have a picnic."

"Well, that's nice, but, Sara…"

"In the car." Sara took Velma by the hand, leading her to the steps. "Just like we were going on a real, live trip."

Velma flattened her feet out, willing them to be fat and full of gravity, to stick to the pine floorboards, and they did.

Sara turned back to her. "That's why I gave you the keys. No tricks. Nothing to worry about. And look." Sara walked to the edge of the porch, lifted a thread from the end of the railing on the stairs. "You can take your towrope with you all the way into the car. To the inside."

Velma stood watching her, contemplating. "Why would you do all this?"

"Because you are my one and only friend, Velma. My one and only. And if this is the way that I have to share something with you, then so be it. Today we'll take a little step. We'll take a ride in the car. Only we just won't be going anywhere." She opened the passenger side door, which faced the stairs. "Your chariot awaits, madam."

Velma smiled. She dropped the rock into the pocket of her housedress and clutched the keys in her fist and walked down the three stairs, took the green thread at the end of the railing, and slowly, ever so slowly, stepped into the car. Sara closed the door as quietly as she could, but the clicking of it still made Velma jump. She sat very still and stared straight ahead. Then Sara was beside her, behind the wheel.

"No tricks?" Velma asked her.

"No tricks."

"No hidden keys?"

"No hidden keys." Sara reached her long arm into the backseat, where she picked up a sack that said City Diner on it. She took out little boxes that held fried chicken, macaroni and cheese, coleslaw, and potato salad. She passed Velma a box and a tiny plastic bag with a to-go spoon, fork, and knife, salt and pepper. "Got you a really nice big slice of that apple pie they make. I know how much you used to love it."

Velma raised her hand, the one holding the thread, and

rested it on the window of the car. "That's good," she said. "I like their pie."

Her friend could hear the smile in her voice. And she knew she had done the right thing.

At 2:30 p.m. Rudy was delivering mail on the part of his route that included his mother's house. She only had the circulars from Piggly Wiggly and Walgreens, and he hadn't planned to stop. He could give them to her later. Stopping might open a can of worms he didn't want to deal with. He was concerned that Mr. Springer and his mother hadn't hit it off so well. That Eddie might decide, quite forcefully, to get in the truck and leave with him. Oh well, he was sorry if that was so, but he wasn't taking any chances with his mama. Eddie was there until Rudy could figure some things out. Just to give him time to think things through today and to watch until he saw some color come back into his mother's face.

"Maybe I should stop anyway," he mumbled under his breath, "just to check on them." About the same time, he passed the pine trees. He was so taken aback by the sight that waited for him that he forgot about stopping. There in the front yard, almost run into the house, was Sara's convertible. And if that wasn't strange enough, sitting in the car was Sara behind the wheel, his mother in the passenger seat, and Mr. Eddie Springer sitting sprightly in the middle of the backseat.

Rudy could swear they were having a party. Rudy put on the brakes and rolled until he was even with the mailbox.

"Hey," his mother said, waving her hand up high.

Rudy lifted his fingers and waved a less enthusiastic reply. He leaned forward as if another look would change the landscape.

Sara wore sunglasses and a white scarf around her neck. The breeze caught it ever so slightly and lifted it in the air, keeping perfect time with his mother's colored threads. Rudy thought Sara looked like a pilot, like she was flying over the Atlantic Ocean or some exotic landscape.

Mr. Springer smiled at him and lifted a glass toward him in salute.

Rudy decided then and there that whatever they were doing, they were fine. Well, if not fine, at least safe. Out-of-their-minds senile or maybe even drunk—which was highly implausible for his mother—but whatever it was, they looked happy. That was far more than he could have said about his mother when he had left her this morning.

Rudy honked the horn twice as he drove away. He had to get his route finished, get home and cleaned up, and get over to Rose's Place. Whatever story was developing in that blue convertible was just going to have to wait.

Twenty-Three

Rose and Annie danced around each other the rest of the day. Rose kept Annie busy and tried to keep herself busy as well. She didn't know exactly what to do with Annie. And she didn't know what they were up against, though, for whatever reason, they seemed to be up against it together.

Rose watched as Annie washed the windows on the outside of the restaurant. *It's keeping her busy anyway. Keeping her mind off things chasing her.*

Rose let out a heavy sigh as the image of the man's face in her backyard returned. It was a pale face—too pale—like a person who never, and she meant *never,* ventured out in the daylight. But it was the smile on that face that bothered her the most.

Rose moved from the desk to stand behind the bar, watching Annie, who sprayed and wiped with all her might. "What am I going to do with you?" Rose asked herself. "And what are you doing in Echo?"

Annie held up two fingers. "Peace," she said through the window.

Rose raised her fingers and returned her peace sign, but her lips remained a tight, flat line.

❧

Rudy stepped into the bar at close to seven that night. Rose was leaning on the bar and talking to Mernie Walker, who was no doubt drinking sweet iced tea, straight. Mernie was a fixture of Echo, its unofficial guardian mayor, and always busy looking out for the people of the town, down in the nitty-gritty where it mattered most. If Mernie had instructions to take care of something, come hell or high water, she'd see to it. That's just the way she was.

When Rose saw Rudy walk through the door, she moved to get her purse and freshened up her lipstick in the little mirror hanging by her office door. When she returned to the bar, Rudy was waiting on the other side. "Would you like a beer first?" she asked.

"No time," Rudy said and then added to Rose's surprise, "Not that there's a rush—or at least not a real rush. But I've got to get home to Mama."

Rudy and Rose looked at each other and laughed at the absurdity of a man his age saying he needed to get home to Mama. It was particularly absurd to think of the very single, skirt-chasing, cigarette-smoking, beer-drinking Rudy having to get home to Mama.

It struck Rose so funny that she had to wipe tears from her eyes. She then turned and said, "Mernie, it's all yours for a little while."

"That's all right." Mernie got off the stool and walked behind the bar. "It'll be right here waiting on you, just like you left it, when you get back."

"Hey, Annie," Rose said to the girl who sat quietly at the corner table. "Help yourself to the pizza. All you can eat." She added with a wink, "You've earned it."

The sun was just setting when Rudy and Rose stepped out of the bar. "Yours or mine?" Rose asked, and Rudy answered, "Mine."

They climbed into his truck, closed the doors, and backed out of the parking lot.

"So it's Annie, is it?" Rudy asked.

"Yep." She rolled the window down. "I made a call to Texas this morning. To an aunt of hers. She'd left Annie a personal message about picking up the rest of her belongings." She put her arm out, feeling the warm air beginning to cool a little.

"She doesn't look sixteen." Rudy turned the truck northward and pressed the accelerator.

"She's not. She says fifteen. My guess is closer to fourteen."

"Fourteen's awful young to be picking up your stuff."

"Awful young for a lot of things." Rose's voice trailed off as she watched the sky turn a misty purple. Humidity cast a hazy net over the town. "It's been hot today, hasn't it?"

Rose looked just as green-eyed good now as she did standing behind the bar in the late of the night. Even better. More touchable and real. For a minute he didn't know how to talk to her, felt teenage awkward. It occurred to him that this green-eyed, good-lookin' woman had sure 'nuff got a hold on him.

He pulled into the lot at the park next to the elementary school—the one he had attended as a boy. Just beyond the slides, the swing set, and the monkey bars was the Little League baseball field. White fence boards that read Piggly Wiggly, Red Man Chewing Tobacco, and Page's BBQ surrounded it. He turned off the truck, put his arm over the back of the seat, and turned sideways to face Rose. "I wanted to take you for a long ride—somewhere out in the woods to watch the lightning bugs." He winked. "But my neighbor is sitting up with my mother, and I think I'll have to collect him soon. From what I witnessed when I passed by there today, there's no telling what's become of him." He slapped his hand on his thigh. "Now, how about I buy you a hot dog, and you tell me what happened this morning?"

They got out of the truck and walked through the playground toward the baseball field. In the distance they could hear the pop of a ball. Rudy called, "High fly," knowing by the sound, without being able to see over the fence.

At the edges of the field, where the trees began, lightning bugs danced in the dark, lifting higher and higher into the trees. Rudy watched them and then looked up into the branches in the distance, searching for that same flash of something he'd been seeing. The thing he didn't want to tell anyone about.

Rudy put his hand on Rose's elbow. He steered her around the bleachers to the back of the hot dog line. He found he needed to learn to navigate his way around her without the accompaniment of background music and constant interruptions of drinks being served, of people calling out, "Hey, Rose," or, "Hey, Rudy."

As if reading his mind, she said, "This is nice. Being here with you, I mean. I don't really get out enough."

Rudy pointed to the hot dogs, held up two fingers.

They moved to the edge of the counter strewn with relish, mustard, and ketchup bottles. "Now," he said as he smeared mustard and relish on his, "tell me about your weirdness, and I'll tell you about mine. I'm beginning to get the feeling that they might be related."

"Could be." Rose put ketchup and mustard on her hot dog, grabbed a handful of napkins. Rudy motioned for her to follow him to the edge of the bleachers.

"Well, my weirdness started out when Little Orphan Annie showed up at the back of the bar, and then I'm shooting at wolfy-looking things. This morning it got a whole lot stranger. I had gone to the bedroom to get dressed, and then I heard Annie calling me to come quick and see something. I could tell from her voice that it was no ordinary thing. I mean, I don't know her from a hole in the wall, but that kind of fear you'd recognize in anyone's voice." Rose paused, thinking hard for a moment.

"Go on." Rudy put the rest of his hot dog in his mouth.

"I stepped up behind her, and there was this creep, and I mean a grave-digging creep, standing not two feet away from the kitchen window, staring at her." She watched a little kid step up to bat. "That's what bothers me most, Rudy. That guy didn't look at me. When I stepped behind her, his eyes never moved. He only looked at Annie."

"Do you think someone followed her here?"

"She thinks some*thing* followed her here." Rose lifted the hot dog and took a small bite. "I don't know." She fought the urge to jump to her feet and cheer when a kid's bat connected with the ball. He took off fast for first base as parents around them screamed. She forced her attention back to Rudy and the topic at hand.

Rudy took a cigarette from his pocket and lit it. "If that's the case, if the girl's been followed, I can understand why she's scared."

"This guy"—Rose took another bite—"ishnotnormal."

"I'm sorry?"

Rose swallowed and repeated, "I said, he's not normal."

Rudy's skin began to crawl. He could feel a thousand bugs run up his back and reach his neck. He shivered a little, closed his eyes, and forced himself to stay calm.

Rose put her hand on his back and made small circular motions, and he could feel the bugs begin to detach and fall away. This was new to him. Company had always helped, at least for a distraction, but nothing and no one had ever put the bugs on the run.

"Rudy, you all right?" she asked as she kept rubbing.

He looked over at her and smiled a weak smile. "Yeah, I'm all right."

Then he leaned over and kissed her. Like he meant it.

Twenty-Four

Velma sat in her porch rocker, watching the lightning bugs take off from the grass, rise and hover above the ground, small green lanterns flitting back and forth ever so slowly. "Not in much of a hurry, are you?" she asked, but the lightning bugs were oblivious. They simply continued their dance. It was just past twilight, and it had been an eventful day. She was a little tired by all the visiting and conversation. And if not full of peace, she was at least touched by the hope of something. Right now she didn't know what. It was just the seed, the sense that something good really might be on the way.

She had asked Sara to take Mr. Springer home on her way back to the east side of town. Mr. Springer, being the gentleman that he was, tried to protest, to claim that he would wait for Rudy. Waiting on Rudy could mean never or forever, whichever came first. It was just the way things were. Or, at least, had been. Velma had seen some signs of change in him recently, but they were early signs, to be sure. She would have to stick around long enough to know if the tide was gonna turn where Rudy was concerned.

And she hadn't been oblivious of all that chemistry going on between Sara and Mr. Springer. Mr. Springer had finally awakened from his nap in the rocking chair and with a big stretch and a smile had come to the edge of the porch and looked down on them as if he were the gentleman of the house, pleased that they had come to visit. Then, at Sara's beckoning, he had joined them in their car picnic without any hesitation. He had been delighted with his box lunch, delighted with the convertible, and more than delighted with Sara. "A retired schoolteacher? You don't say!" And Sara had lifted the lever to lean the front seat forward so he could step into the car. During the "ride" they discovered the many things they had in common. These included moving to Echo from other parts of the world and being retired from the same esteemed profession.

Velma had loved every minute of it. Of listening to them chatter back and forth about geography, and then moving on to history, and then to political science, and then off to discuss the current state of affairs in the nation. "Ahh," she breathed a little and put her head back, closed her eyes. It was good to finally see that Sara had somebody she could talk things to death with. It was just what Sara needed. All Velma wanted was the sounds of the coming night.

For a moment, but only the shortest moment, Velma heard music. She thought she heard it coming directly out of the sky. Then the air shifted. A breeze blew in, coming from the south. Without opening her eyes, she said, "About time you showed up," to the man sitting in the rocker beside her. He wore the same jacket, the same trousers, the same boots, and the same hat on his head. "I've had a rough time around here, in case you didn't notice." She turned and looked at him. He appeared too big somehow for the chair, yet it held him.

"Well, now," he said, echoing her tone for tone. "It's been a little tough to catch you alone of late."

Velma tightened her lips. "I was pretty well alone down there in the bottom of that water yesterday. You like to have killed me."

"I did no such a thing."

"Then your rock tried to drown me." She pushed off the floorboards hard, remembering and getting righteous.

He leaned over toward her, his arm on the rocking chair arm. "That rock is a part of you, Velma. As goes the rock, so go you."

She took the rock from her pocket. It came alive, the colors changing from red to green to gold to blue. "I think it likes you," she said. She held it out to him. "And I think you should take it back."

"Can't do it." He sat back in the chair and pushed his feet off hard from the floor, mimicking her stubborn streak. "It's not time for you to put it down."

"Sure feels like time to me." She leaned toward him so that they looked just like good friends sharing a deep secret. "In case you don't know, besides near drowning, I've had someone come looking for it. Tried to take it from me in not a very nice way—if you know what I mean."

"I told you Old Slink would be coming along."

"Is that what you call him?" Velma loosened up a bit. "What's more, that thing came in looking just like my son." She leaned back in the chair as if to make her point.

The man reached out and patted her on her hand. She looked down to see traces of light where he had touched her. The traces slowly disappeared as the man began to speak again. "He likes that sort of thing." His voice took on a confiding tone. "He thinks it's such a big disguise. If you look between the lines, Slink always looks the same. Just like Slink." He tapped her hand again. "I'm sorry you had a run-in though. I know he is a nasty thing."

"Well, he didn't fool me. It wasn't Rudy, and I knew it."

"Of course not. You'd know Rudy anywhere."

Velma became still. "So you know my Rudy, do you?"

"Knew you, didn't I?" The man took the hat from his head, ran his hand through the white hair. Put the hat back on. "Of course I know Rudy." There was a touch of sadness to his voice.

The lightning bugs climbed higher and higher and were now lighting in the trees. The breeze picked up so that Velma could hear the tinkling of her tiny glass wind chimes. She had three scattered out in different trees. Little pieces of glass strung together just so. Joe had made them for her the year before he died. She turned to the man and asked him, "Where's my Joe?"

"Right where you think he is."

The owl called out an answer from the trees, "Who-who-who."

"It's all very confusing to me."

"Just pockets of time, Velma." He settled back in the chair. "It's all pockets of time."

Velma worked her gumption up, leaned over, and held the rock before his closed eyes, shaking it. "See this?" she said, shaking it until he opened his eyes. "You know, my very special birthday present?" She stopped shaking it and leaned back in her chair, her voice lowering. "Well, I think it's making me sick. One minute I've got my Joe, and the next minute…"

"What?" The man's voice was full of liquid fire. "A gift such as this, a gift of time and remembering? What makes you sick is the forgetting."

When she looked back at him, she had to tilt her head up a little more, as if he had grown larger.

She tugged at the edge of the pocket on her housedress. "I don't know. I guess I feel that I'm in limbo, between what was and what is. And it's making me dizzy."

"Velma." His voice became so soft now, so smooth, that her eyelids grew heavy. He leaned back, closed his eyes again, but the voice continued spreading out before him. "Velma," he said, "you're caught right in the middle of what you have and what you want. Of who you are and who you could be." Then he opened his eyes and looked at her with a smile tugging at the corners of his mouth. "Saints in limbo." He winked at her. "That's what you all are."

Velma rocked and thought about what he said. The man stayed quiet, rocking beside her, and she could hear him humming under his breath. He appeared to have all the time in the world, not in a rush for anything.

He put out his hand, and Velma held her palm up, the rock ready for the plucking. But instead of taking the rock from her, he wrapped both his hands around hers and closed her fingers over it. "There was a very old story once told, and some tell it still." His voice had taken on that rumbling sound that she had heard before. "The name of the story was *Unus de Tribus Sanctis*. It means 'one of the holy three.' Seems you have yourself a piece of heaven." He crossed his arms and leaned back. "The big story goes that in the time before there was any time, no conception of time, no shutters in eternity, there was a great war in heaven. One of an age-old struggle for power. And the army that plotted against the King was overthrown and cast out of heaven. But three of the angelic beings that were kicked out grabbed a piece of heaven as they were cast down, trying to hang on to something they wanted to own and possess, not leave behind."

Velma was so still she thought just maybe she had stopped breathing, but she managed to whisper, "And then what happened?"

"Well, at first it appeared that they had succeeded. But not for long. The beings with the stones were hunted and tracked. Then the stones were recaptured and returned to heaven. But a new problem emerged." He leaned toward her just a little bit. "Or so the *story* goes, you understand. These tiny pieces had been ripped out, but heaven being the place full of creative power that it is, when the great angels returned them, they simply didn't fit. Heaven had already rebuilt itself." He leaned back again in the rocking chair. "So according to the old story, the three stones were scattered, and occasionally they seem to show up in a pocket, or on a doorstep, without warning or explanation. And they always have those old castaways slinking around, trying to get them back. But the rocks are said to serve a purpose, to bring good medicine for the soul, and when it's the right time, and without any fanfare—*poof.*" He ran his right hand slowly through the air. "Just like that they disappear as if they were never there."

The light inside the rock exploded between Velma's folded fingers. She closed her eyes again, shielding them from the rays.

"Velma." The man wasn't saying it; he was singing it. In that moment Velma thought the man should have a name too. She thought she might give him one, but then he called her name that way again—in melody, in song. "Velma," he said, "she's coming."

"Who?" Velma said, or she thought she said. It could have been the owl. She still couldn't open her eyes against the bright light. And then the light was gone as quickly as it had come, and with it, the man. Velma was alone with the rock, which lay plain and cold between her palms. The porch was deeply dark now. The wind shifted, came out of the north, and with it the sound of Rudy's truck as the light from his headlights approached in the distance.

Twenty-Five

Rose watched Rudy's taillights until they turned the corner at the signal and disappeared. She felt like a schoolgirl with a bad crush. And she wasn't that at all. She had been dealing with her feelings for Rudy from afar for a long time. She had determined not to be one of his conquests, one of the women who passed through his nights. And now, here they were, thrown together by strange occurrences with a common theme. She and Rudy and Annie and Rudy's mama. Weird appearances night and day. Just plain, all-out weird. But she wasn't going to let that or all the desire she had kept locked up tight come pouring out into Rudy's lap. He had plenty of that for the taking. So she had offered him lunch instead. Someplace public. No picnics in the woods. No moonlit walks down by the creek. No sir. Public. Daytime. Witnesses. Chaperones. That's what she needed. She turned on the adding machine on her desk and was getting ready to add up her week's invoices when the sound of music erupted from the stage.

She wondered who had the microphone. Even though her sign outside said Karaoke Night Every Night, rarely did anyone get up and sing on a weeknight. She guessed most of her customers needed a few drinks to warm up their courage, even when they knew every soul in the bar and were most likely blood kin to many of them. Then, as the night wore on, if people had a few drinks too many, Rose would have to demand their car keys and the microphone. They didn't mind giving up the keys but clung to the microphone, wanting to sing all night. Rose opened her office door so she could hear better.

"Hey, Mernie, sounds like we got a real singer in here tonight," Rose yelled out the door, impressed by what she was hearing.

Mernie sat on the stool behind the bar, sipped her iced tea, and guarded the cash register. "You might say that. You should come take a look at this."

Rose got up from her chair and peeked her head around the door and looked out across the bar.

It wasn't a karaoke singer at all. It was Annie up there on the stool, the microphone on the stand in front of her, her guitar in her lap. Her eyes were closed, and her heart was in her voice.

"Well, I'll be," Rose said and went behind the bar, lifted a Bud Light, and opened it. She never really drank much. It was one of the many choices that helped her make a profit in the business. "She can really sing."

"She can play too," Mernie said dryly and took another sip of her tea. "You should have heard her beating on that guitar earlier."

"You mean strumming it?"

"No I don't." Mernie was firm. "She was beating on it."

Annie's voice rang out strong. Tested. And on the backside of that voice was more experience, more of life's hard knocks than Rose wished she could hear. And she could tell that right now Annie was a long way from Texas, a long way from things chasing her and her not knowing where she would sleep that night.

Eyes closed, Annie finished the last verse of "Knockin' on Heaven's Door."

When she looked up, she locked eyes with Rose. Then Rose began to clap, and Mernie joined her. The lone man at the bar clapped, and the three people in a booth clapped. Annie rushed off the stage and straight out the back door.

Mernie asked, "Is she all right?"

"Yeah, she's all right." Rose nodded at the table signaling for another round. "If you don't mind, would you get their drinks before you take off? I need to get her out of that alley. She can shake off her stage shock inside."

Rose opened the back door. Annie was trying to collect herself, to wipe the tears away with her hand. "Hey, you," Rose said as she leaned against the wall next to Annie. "I figured you could play, but you didn't tell me you could sing."

"You didn't ask," Annie said.

"Yeah, well, I've been a little busy on other things that you might've noticed." She hooked her thumbs in the belt loops of her jeans. "I now see why you keep dragging that guitar around."

"How was your date?" Annie didn't want to talk about her singing or the guitar or how she learned to play alone in her room. She didn't want to talk about any of it right now. She twisted one of the earrings in her ear and waited for Rose to answer.

"It wasn't a date."

Annie didn't reply, and they looked across the empty, overgrown, weed-eaten lot behind them, then turned in unison and looked up and down the alley. They didn't see anything, but they felt something.

"Did you hear something?" Rose asked.

"I don't think so." Annie thought of her first night, of the animal in the alley, and the man in the backyard the next morning. "Want to go inside?"

"Yeah, why don't we do that." Rose opened the door, stood back, and waited for the girl to enter. She looked over her shoulder, squinted into the darkness at both ends of the alley before she stepped inside.

As the door closed, a figure stepped out of the shadows at the corner of the building. If Annie and Rose had turned around, they would have seen him outlined there against the dying light of day. But they didn't, and the shape disappeared back into the shadows.

Twenty-Six

Rudy's truck drove into the dark yard. Out of habit he parked where his daddy used to, there beneath the oak tree. He cut the lights and turned off the engine. When he stepped onto the porch, he was startled to see Velma in the darkness.

"Mama?" He put his hand over his heart and leaned against the railing. "What are you doing out here in the dark?"

"Did you see him?"

"Who?" Rudy walked to the screen door, peeked inside. He didn't see anyone.

"Who? Who? Who do you think? The man!" she said, shaking the rock at him.

"You're funny, Mama. Why are all the lights off in the house?"

He reached his hand inside the door and turned on the porch light. Velma flinched when he did, tossed her arm up in front of her eyes. "Son, what are you thinking? Turn that off before you blind me. Besides, it'll draw the moths."

"Okay, fine. I'll turn on the inside light then." He walked into the living room and turned on the lamp next to the porch window. The light spilled out in a yellow glow through the pane, casting rocking-chair shadows against the edge of the porch. Rudy walked out and sat down on the porch swing, one arm resting across the back.

"You never did like the dark."

"I still don't, Mama." He took out his cigarettes and lit one.

"Why is that?" Velma waited for an answer. When he didn't offer one, she pressed on. "Well, do you know, or don't you?"

"Yes ma'am, I think I do." Rudy smoked and pushed the swing, but he still didn't answer her.

"You're a stubborn old mule, boy, even if you are my joy." Velma shook her head and opened her hand to look at the rock, content and colorless.

"It's lonely, Mama," Rudy said. "The dark just feels so lonely."

The dark was different for Velma. It was a blanket of quiet and simple dreams. Or at least it used to be. And it was for so many years with Joe by her side. Night after night, them together, nesting in a sea of dark. It was a good thing.

"Rudy, I wish I could have made things different for you somehow." She looked at the man-child of hers sitting on her porch. He was a good-looking kid, and he had become a good-looking man. Movie-star good looks. Not the kind you see now on the movies or television. She didn't understand those men. They all looked like boys to her. But he had a Cary Grant kind of look. A little rougher around the edges but similar to that. But now those looks were on the verge of fading. And she could see—when she looked under the rug of love she kept him wrapped in—that with the drinking and the smoking and those late nights of carousing with God only knew who, well, it was a wonder he hadn't caught that horrible disease there was no cure for. But he still had enough looks and good sense to turn that boat around. Okay, maybe not good sense. Maybe looks and luck. She didn't believe in luck for herself, but Rudy had a touch of that old "seven come eleven" kinda luck. Gamblers' luck really. The kind of luck that could run dry in a hurry. Leave a man desperate or dead. She knew about that close enough.

"Sometimes you remind me of my daddy," Velma said and wished she could snap it back.

"Oh really?" he stopped rocking and leaned forward, his elbows on his knees, looking at her narrowly through smoky, squinted eyes. "You told me your daddy was dead. That you never knew him."

A breeze drifted toward Velma; the wind chimes tinkled in the trees. For the first time Velma got a scent of man cologne. In the lazy light she noticed that Rudy was wearing a button-down shirt, with cuffs turned up neatly on his arms, and that he was wearing new jeans.

"You had a date tonight, and you still came out here? This early?"

"Oh no. You're not changing the subject." Rudy got up and flicked the cigarette into the yard.

"You're gonna have to pick that up."

"Yes ma'am, I will." He looked across the dimly lit porch at his mother's profile. "Tell me about this daddy you never knew."

Velma hesitated. She rolled the rock around in her hand. "I knew him," she said quietly. "There just wasn't much worth knowing."

"And that's who I remind you of." Rudy sat back down on the swing.

"Not in those ways." She got up and moved to sit next to him. He slid over, adjusted his weight for her. She patted him on the knee, then sat back and looked at him. "Not in those ways," she repeated. "But in others. I guess in some things it must be obvious to you that you don't take after me, and you don't take after your daddy."

"To tell you the truth, Mama, I never thought about it much."

"Well, that's Mama business anyway. I can tell you this: you got my daddy's charm. You got that kind of magnetism that just draws stuff to you."

"Like women," Rudy said with a slight smile.

"Oh, I'm sure that's part of it, but here's the thing, that kind of gift." Velma wanted to pace, to wring her hands a bit, to walk back and forth on the porch, but she knew that she had to sit still to try to keep Rudy calm. If she started pacing, he might have one of those bug episodes, and she wasn't in the mood for that.

"Your granddaddy didn't do much with it. Matter of fact, it's what got him killed. And I never should have been put through that."

"Through what?"

"The ruination of everything, of my life. What it brought on. His trouble. It started like a train reaction."

"Chain reaction, Mama," Rudy corrected her.

"No, weren't no chain; it was a train reaction." Velma shoved her fist forward, trying to show what she meant. "He got killed, and then everything happened all at once like a steam engine off the tracks and going crazy. People came and took what little we had, and it killed Mama but not for three more years. Her heart broke in half, and she died." Velma touched the tip of her white tennis shoe to the porch and pushed slightly. "I was eight years old then. Solid orphan."

"I know, Mama." Rudy got up from the swing, put his hands in his pockets, and paced the floor. "You told me over and over. You were an orphan." He patted his pocket a few times and counted the cigarettes in the pack, put his hands back in his pockets. "They sent you to live with some aunt and uncle you didn't know."

"Well, because of him—Daddy, that is—we'd been pretty much outcasts is what I could get out of Mama, but you can't get much from anybody when you're eight and asking questions. Reckon people didn't like all his drinking and his gambling and running up debts we couldn't pay. Apparently, every good start they tried to give him, he just let it slip away. Guess they got tired of it—all of them, from both sides of the family, so we became just outsiders, you know. Living on his whims and bad fortune. But that's what I picked up later, you know, the way that children overhear things they shouldn't."

"Why is all this on your mind tonight?" Rudy crossed his arms, held them tightly, and hung his head down, his chin almost touching his chest.

"I don't know. I really don't. I guess I was thinking about you. Wondering what was going to happen next."

Rudy thought of Rose, of that kiss at the ballpark, and he grinned in the dark in spite of himself. He knew what he would like to have happened next. But when he had taken Rose back to the bar, she had said something about how they could maybe have lunch sometime real soon and figure out what to do with their common problem. *Lunch?* He didn't do lunch with women. He did other things. Lunch would be a new one for him. For the first time tonight he remembered that he had dropped Eddie Springer off to sit with Velma.

"Mama, where is Mr. Springer?" Rudy went to the screen door and peered through it like he expected Mr. Springer to be sitting where he left him this morning, like he had just overlooked him.

"Sara took him home."

"And speaking of that"—Rudy pointed to the place where Sara's Olds had come to rest at the foot of the porch stairs—"what in the hell was she thinking, almost driving through the house?"

"She was picking me up, and you know you aren't to be cussing around me."

"But, Mama," Rudy started to protest until she rolled her eyes at him. "Sorry, sorry, but you have to admit… Picking you up? For what? Where did you go?" For just a second there was hope in his voice that Velma might actually have tooled off with Sara in the car and made it down the road.

"For a picnic."

Rudy remembered the scene, the sunshine, the three of them waving, laughing, and drinking something. "In the car?"

"That's right. In the car." Velma walked past him and into the house, talking as she went. "And it was lovely." She dropped the rock inside her dress pocket, patted it, and whispered under her breath. "You and me's got business. But first things first."

Rudy looked out into the woods, then down to the water. There was nothing on the horizon, nothing out of the ordinary that he could see or hear. He walked down the porch steps, walked quietly around the south side of the house, around the rosebushes and the wisteria vine that was now six feet high and just starting to bloom, and stood in the back looking out across the field. The crickets were chirping loud enough to drown out anything else that might even think of competing with them. Everything appeared normal. He checked out the back of the house, walked up the steps and through the back door.

Velma sat at the kitchen table, and she gave him a little wave. It was a bit of a little-old-lady wave. She had a plate of cold fried chicken, macaroni and cheese, and a huge slice of apple pie parked in front of her. A glass of milk sat beside the plate. She smiled at Rudy and then took a bite of the pie. She ate it along with her leftovers like it was a vegetable, not a dessert. And she hadn't even asked him if he was hungry. Had actually sat down and started eating without him.

The sight of his mother with her mouth full of pie made it all come flooding back to him. In one day he had found out about the lost babies, the murdered grandfather, the pasty pervert in Rose's backyard; had seen Dave holding Rose; and had heard about how he hadn't turned out to be much of a man. And now his mother had plopped down to eat—just as sassy as you please—without even inviting him to the table.

"Mmm-mm," Velma said as she swallowed another bite of pie, took a sip of her milk, and looked up at him with a childlike smile.

Out of all the peculiarities in the day, in Rudy's book his mother eating everything in sight and not offering him one single bite...well, that topped them all.

Annie had gotten over her butterflies and tears. She'd gotten so far over them that she was now wolfing down the largest cheeseburger the City Diner offered, a large plate of fries, and a Coke, talking nonstop all the while as she shoved food into her mouth. She chattered all about music, and who she loved and why, and who she hated and why, and how she would love to open for U2 on tour. When she stopped long enough to look at Rose's expression, she added, "No, really, I mean it." Then after stuffing another fry into her mouth, she said, "But not solo, of course. With my band."

"Of course," Rose said and took another sip of her coffee. "An all-girl band, I suppose."

It was Annie's turn to make a face. "That has so been done." She sipped the Coke through the straw until the glass was empty. "I mean, not that it wasn't cool and everything in your day, but it's really over. I was thinking a mixed band. Totally mixed. You know, Asian American, Mexican American, Euro American, African American, Native American."

"Kinda like the Village People, huh?"

"Uh, no." Annie twirled a piece of her hair around her fingers. "It will be totally visual but very *not* Village People. Give me a break. I'm talking about real music. I'm talking about opening for U2. Be serious."

Rose smiled. "Well, of course if that's the case, you left out the Irish American."

Annie rolled this over in her mind a bit. "I met all the others in school. I don't know any Irish Americans."

"Well," Rose said, "you do now."

"Oh." Annie leaned over and stared at her face long and hard.

"What are you looking for?"

"Signs. You know. Genetic things. That DNA stamp."

Annie sat back, a little more satisfied. "At least that way I'll recognize your type."

Rose thought Annie had the strangest combination of things. The old with the new. She was part this world and part the past and part the future and anything but standard for a girl at whatever age she really was. "I don't think it's politically correct to say 'type,' Annie."

At that Annie grinned in such a way that Rose had another flash of déjà vu.

"Oh, I'm not worried about being PC. I just want to be sure if I see the right face dragging a set of drums behind him, I can say,"—Annie rose just a little in the booth and took on a more powerful voice—"'Hey, you Irish American dude with the drums. Yeah, that's right, I'm talking to you. Wanna try out for my band?'" Annie relaxed again and smiled at Rose.

"So you're gonna be the leader of this band—The Americans—are you?"

"The New Americans," Annie corrected her. "And absolutely." She tapped her finger on the menu picture of a milk shake with whipped cream on top. "You did say to save room for a chocolate milk shake, right?"

Rose waved at Wanda to come over. "So what's your hyphen, Annie? What kind of American are you going to be?" But she didn't wait for her to answer. "Hey, Wanda, honey, I know you're ready to call it a night, but this hardworking girl thinks she'd like a chocolate milk shake."

"I'd like to see where she's gonna put it after what I've seen her eat. But if she wants a milk shake, she's got a milk shake coming."

Annie kept talking after the milk shake arrived. Rose played with her cigarette that she wasn't allowed to light in the diner. Annie took the hint and asked for the rest of her milk shake to go. The two of them wandered into the late-night air.

The midnight birds were calling. They were the strangest things. In the middle of the night, they woke up in the dark and called out to one another, chirping like it was daybreak. Then they would settle down and go to sleep again. "I like 'em," Annie said as she got into the car.

Rose didn't have to ask her what she was referring to. She knew.

They drove to Rose's in silence with the car window down, Rose smoking a cigarette and Annie drinking the milk shake. They didn't turn on the radio, but they didn't talk either. They soaked up the humidity, listened to the crickets chirping in the grasses while they waited at a stoplight. The sound of night birds singing followed them all the way home.

They pulled up at the house with the palm trees out front and the lights shining on them. It looked like a happy home. A small but well-kept happy home. And again, Annie felt so relieved to be here. So happy to be able to go inside, knowing that what waited for her was clean and orderly—and didn't have yet another new, unexpected boyfriend who had just moved in.

She had looked at Rose, caught the profile of her Irish

American face in the darkness—the sharp nose, the tilt of the chin, the flashing eyes, that long, dark hair. Rose could have boyfriends and men by the dozen, but Annie knew from hanging around for just a little while that Rose wasn't that type.

Twenty-Seven

Rudy heard Velma humming "Amazing Grace," smelled coffee brewing and biscuits baking. But then he thought he was dreaming again. He opened his eyes, trying to remember what day it was. *I'm the rural-route man,* he thought and rolled over and closed his eyes. *No need to rush.* Then the image of Rose, the story of her being stalked by a stranger, woke him up. He wondered if she was safe or if she'd had another visit from some unexpected man or beast in the night. Rudy rolled out of bed and reached for his jeans. Right now Rudy wished he had his old Levi's handy—not brand-new ones. He wanted the ones so worn they were like a second skin. He stumbled slightly into the kitchen and looked at his mama, who had been up since sunrise.

"Look at that." She put one hand on her hip, pointed a butter knife at him. "You look just like you did when you were a little boy. I swear, just about the same. Same sleepy face."

Rudy saw the biscuits on the stove, the steam still rising from them, and the butter melting on the tops.

"Coffee?" Velma asked, and Rudy nodded a sleepy head. He glanced at the stove, searched for any sign of grits and eggs or a piece of meat. Velma caught his roaming eyes. "What you see is what you get. There're some figs for those biscuits if you want them." She pointed to the jar of figs on the table, then handed him a cup of coffee as he took a seat.

"This is just fine, Mama. This is great," Rudy said and meant it.

Velma took her coffee and sat in front of him. Rudy took a big bite of a biscuit and declared with a full mouth, "Nobody makes a better biscuit than you."

"Well, I hope it suits you, because I've run dry of everything. And I do mean everything."

"I meant to pick some things up for you." Rudy took another huge bite, reached for the fig jar. "I'll go to the store today on my way home."

"Now, Rudy,"—Velma reached for a biscuit, sliced it open, and spooned figs in the center of it—"I've been managing for a long time."

"It's okay, Mama." Rudy took a sip of his coffee, leaned over, and touched her on the back of her hand. "I should have taken more notice."

Velma spooned another bit of figs onto a second biscuit and took a bite. She didn't argue with Rudy. Taking some notice would do him good. "Rudy, I've got a confession to make." She lifted her cup and sipped. "I think I was just a little…just a pinch tipsy last night."

"Mama, have you been nipping at Daddy's bottle?" Rudy pointed his thumb over his shoulder to the cupboard above the refrigerator.

"Don't be silly. You know better than that. Like I said, I was kinda like tipsy. Kinda. Maybe just like it."

"Well, that would explain a few things," Rudy said, thinking about the fried chicken.

"It was 'cause of the man," Velma said.

"Everything is 'cause of the man."

"You know, the man who gave me the rock." She lifted the rock from her apron pocket and held it on her open palm.

"What other man is there at this point, Mama?" Rudy reached for another biscuit. "I just never get to see him."

"Well, he was here. Right there on the porch."

"He was on the porch when I was out there with you?"

"No no. If he had been, you would have seen him."

"I'm not so sure."

"I'm not crazy, Rudy." She turned to face him. "He's a real man. Like I said, I'm not crazy."

"Mama, I have never thought or said to anybody that you were crazy. Peculiar maybe, but not crazy." Rudy took another bite. "Did he show up in a car this time?"

"Well, he doesn't exactly come around like that." Velma twisted her lips to the side while she was thinking. "It's not the way he travels. I don't think he's a human being."

"Thought you said he was a real man. Mama, make up your mind."

Velma tried to do that, to make up her mind. "He is a man. But he's not like another man. You might say he's not from around here." And with this she giggled a little at herself.

"So let me get this straight." Rudy stretched his arms above his head and yawned big, stood to pour himself another cup of coffee. "So you and this alien were nipping something last night that made you tipsy."

"I'm not a nipper, Rudy. And he's not an alien."

"How do you know? You said he's not from here. He might be from Mars."

"Rudy, I watch television, so I think I would know what an alien might look like." Velma dropped the rock back into her pocket, ran her finger around the edge of the cup. "Well, you know what I mean. From what those UFO people claim—but now that's just crazy talk."

"Now, Mama. You're telling me my idea is crazy, but talking about a man who gave you a rock that makes you flip-flop through time like a fish out of water—that's not supposed to sound crazy?"

"It is what it is. I was trying to tell you that I think I was punch-drunk last night."

"Tipsy," Rudy corrected her.

"Yes, tipsy." She took another sip of the coffee and a bite of the biscuit that had gone cold. "He has that sort of effect on you. Makes you not worry so much."

"Then you had to be sure 'nuff tipsy last night, because normally you worry about everything under the sun." Rudy looked up at the phone on the kitchen wall. "Can I make a call?"

"What kind of question is that? You don't have to ask me if you can make a call unless you're calling Japan."

"Why would I call Japan, Mama? I don't know anybody in Japan." Rudy had already picked up the phone and started dialing the number he knew by heart. The bar phone rang without an answer. Finally he hung up and dialed information. "Echo, Florida," he said.

Velma sipped her coffee, listening intently. She got up from the table, walked nonchalantly around to the kitchen window, pretended to be looking at her flowers.

"Rose...," Rudy started to tell the operator. He stopped midsentence. He didn't even know Rose's last name. At least he couldn't remember it. "Never mind," he said and replaced the receiver. He'd been amazed lately at the things he didn't know.

Velma twisted up her lips. Thought about how to pose her questions about the phone number, the new jeans, and the pressed shirt.

Rudy's cockiness had paled a little.

She wondered who to credit for that. "You lose a tail feather?" she asked, which was exactly what she wanted to say, but it didn't translate very well.

"What?" Rudy asked, but he didn't really hear her. How could he not know Rose's last name? How could he ask her after all those nights of standing in the bar talking to her?

"Just wondering what you been up to lately," Velma said,

but what she really meant was what women was he hanging around. She put her hand into her pocket, wrapped her fingers around the rock. She was thinking she had figured something out. *"A piece of heaven,"* the man had said.

Rudy looked at Velma, studied her face, and was happy to see that her color had returned. As a matter of fact, it was the first time he'd really looked at her all morning, and dang if she didn't look younger. Seriously younger. As if ten years had been rewound.

She knew what he saw, the mystery. That bright light that had been in her hands. It had disappeared, and when she woke up this morning, she had it figured out. Like the answer had come to her while she was sleeping. She knew where the light went—inside of her. "I got this here rock," Velma said, lifting it from her pocket and holding it up to Rudy.

"Yes, Mama, I know about the rock, but—"

"You don't understand." She put the rock back into her pocket. "I've got the rock, and it's got me, and it's a piece of heaven."

"I'll see you tonight," he said. "I've got to run."

"Suit yourself." Velma bent over and picked up Tomcat True, who had been winding himself about her ankles. "We'll be all right."

"I'll bring groceries, Mama."

"I didn't make a list." She followed him down the hall and out the front door as he went to his truck. "You don't know what to bring," Velma yelled.

"Everything," Rudy said as he got inside the truck. "I need to bring everything."

He held one tan arm out the window and waved good-bye.

Twenty-Eight

Rudy pulled into the driveway of his duplex. Time was taking on a new significance for him. He looked at his watch, thought about showering, changing, taking extra clothes to Velma's, seeing Rose, finishing his route, buying groceries, and somehow discreetly talking with Tom down at the station about what had been going on around town without making it sound like something from *The Twilight Zone.*

Rudy wondered how his life had suddenly become so complicated. He threw his truck into Park, jumped out, and was heading for his front door when he was stopped dead in his tracks by what he saw. He was so taken aback, so surprised, that he forgot all about his worry and his hurry.

Miss Sara Long was slowly, carefully, backing out of Mr. Eddie Springer's front door and pulling it closed. He had just enough time to cross his arms and plant a satisfied smile on his face before she turned and began to go down the stairs. She had almost reached the bottom, tiptoeing all the way, when she looked up and saw him standing there.

"Morning, ma'am," Rudy said with a nod. He couldn't have wiped the grin off his face if he'd tried.

"It's not what it looks like," Sara said as she walked around him.

"Oh, it never is. Here, here." He rushed past her. "Let me get that door for you."

"I can get my own door, thank you." Sara held out her keys. "Besides, it's locked."

Swift as Tomcat True, Rudy plucked the keys from her fingers, unlocked the door, and opened it with a flourish. Sara stepped inside and took the keys back from him. "'Appearances are often deceiving.' Aesop," she quoted. She put the key in the ignition and started the car, waiting for Rudy to close the door.

"And it burns, burns, burns—that ring of fire." He shrugged and said, "Johnny Cash," as he closed the door.

Sara backed out of Eddie's driveway with Rudy still standing there smiling and waving at her. Then he turned and picked up Eddie's morning paper from where it had missed the porch and tossed it full force at his front door so it hit with a resounding slap. Then he began to laugh.

Rose knocked on Annie's door. *Annie's door,* she thought. How did she move in and take over so fast? And why wasn't she up yet? "Annie?" She opened the door, but Annie wasn't sleeping. She was lying on her back, wide-eyed, staring at the ceiling.

"You awake, huh?" Rose walked closer and sat on the edge of the bed, coffee mug in hand, her robe on, her dark hair in a ponytail at the nape of her neck. She smelled of tangerines and spices, some kind of soap, and Annie wanted to throw her arms around her and beg her to keep her. Instead, she willed her arms to stay locked behind her head, her face to remain impassive and unemotional.

"No bad guys in the backyard." Rose laid her hand on Annie's foot buried beneath the covers and gave it a tug. "It's okay to rise and shine."

"You can't keep me," Annie said, "not forever, I know." Then she did that quick-moving thing where suddenly she was in an entirely different position. She sat up in the bed, her back against the headboard, her legs crossed in front of her. "I mean, I appreciate everything you're doing, that you've done, but I know it's going to end." Annie put her elbows on her knees, her chin resting on her upturned hands. "I mean, I know you have your own life, like before me."

Rose wasn't prepared for this. Yes, she knew that a teenage girl on the run couldn't suddenly take up residence in her house without structure and direction. And taking in a kid hadn't exactly been something she had been planning. Owning a pizza place, a karaoke bar—whatever you wanted to call it—wasn't very conducive to surrogate motherhood.

"Look, Annie. I don't mind you hanging out, helping at the bar." She stood, tied her robe around her tighter. "After all, it's summer, and you're not missing school."

"Well, technically I am AWOL from summer school. I missed passing by about that much."

Rose sat back down on the corner of the bed. Everything related to Annie was always messier and more complicated than she expected. "Okay, kid, you're missing summer school, and you're flunking."

"I don't mind flunking out, Rose. I really just want to keep playing my music and find my band."

Rose bit the inside of her cheek, trying not to say the wrong thing. "Annie," she said, and the green eyes fastened on her. "Bono graduated." She leaned forward. "And he met his entire band in high school."

"Really?" Annie said, her eyes opening a little wider.

"Yes, really." Rose got up from the bed. "Can you imagine if he'd just dropped out? No U2." She walked to the bedroom door. "They're from Ireland, you know."

"Everybody knows that."

"Get up and get dressed," Rose said and closed the door. She decided career counseling did not go with the first cup of coffee. She walked down the hall to get dressed. But she was smiling as she went.

Twenty-Nine

It was a beautiful morning. The sun was shining through leaves that were now in the fullness of their glory with a thickness of green comfort.

Rose drove while Annie rode shotgun. The guitar had taken its position in the backseat. Rose rolled down the window, started to light a cigarette. Annie coughed a little, rolled her eyes at her, and pointed to her throat. Earlier Annie had claimed Rose's secondhand smoke could kill her entire singing future. "Just *kill* it," she'd said.

Rose rolled her own eyes but laid the unlit cigarette on her lap. Annie turned on the radio, punched the buttons. "One station?" she yelled over the sound of the wind. "You only have *one* station?"

"Two," Rose corrected her and pushed another preset. "There's country,"—she switched the radio back to its original station—"and this is the other one."

Annie turned it off. "You know, neither one of them is very good." She began to hum a familiar tune.

Rose listened to Annie's low humming, caught a few words when Annie suddenly switched gears and sang a line or two and then retreated again to a hum. Rose glanced at Annie.

A little food, hot water, sleep, protection. She was starting to shine, Annie was.

It appeared to be a perfect day, Rose thought. But she kept looking in the rearview mirror, feeling something was out of place, searching for something that didn't seem to be there. Her eyes darted from one side of the road to the other. She took her foot off the accelerator a little, slowed down to the speed limit. Something definitely wasn't right. She began to scan the buildings along the road. She turned to look down the alley that ran between the Mapco gas station and the Suds and Stuff Laundromat. She only saw a brindle-colored dog looking solemnly at her.

Everything appeared to be quiet. Yet that persistent feeling caused Rose to glance in the rearview mirror and slow down even more as they approached the front of the bar.

Annie unlatched her seat belt and reached over to the backseat to pick up her guitar.

"Wait, Annie," Rose said. "Put that belt back on." Rose drove past the bar, around the corner, and pulled into the alley so she could see behind the building and across the empty lot.

Something…is searching for us, she thought. Rose looked over at Annie, who seemed impervious. *No, something is looking for her. Something is searching for Annie.*

"I don't need a seat belt just to circle the building."

Rose was a hardworking, down-to-earth, logical girl. But

she knew something wasn't right. When she drove around to the front of the building again, instead of pulling into the driveway and parking in her usual spot, she took a hard right and then a fast left at the green light where the road opened up to the barrenness of Highway 155.

Annie stopped singing. She sat up straighter in her seat, threw both hands on the dash, and looked backward at the bar. "What's going on?" she asked.

"I said put that thing back on!"

Annie grabbed her seat belt and snapped it across her lap. "Okay, okay, but what is going on?" Annie craned her head and looked out the rear window, searching for something, anything that had Rose on the run.

She didn't see anything, and Rose didn't answer. Instead, Rose adjusted the side windows, then the rearview mirror, and pressed the accelerator. The speedometer climbed to eighty in a fifty-five-mile-per-hour zone.

Annie wished she could reach for her guitar and hold it in front of her for protection. "Rose?" There was a question mark in her voice, but she was yelling to be heard. She attempted to hold her hair with one hand to keep it out of her face.

"Something's chasing us, Annie."

"But I don't see anything." Annie wanted to change positions, to get up on her knees, to hang on to something. The telephone poles blurred past so fast that Annie got dizzy trying to focus on them. When they sped past the sign that read

"You are now leaving Echo. Drive safely and hurry back," Annie watched it shaking in the side mirror.

"Neither do I, Annie. I don't know what it is, but I know it's out there."

But it was Annie who changed her focus from the sign to the backseat and saw a familiar face—the leering, pasty one from the backyard. She wanted to tell Rose, but all Annie could manage was to grab her arm—hard.

Rose pressed the accelerator, watched the needle climb to ninety-five.

"Rose." Annie tried to yell, but it came out a whisper. The apparition in the mirror smiled wider. "Rose," Annie said, clenching her arm even tighter and raising her voice. "He's here."

"Where?" Rose glanced at Annie, whose eyes were still glued to the side mirror.

"He's in here," Annie said harder, more intensely.

Rose glanced in the rearview mirror in time to catch the eyes, the pale lips curved up in a slice of satisfaction. Just as she slammed on the brakes, the face changed into something different. Something smoky. Something winged. As rubber burned the road for twenty feet, as Rose threw the car into Park, as she and Annie threw open the doors and poured out into the emptiness of Highway 155, the wings rose through the roof of the car, hovered there, and then melted into nothingness before their eyes until they were surrounded by only blue skies and the hot smell of smoking tires.

With the car still running, Rose paced back and forth, yelling, "What was that?" She screamed again, "What was that?" She reached into the car, grabbed her cigarettes, and took her lighter from the front pocket of her jeans. She lit one with a shaking hand, took a deep drag, and leaned on the roof of the car. She stared at Annie, who was still turning in small circles like a dancer on a music box, trying to shake off the wild shivers that were running up and down her body.

Annie finally slowed down long enough to cross her arms tight across her chest, look hard at Rose, and say, "*That* was the thing I told you about in the trees. I'm sure of it."

Rose took another drag of her cigarette. The thing in the dark alley that night, the thing in the yard, the thing in the backseat all had one thing in common: they were all looking for Annie. Rose was certain of that, but she sure didn't know why.

"Get in the car," Rose said.

Annie reached into the back, took her guitar case, and held it in her lap. Rose made a U-turn in the middle of the road. She lit another cigarette.

Annie didn't complain.

The speedometer climbed once again as they raced in the opposite direction, back inside the borders of Echo and back toward something that was playing hide-and-seek with them every step of the way.

"Ready or not," Annie whispered, "here we come."

Rudy had passed by Rose's Place in the morning but hadn't seen her car parked in front. He had stopped at the Piggly Wiggly to get his mother's groceries and had planned to drop them off before he started his route. His deliveries were in the truck, and he had the day synchronized down to the minute, including making special arrangements for his lunch date with Rose. This morning's surprise of running into Sara as she was sneaking out of Mr. Springer's had given him a glorious idea. And he was hoping that if his charm couldn't get him what he wanted, the threat of blackmail would. Maybe he could talk her into loaning him that fine convertible for a little drive in the moonlight some night with Rose.

His buddy down at the post office had told him Rose's last name was McClarney. Now all he needed was her home number. He pulled open the faded yellow phone book at the pay phone in the parking lot and turned to the *m*'s. He ran his finger down the lines, but before he could find the name and number, a car whipped around the corner, burning rubber and driving past him at the speed of light.

Rose.

Rudy jumped in the truck and drove into the street behind her. He was trying his best to turn over a new leaf. To not be a man full of regrets for the choices he'd made. He didn't want to be a country song—all about ending up alone and drunk and broke. It was dawning on him that he needed to make amends. To stop running from the things inside of him. To stop chasing women.

And here he was, chasing one at high speed.

He tried to catch up with Rose's car as it fishtailed slightly. Then it turned right on Main Street. Rudy let out a low whistle and stepped on the gas.

Rose drove up to the police station and parked in a space behind the building.

"You want me to wait here?" Annie asked.

"Get out." Rose stopped and turned around. "Don't leave my sight. You understand me?"

Annie nodded, her eyes growing larger, but inside she was actually breathing a sigh of relief. *No problem,* she thought but then asked, "Can I bring my guitar?"

"Suit yourself, Annie, but hustle," Rose said, then walked around the corner of the building.

Rudy glanced down Main Street but didn't see the car. *Strange,* he thought. He started singing along with the song on the radio, "My baby…she's one of a kind…" He continued singing the old Tim McGraw song, beating his fingers on the steering wheel, looking up and down each street for any sign of Rose's car.

Finally he caught a flash of a pair of very determined Levi's walking up the steps to the police station, followed closely by a girl with her arms wrapped around a guitar. "Aha," Rudy said and turned the wheel just before he passed the road. He parked on the side of the street in front of the City Diner.

He jogged down the sidewalk toward the front steps of the one-and-only police station. He'd check in on Rose and have that talk with Tom he'd been planning. Mail delivery was now really running late. Good thing his customers loved him. Good thing he was on the rural route or else he'd be on no route at all. He could see himself making those explanations to Brenda, could see her crossing her arms and grinning at him, saying, "One more chance, Rudy. Just one, and then you are outta here." She always said the last part like an umpire at a baseball game. Rudy figured that he had struck out at work at least nine times, and he was still sliding into home every time he cashed his paycheck.

When he ran up the steps and through the lobby door, he saw Annie parked on a wooden bench, her guitar across her lap. "What are you doing here?" she asked. Rudy looked through the plate-glass window behind the counter and saw Rose pacing in front of the chief of police, throwing her hands up, shoving them inside her back pockets, throwing them up in the air again.

"What's going on?" Rudy asked.

Annie looked at him and twisted her lips up tight to one side. "We had a little situation."

"Another visit?"

"Yep." She tapped the toe of her shoe on the hard floor. "Something like that."

"Same spooky guy?"

"Oh yeah." Annie ran her fingers through her hair. "But a whole lot spookier." She stared at her nails, then tore at one with her teeth.

Rudy sat next to her on the bench to wait for Rose. From the looks of things in the office, he didn't want to go in there. He looked at the girl, closely studied her for the first time. She had a special spark to her that he liked. For a flash of an instant, there was something so familiar about the girl, about the tilt of her chin, but then it was gone.

Annie kept talking, seemingly not needing any encouragement to do so. "You wouldn't have believed it. You just wouldn't have believed it." She punched him lightly on the arm. "I'm telling you. I was there, and I'm having a hard time believing it!"

"Doesn't look like she's having a hard time believing," he said, pointing at Rose, who was now leaning with her fists on the chief's desk, looking into his face.

"She knows what we saw," Annie said, but then she added as an afterthought, "but it won't matter." She waved her hand in small circles toward Rose and the chief. "All that won't matter at all."

"Why do you say that?"

She didn't answer. Just ran her fingers softly up and down the strings of the guitar.

Rudy watched as Rose stomped out of the chief's office. She stood in front of him, her green eyes blazing. He could feel the heat coming off her body.

"What's up, Rudy?" Rose had her arms crossed. She looked like she was trying to keep herself from exploding.

"Actually, Rose,"—Rudy stood, softly placed his hand on her elbow, and leaned into her slightly—"I was checking on you."

Annie stood up, used the strap to hoist her guitar to her shoulder. But she was silent, alternately watching the ground and the people milling about the station. She caught the eye of the chief watching them from behind the counter. His arms were crossed too. Annie looked away, and after a few moments she could see the bulk of the man retreat back into his office and close the door.

"I was going to call you," Rudy continued, "but then I saw you drive straight past me like a bat out of hell, so I followed you to see what was happening."

"Bat outta hell." Rose pointed at him. "See, that's exactly what I'm talking about." She turned and walked out the door. She stomped down the steps still mumbling, "Bat outta hell."

Rudy walked with Annie, keeping pace with her as they followed Rose to the parking lot. "You were about to tell me something," he reminded her. "About why none of this was going to matter."

"There is something happening that is…oh, I don't know"—she made those circles in the air again with her hands, only this time using both of them—"peculiar." She glanced at Rose's retreating frame. "We shouldn't let her get out of sight."

"Annie." It was the first time Rudy had called her by name. He laid his hand on her shoulder so that she had to slow down. "Aren't you afraid?"

"I am afraid," she said as she looked back at him. "I think I'm the most afraid."

Purple wisteria petals floated softly around them, a few landing at their feet and then getting blown along on the pavement.

Rudy searched her face for that sense of the familiar, but it was gone. "C'mon." Rudy started walking again. "She'll be waiting on you."

"She'll be waiting on you too," Annie said with a smile.

They both trailed after the only footsteps either one of them wanted to follow.

Thirty

Eddie Springer stepped out onto his porch. He was normally a light sleeper, at least within reason, but Sara had been exceptionally quiet in sneaking out the front door. He had been awakened by a loud thud and had found the paper waiting at the door. It was then he had seen the blue Olds already far down the road. He had smiled without even picking up the paper, closed the door, and gone back to bed. That wasn't his way. But yesterday had been a long and interesting day. A life-changing day. And sometimes a life change required a little more sleep. Like this morning.

It had been enough of a challenge to circumvent the muddy waters of Rudy's mother. She hadn't wanted him to keep her company, and he could see that. But then she had shown him her rock. And a day of wonders had begun.

He had fallen asleep sitting right there, on a stranger's porch, in a stranger's chair, in broad daylight. At first he had just been aware of resting. Of closing his eyes and listening to the sounds around him, feeling the breeze run over his skin. He had listened to the sounds of insects in the trees and of the wind chimes hanging somewhere in the distance. Those were the first sounds he'd heard, but then he could hear sounds below that, beyond that. He could hear a special sound, the low whistle of the wind as it rustled through the pines. He could hear Velma somewhere in the house, slowly moving about. Eventually he'd heard the water moving along with a lazy rhythm, carrying things downstream and beyond as they slowly made their way to the brackish water below and then out into the Gulf of Mexico.

And then the listening had become something else. He had begun seeing these things as if he were among them, even from the porch, from the chair, and with his eyes closed. He'd watched a leaf floating there on the sunny surface of the water while being carried slowly farther and farther downstream, turning on the surface of the water, resting and turning. And in that moment he had known everything that lived and moved beneath the surface. The fish swimming there in the deep cold. Before, he had not known their names, but sitting there resting, he had known the local names, the old names. He knew that they were mullet, bream, shellcracker. He had known that something was there, deeper and darker, sliding through the shadows, something long, called a garfish. More eel than fish, baring razor-sharp teeth. He had seen turtles sunning farther down the creek on the wet trunks of old, fallen trees that protruded from the water at strange angles. He had watched as the alligators nested, sunning themselves on the banks, slipping silently in the water when they heard a boat motor approaching.

And little by little he had seen the birds that nested in the trees along the water, the clear paths where the deer made their way in the cool of the night to drink. He had seen the nest of an old owl. And somehow, in his half sleep, the owl had turned and looked at him without making a sound. Just watching Eddie Springer, craning its neck slowly, watching him pass.

He had known that squirrels filled the tree branches and that field mice slept safely in the holes near the trees. That raccoons feasted richly, eating the things the earth produced, and that there were opossums and all manner of small creatures fat with the good provisions of the earth. He had heard the movement of the creatures beneath the water, the collective breathing of the animals in the woods, until finally he had heard his own breath. And then he had opened his eyes, and it felt as if he had taken a journey of a lifetime. A long and momentous occasion. And when he'd stood, there had been the convertible, like a chariot from a dream, waiting for his descent, the smiling faces of the women in the car, and an invitation for another adventure.

That's when Rudy's mother had introduced him to Sara, the striking woman with the gray hair and the flight jacket. The one who looked as if she could carry him to the four corners of the earth and safely return him home again.

"My friend, the teacher," Velma had said, as if Sara were a prize from the county fair. "Retired," Sara had added in a voice he found rich with intelligence.

Mr. Eddie Springer had stood a little straighter as he'd walked down the stairs. "You don't say?" He had looked into

Sara's eyes as she had opened the door and ushered him to the backseat. And they had talked about everything. Talked like he hadn't talked to anyone—not since having heated discussions with his colleagues. Even those had grown cold and stale in the final years before his retirement. But the conversation in the car yesterday—now that had been a celebration.

It was the late night that had been the icing on the cake. A simple ride home was all that it was supposed to be. But then he had invited Sara in for coffee. "I grind my own beans," he had said and then added with a smile, "from Seattle."

Sara had smiled back and turned off the car.

Thirty-One

Velma sat on the back steps, looking out over the barn, the back field, and down by the water. The sun had risen, but it was still on the other side of the house. It was cool here in the shade. She held a cup of coffee, sipped from it while watching the wind pick up the dry dust from the field and toss it like a handful of scattered wishes.

"We need some rain, Tomcat," she said, but the cat wasn't nearby at all. He was asleep in the sun on the front porch. She took the rock out of her pocket and held it up to the sky, expecting to see through it. The rock remained breathlessly solid. "I get you," Velma said, "at least part of you." And as if the rock heard her words and understood her, a soft glow began at the center, a vibrant, good-times, eternal blue. Velma laughed. "Yeah, that's right," she said, "make me promises you can keep." She pushed her hair back where a long strand had fallen beside her face, set down her coffee cup, stood up, and stepped off the stoop. Velma True had figured out a thing or two. Like how to remember. And how to forget.

She free stepped into the backyard, making her way out into the open field with the blue star shining in the middle of the rock.

What she didn't see was the shadow that passed over her

house, the wisp of smoke that was making its way to the edge of the trees. She was being watched now from the tree line—intently.

Velma walked toward the barn, her feet snapping sprightly as she went. She sat on the magnolia stump and leaned against the barn. Then she held the rock up in her palms, looked deeply into the blue that was rolling into green like the sea, into a white like diamonds. "Take me," she whispered. "Take me to him." For a moment there was nothing. Only the sun and the heat and the dry, dusty field beside her. But then the sky split open, rolled back until it touched the ground beneath Velma's feet.

She held the rock tighter as she felt herself rolling, rolling, rolling through shadows and shades, through pulses of light and movement of things certain and uncertain. Time was being ripped from its shutters and rearranged. She laughed, but the sound of the laugh was lost between walls that no longer existed.

And then it was quiet.

She sat by the creek, down by the landing at the base of the big cypress trees, their roots sticking out of the water. The cicadas hummed in the breeze, stopped, hummed, stopped, then hummed again. "Of course," she said and stood, shading her eyes with her hand and looking far up the creek to the bend in the water.

Velma saw the boat as soon as it cleared the bend, just the bow of it sliding out of the green and into view. She smiled and walked into the water, the hem of her dress tugging at her, lapping against her legs. The first sight of him almost brought her to her knees, but she told herself, *Toughen up, old girl. Toughen up,* as tears rose in her eyes. She rubbed them away with her fingers, watching as he expertly sculled the boat, silently moving the oar back and forth under the water.

The boat floated against the bank, the tip of it sliding slowly into the mud. Velma stood next to the bow, let it run up just past her.

"Hey, Velma," Joe said.

"Hey, Joe," Velma said. He wasn't her old Joe. And he wasn't her young Joe. She laughed a little and said, "You're Joe in the middle."

"C'mon, I'll take you for a ride."

Velma looked over her shoulder at the house. It looked the same but a little brighter, a little straighter.

She stepped into the boat and sat on the front bench. Joe smiled and shoved the oar down to the bottom of the muddy creek bed, and with one great push they were free and floating backward. He dropped the paddle in the water behind him, began to silently scull the boat, twisting it back and forth, back and forth in the water. They moved in reverse, away from the bank and out into the middle of the creek, where the sunlight fell on Velma's arms. She closed her eyes, turned her face up to the sun, relaxed, and waited for Joe to turn the boat, to begin the journey upstream. Around the first bend to the right, the next bend to the left. It was the watered path he had always taken. The cypress trees stood tall at the water's edge, their limbs towering above the smaller trees: the small magnolias, scrub oaks, and early pines.

Velma looked at Joe, saw the red color of those arms from too many days in the sun. She watched the sweat breaking through the pores so that he glistened as he rowed, admired the cut of his jaw, the shape of his neck, the curve of his shoulder. She loved those hands—the power of them while they were moving, the silent strength of them when they were resting. Mullet jumped in unison to the left and right of the boat and landed with lazy plops back in the water. Joe lifted his finger, pointed in the direction of three big turtles sunning on a fallen log. The cicadas chimed in with the breeze, held their breath for a moment, and then returned again in full force.

Joe smiled at her like he loved her more than air.

This, right here, right now, Velma prayed silently. *Let this be forever.*

Joe gave her that wink Rudy got from him. "Velma, didn't you know? This was forever."

"You knew what I was thinking?"

"I've always known what you were thinking."

She laughed. It was a young girl's laugh. "Not always, Joe." She slapped her leg and shook her head. "Not always at all."

"I've always known."

She could see he was serious.

"You called me out of that fishing hole back there"—he pointed through the trees—"because you had questions."

Velma looked at him, thought of all that he was to her. This man of hers, both lost and found. "It's true." She took the rock from her pocket, held it up to him. "This is it, Joe. This is why I'm here."

"That's not your question." He took the oar, pushed them away from a log jutting into the water.

"I was just showing you. This is how I got here."

Joe sculled into the open circle where the blue springs were.

Velma stopped speaking, leaned way over the side of the boat, and watched her reflection and the boat's reflection in the water. When her eyes adjusted, she could see far, far below the surface where there were big fat fish that moved slowly in the cold water. Then she could see the underwater lilies blooming, moving in the current of the underwater springs. She sat back and looked at him. "Is this heaven, Joe?"

He still wore that smile, the one that was knowing but not telling. "Well, if it ain't, it should be."

"Oh, well, you would say that." She almost giggled but placed a hand on her stomach, willing the giggle to stay put. "I did come to ask you something." She pushed her hair back from her face. "It's about Rudy." She expected his face to make a sudden turn, expected to see that old shadow of frustration pass across his eyes. But it didn't come.

"He'll be all right, Velma." Joe lifted the paddle out of the water and let them drift, caught in the crosscurrent from the springs blowing from the underwater cave beneath them. They languidly floated in slow, concentric circles. "Just don't worry so much, and he'll be fine."

"But, Joe." Velma trailed her fingers in the water, busting up the perfect mirror on the surface. "He's got them bugs again." She nodded seriously at him for effect. "You know."

"Velma,"—Joe lifted his chin—"just because you're his mama, you don't have to be the one to fix him. It's not your fault."

She looked through the cypress trees and the trees beyond them into the shadowy darkness, into the swampiness of the creek.

"And it's not his fault either. That's what you need to tell him. It's not his fault," Joe said.

"What's not his fault?"

"Look," he said, pointing at the clear water.

"I been looking, Joe. I see the fish and the lilies and where the sand is bubbling from the opening of the cave. Like I said, I've been looking."

"Look again, Velma."

She leaned way over the boat, her hands clinging to the sides, the tip of her nose about to touch the water. At first it was only the surface mirroring the sky, the magnolias, the cypresses. For a moment she even thought she saw the old owl sitting in the cypress high above her, watching her reflection. She looked way up into the trees, but there was no sign of him.

"Look, Velma," Joe said again, and she returned her gaze to the water.

She began to see that the surface was peeling back, as if a current were ripping through the middle of it, parting the images on the surface as though it were a curtain. What lay beneath was their kitchen from long, long ago. It was she and Joe, the white kitchen curtains blowing in the breeze behind them. She could even see the changing colors of the little red-leaf maple that she had planted by the window.

"I see," she said. Then she could do more than see. The noises in the woods faded, replaced by Joe saying, "Velma, it's not your fault."

But it was not Joe in the middle, not Joe in the boat—it was the younger Joe. A younger Velma was crying, and the younger Joe tried to comfort her. They had lost another baby that day—the last, the one she had named Mariah. "But it is," she was saying. "I just can't hold on to 'em."

"If you want to go blaming someone, Velma, blame Rudy's birth," Joe said.

Velma's head snapped up.

"Or for that matter blame me for not being there that day. But just don't go blaming yourself."

"Joe, Rudy was just born, that's all. It was no fault of his that he was turned and trouble."

"Of course not. That's not what I'm saying. I just mean…" He paused, ran his hands through hair thicker than night. "I'm just saying Rudy's what done it. His birthing scarred you,

Velma, and that's that." He sat down heavy and looked at her with logic and love. "There won't be no more babies now, Velma. You need to accept that."

Something rustled, like leaves rolling. Velma had been too broken to really pay attention. But now, from where she sat in the boat, she could see her young tears fall on her hands, which were folded on the table. She could see Joe's hands reach out and cover those tears. What she hadn't seen then, what she could see now, was that below the window, under that little tree, sat Rudy. Six years old and just home from school, sitting there in the afternoon light. And even from this far, far away, she could see him shiver.

"He heard it all," she said to Joe but not moving her eyes away. "Everything."

"He did."

A shadow covered the sun so quickly that Velma caught her breath, looked up, and saw the sun blotted out, then released again.

"Hearing it stuck with him somewhere, Velma. It's why he gets those bugs."

"And we never knew." Velma felt wistful, full of if only's.

"Sugar," he said, "nobody ever knows." Joe put the paddle in the water, began rowing back down the creek. "We just do the best we can."

The boat moved seamlessly away from the circle, moved into the current, and turned on its own accord to head downstream.

"I can come back tomorrow," Velma said. She was watching Joe, and she knew ahead of time. She knew and he knew that there would be no tomorrow for them here. Not now.

"This was special. Just for today," Joe said.

Velma nodded, watched his arm turn the paddle, and watched the muscles move under the skin, the hair glistening. Fresh tears came to her eyes. "I love you, Joe."

"I love you too, Velma girl." He gave her that look she knew so well. "I always will."

She tried to ask when she would see him again, but "when" was the only whisper that escaped, and she put her hands to her eyes.

"Due time, sugar," Joe said. "All in due time. And I'll be waiting."

The boat began rocking back and forth so much that Velma closed her eyes, held on to the sides with both hands. The rocking stopped, began again—more violent this time.

Velma opened her eyes to see the shape of a man. His hand was on her shoulder, shaking and shaking.

"Stop that," she said. And the hand stopped. She looked up and for just a moment thought it was Joe. Then she realized she was just stump sitting and it was Rudy's hand on her shoulder.

Velma's eyes were still not focused. "I thought you were your daddy." She covered her eyes with her hands. "For just a second you looked just like him." She stood slowly.

"I thought you were dead, Mama."

"Well, I'm not." Velma put one leg out in front of her, shaking it, then the other. They had both fallen asleep.

"But you *are* sunburned. Just look at you." He stood back and put his hands in his pockets. "You could have found a better spot to nap."

Velma looked down at the pinkness of her legs and arms.

"What are you doing out here, Mama?"

"What time is it?"

"Time for you to put some groceries up."

Rudy had been so excited to rush into his mama's house with his arms full of bags, to say, "Look, look, I've got everything." He had imagined making trip after trip for more bags, his mama following him back and forth, blustering and clucking all the way. But when he had got there, the house had been empty.

So he had made the back-and-forth trips alone. When he had placed the last of the bags on the counter, he had glanced out the kitchen window and had seen her sitting on the stump, leaning against the barn, just like her heart had stopped for good. He'd gone flying out the back door to reach her, to check her pulse, to see if she was alive. He knew what the answer would be one day. Her dying was inevitable. But he hoped it didn't come along before he got some things straight.

Velma walked up the back steps and opened the kitchen door. Brown paper bags took up every inch of the counter, covered the table, and filled two of the kitchen chairs. There were two more bags on the floor by the refrigerator.

"Lord, Rudy, what have you done?" she said. "I'm never gonna have room for all this."

"Look, Mama!" He almost danced around the kitchen. "I've got ham, bacon, and pork chops. And there's Crisco, sugar, flour, butter, cheese, dried beans, and peas." He pulled things out of the bags and tossed them on top of other bags. "Tomatoes and fresh okra and squash. And just for the fun of it, you know, so that you eat something a little healthy, I got you apples and oranges." He stood back, grinned at her, and winked. "What do you think?"

Velma pulled out an empty chair and said, "Well, I've got my work cut out for me now, that's for sure." Then she saw Rudy's face fall. "Oh, but, Son, you did a good thing. Really. Just took my breath away a little, that's all. I just haven't seen this much food all at once since…" But she didn't finish her sentence.

Rudy walked out the door and sat on the back steps. He lit a cigarette and talked to her through the screen. "I hope you don't mind,"—he kicked the dry dirt with the toe of his shoe—"but I invited company for dinner."

"Really? What kind of people?"

"Just people. Nobody you know."

She turned sideways in the chair, looked at his back.

"A couple of friends."

"Men or women?"

Rudy grinned. "A woman, Mama. And a girl."

"Who are they?"

"I told you, you don't know either one."

Velma ran her fingers through her hair. She stood up and started putting things away. "I don't cook fancy, you know."

"Mama, home cooking will be just fine." Tomcat wandered over and rubbed against Rudy's leg. "Hey, old man." Rudy stroked the top of his head, scratched behind his ears. He looked across the field, let his gaze roam beyond the dirt, the dust flying in wisps. He scanned the tree line, squinting against the sun. He stood, put his hands in his pockets, and walked to the edge of the dirt, never taking his eyes from the trees. Tomcat languidly followed him and sat down again at his feet.

"Mama?" he called. "Mama!" he called in a louder voice.

"What, Rudy, what is it?" Velma yelled back.

"Come out here, would you?"

A cloud of dust lifted and circled, settled back into the field. Velma opened the back door, walked down the stairs and out into the yard to Rudy's side.

"What is it, Son?" Velma followed his gaze out to the trees.

"What do you see out there beyond the trees, between us and the water?" He pointed but to no distinct spot.

Velma looked harder. "You know I don't have my glasses on."

"You never have your glasses on."

"Well, I already know how things are." Velma pushed a piece of hair away from her face. "But I don't see anything."

"Something's not right." Rudy looked at the sky. It was blue except for a few wispy clouds caught by the wind. "Why don't you ride along with me to deliver the mail?"

"Now, Rudy…"

"Just for today." He turned to her, laid his hand on her shoulder. "I'm asking you to do this for me."

Velma put her hands on her hips, planted her feet hard on the ground. "Well, you're asking too much. Besides, I got work to do and dinner to make. For company."

"Well, all right then, Mama, all right. But listen to me." Rudy paused and pointed out toward the woods beyond the field. "Don't go out there today. Don't go down by the water."

"Okay, Rudy," she said. "I wasn't planning on it anyway."

Rudy put his arm around her shoulder as they walked toward the back stoop, up the steps, and into the kitchen.

Tomcat True remained where he was, his green eyes watching the thing that moved silently through the trees. The cat twitched his tail twice against the dry ground, then he rose slowly and walked toward the house.

Thirty-Two

Annie wiped down the tables, even though they didn't need cleaning. She'd washed them before closing last night. But she'd come to the bar and needed to do something before it opened.

She finished the last table and sighed, walked to the window, and parted the blinds. She looked up and down the street. Nothing there. She sighed again and dropped the blinds.

Things weren't going according to her plan. Not that she ever had much of a plan. She'd had a little plan—better than nothing, right?

She looked over her shoulder to where Rose had gone into the office, saying, "Just let me think, Annie. Let me think." Rose had closed the door behind her.

Annie picked up the wet rag and tossed it in the air a few times, then dropped it over the glossy bar into the soapy dishwater. She walked around the bar to get her dirty green backpack. It had seen better days, but it was still with her. The most constant things in her life were her backpack and her guitar. In her heart Annie was always one step away from being homeless. She had always been reminded that she was the orphan child of the better sister and an inconvenient happenstance. She hadn't had a better place to go until now. By accident she had found Rose. Had found her while looking for someone, anyone, who had once belonged to her mother.

She unzipped the pack, took out a worn notebook, and silently turned the pages until the photos slipped onto her palm. On top was the faded photograph of her mother, smiling and not yet touched by Annie's birth. Sitting on either side of her were two people Annie didn't know. Although the picture was well-worn—first from when she and her mother lay on the bed and flipped through the few photographs, and later from when Annie looked through them alone—her mother had never given an explanation about this one. There were other pictures, of course. Photos of her mother's life before Annie and a few of Annie before she turned seven. This picture was the one that meant the most, because in it her mother was happy and laughing. Alive. Annie's only clue was the words printed carefully on the back: "Christmas in Echo."

There were no words to explain what had happened that morning months ago in Texas when she had been lying in her bed, staring at the ceiling, thinking of summer school, thinking of how many years she had left to tough it out with Trudy. But then what? What would life hold for her at eighteen that it didn't have now?

And there, in the middle of her thoughts, the photo came to mind. Looking at the smiling face of her mother, at two people she didn't recognize—then the picture came alive. Somehow, like an image projected on a screen, the photograph was on her ceiling. It began moving. The people and her mother moved and laughed. The lights from the Christmas tree in the background blinked on and off; the colors from the tree blended, receded, and moved forward again.

She heard the sound of their laughter, their voices rising and falling. There was a man's voice somewhere in the background—a man not in the picture. She heard presents being opened, drinks poured, and dinner served. After Annie had watched this for a long time, she realized she wasn't just using her imagination but that somehow the picture had left its boundaries and come to life. That she was watching a day from years before unfold as if she had been there.

At that moment the older woman in the picture looked up. Annie could have sworn that she was looking directly at *her*, watching her right there on her bed. This was impossible, she knew, but it felt real.

Then the photograph that wasn't really there flipped itself over. The old, inked mysterious words, "Christmas in Echo," grew larger and larger until an address replaced them. Moments later the numbers and letters faded.

Just like that, the images were gone, leaving Annie staring at the cracked ceiling of her bedroom.

But she kept that address in her mind.

That's what began to shift her life eastward. It was the thing in Annie that had broken open and helped her decide life would change. One old photograph, one strange, unknown address had called to her like nobody's business. So she'd written the note, packed her backpack, picked up her guitar, and walked out the door and down the street of her neighborhood without looking back. Now it seemed a million miles, a million days, away.

Annie ran her fingers over the faces in the photograph. It wasn't that she was looking back now. She was just trying to find her way down the road of life without anyone getting hurt.

The office door opened, and Annie jumped, shoving the photograph back into the notebook. Rose tossed her hair over her shoulder and absently asked, "Working on something?"

"Kinda." Annie returned the notebook to her backpack. She dropped her backpack and reached into the soapy water, found the rag, wrung it, and began to scrub the spotless bar.

Rose reached for her hand, stopped the wiping. "What are you not telling me, Annie?"

"I didn't mean for anything bad to happen. I mean, I didn't mean for you to get wrapped up in this, Rose. I didn't even know you."

"You're still not answering my question." Rose crossed her arms.

Annie stopped wiping. "I think somebody here sent me a message." She added, "Like an invitation."

"An invitation?"

"Maybe. Kinda."

"Kinda how?"

Annie laughed, but it was a nervous laugh. "Well, it sure wasn't like the kind you get in the mail in a fancy envelope."

Rose continued giving her a hard, green-eyed stare. Annie tried to figure out what to tell her. And what not to. She decided honesty might be the best option. She slowly picked up her backpack again and took the notebook out of the bag, catching the few pictures as they fell from the pages. Annie slid the Echo photo across the bar.

Rose picked it up and looked at the faces. She looked at Annie, then back to the faces of the older people. It looked like it was a happy day. There was a Christmas tree in the background. "Your mother?"

Annie nodded.

"And these people?" Rose pointed to the others.

"I don't know." Annie reached for the photograph. "But I have this." She flipped the photo over to show Rose the address.

"Rural route. Millers Ferry Road," Rose read. "That's just outside Echo," she said. She picked up the photo, carefully turned it over again, and looked at the faces more closely. Someone there looked familiar to her. The man in the picture. She was trying to remember if she had ever seen him and if so, where. She scanned her memory of people, but nothing. Not exactly. "How did your mother know these people?"

"I don't know."

"She never told you?"

Annie took the photo from Rose, shook her head no, and placed it back in the notebook with the others, then zipped her backpack. "It's just some kind of unfinished business. You know, the kind people have when they die suddenly."

Rose looked at her and nodded. She knew a thing or two about unfinished business. And she knew that death sometimes left a horrendous to-do list that would never get done. Full of big things, like forgiving all the lovely people who had kicked you when you were down. She'd finally get around to that in the afterlife, she had decided. She figured that would keep her busy all the way into the new millennium.

"So what is it you think she didn't finish?" Rose sat on the stool. She looked at the clock on the wall. They were actually supposed to have dinner at Rudy's mother's house. She crossed her arms over her T-shirt, looked at her jeans and sneakers, and thought maybe she should dress better.

She tried to imagine Rudy's mother. Tried to imagine the things he might have said in passing late at night. But all she remembered was him saying, "I've got to get Mama to leave the house." That was all that came to mind. Now she was sorry she hadn't asked for more information, like, "Tell me about your mother, Rudy." But they had never talked like that. Now that she thought about it, what did they really know about each other except that she worked hard and he womanized? And that one big kiss? That was about it.

Rose looked at the clock, walked over, and unlocked the front door.

Annie looked up at the unlocked door, and Rose caught

the look. "Honey, if he can pop in and out of the backseat of a moving car, a locked door doesn't matter too much, now does it?"

"Guess not." Annie picked up the rag and wiped the bar.

Rose went behind the bar, started a pot of coffee. "Hey, put that rag down and play me something on your guitar. Help us both work up an appetite for tonight."

Annie smiled. She started to sit on the stool behind the bar until Rose said, "Uh-uh." She pointed to the stage. "Up there, kid, where it counts."

Annie walked over to the stage, pulled the stool forward, climbed up on it, hugged the guitar to her chest, and looked at Rose. Rose smiled at her and said, "Well, I don't imagine that thing is going to play itself." Then she turned her back and appeared to be busy.

Annie closed her eyes, hummed softly to herself. Her fingers ran up and down the chords as she rocked back and forth, letting the guitar talk to her, letting it tell her what it wanted her to play. That was her way.

Annie began to play. And to sing.

With the first real note, Rose stood up straight, the cream in one hand, her coffee cup in the other. She wanted to turn around but was afraid that would be a distraction. She didn't need to worry. Annie was singing about the ghosts of Christmas past, of an unopened box and a broken heart. She sang of wild things and things worth taming. And something about that singing, about Annie's voice, about the way her fingers pleaded their cause on the guitar made Rose cry. Annie was preaching a Sunday sermon, she was orchestrating a Saturday dance, and Rose felt something inside her break open that had blocked out the past, steeled her to the life left to her, the one she had created with all its careful boundaries holding her in place.

Rose set the coffee cup and the cream next to each other. She opened her eyes and turned to face Annie as she sang the last line, the guitar chords still hanging in the air. Annie looked at her across the space of more than just that bar. She looked at her across the space of truth and time.

Rose placed both her palms flat on the surface of the bar to steady the part of her that was still reeling inside. "Annie,"— she looked down for just a second and then glanced back up at the girl on the stage—"where did you learn to play like that?"

"In my room. Alone," she whispered as a few tears ran down her cheeks.

Rose nodded, keeping her palms in place as her coffee cooled in the cup behind her. As Annie wiped her tears away with the back of her sleeve. As the mystery of the world kept spinning outside the shuttered window. Rose looked at Annie and nodded at her across the bar, then she kept nodding her head, kept saying yes to some deep question that no one seemed to be asking but one that Rose heard loud and clear.

It was the same question being asked over and over and over. *Will you keep her? Will you keep her? Will you keep her?* the voice asked again and again. *Will you promise to keep her?*

And all Rose could do was stand there and nod yes and mean it with all her heart.

Thirty-Three

Sara leaned against her window, the one that looked out over the eastern horizon. The sun had been up for a long time. Sara felt strangely awake, almost electrified, in spite of the fact that she had just made it home, had been up most of the night, dozing occasionally in Eddie Springer's bed. She had listened to him breathing softly out on the living room sofa. What irony, she thought, to find someone like him now. This late in life.

Sara had been visiting doctors. First Dr. Walker downtown. Then to Birmingham. But the doctors said time would do what time would do. They had given her a prescription, given her advice, then given her a picture of her future that she had already known was coming. Now she had to make decisions and find herself a place where she would eventually go. A place where she would live memory free until her death. Her hope now was that she would forget the forgetting. She didn't want to be aware day by day that the brain she had worked so hard to fill with the facts and figures and fancies of life would be depleted. Everything she ever fed into it would be replaced with nothing. Eaten away bite by bite.

The doctors had tried to make her look at the bright side. That with medication, with mental exercises, she would be able to continue living a normal life for an indefinite amount of time.

She wanted to slap them all. Hard. She wanted to tell them that her joy was not in the keeping. It was in the getting. It was in the learning more new, unknown things every day. It was rereading a work of Chekhov after twenty years and getting something new from it. It was understanding that new discoveries were being made by the second and that the universe was unfolding, peeling back layer after layer of mystery until someday they would discover…

And Sara stopped thinking those things because a small shot of hope ran up her arm. The word *discover* rising in her heart. Her tongue rolled over the word, tasted it aloud. "Discover," she said. Then she said it again, and it occurred to her that technology was moving faster than even those who understood it could comprehend. Technology raced forward, determined to usher in a new day, a different life so that even in the backwoods of Echo, it inched its pulsing fingers forward.

"They just might find a cure," she said to the green grasses stretching out under the pine trees. "They might outrace the eraser in my mind. Just in time." It was an outside chance, but it was better than nothing. Better than a dark corridor that would lead into the essence of nothing at the end of her days.

But now here she was with this new friend. This friend who spoke three languages—if you counted Latin. A friend who asked questions and listened to the answers. Who was still curious about making new discoveries after all these years. And that's what they had spent their night doing. Drinking coffee and talking like the words were pure oxygen. Like they had been trapped in the airless vacuum of Echo only a few miles away from each other and not known it.

They had been giddy at having discovered a like-minded person. And that's when Sara had told Mr. Eddie Springer what she hadn't voiced yet even to Velma. About the doctors and about how her mind was racing away from her, pieces getting broken off and lost, lodged somewhere in the nebulous gray world just out of her reach. And Eddie had shaken his head and said, "Oh no, oh no." He had laid his hand on top of hers and squeezed it, then whispered, "Oh no," again because he understood. He fully and totally understood.

Sara stood looking out her window, but what she saw was far beyond the horizons of Echo. Eddie had taken her so seriously when she had told him the news. And then he had said very simply, "Let's go, Sara." When she had asked, "Where?" he had replied without hesitation, "Everywhere. While there's time."

He had jumped up from the table, run to remove a globe from the top of his bookshelf, and brought it to the little dinette and placed it in front of Sara, then taken his finger and spun the globe until it was one big, blurry, changing world. "Choose," he had said, laughing.

And Sara had laughed along with him and said, "Choose what?"

"Choose," he had said. "Just close your eyes, point your finger, and choose." And Sara had done just that. She had looked at Eddie and said, "All right. Very well. All right." She had closed her eyes, lifted her finger high in the air, and then lowered it slowly until she could feel the earth spinning just beneath her skin. She had brought her finger down, laughing all the way until she had stopped the earth. Keeping her eyes closed, she had said, "Well, tell me. I can't stand the suspense."

Eddie had gently, carefully lifted her finger. "Well," he had said, "looks like we're in for adventure."

She had opened her eyes then, leaned forward, and squinted at the latitudes and longitudes until the outline of Africa and the city of Tangier had emerged. Then she had smiled.

Eddie had supervised their moving to his computer, pulling up a chair for her to sit next to him, then signing on to the Internet. There they had researched travel plans and program discounts. "You're a member of AARP, I assume," he had asked, and she had said she was. He had said they should book their trips now.

"Now?" she had asked him, looking at the clock. It had been 1:33 a.m., and she couldn't believe the time had gotten away from her like that.

"Absolutely, undoubtedly now," he had answered, and then he had turned and looked at her as if he had been reading her mind. "How much more time should we let get away?"

Now, with little sleep and a heart full of excitement, Sara had confirmation numbers for what Eddie called "the first leg of our adventure." Their flights, their hotel rooms, and their car rental. An adventure indeed. They were scheduled to leave in four weeks.

Sara turned away from the window and reached for the phone. "I need to tell Velma."

For the third time Rudy had made Velma promise that she'd not go beyond the field and would stay away from the water. Then he'd laughed and said, "Mama, just don't go farther than one of those threads out front will let you."

She wrapped her fingers around a red one that trailed five feet off the porch and waved at him as he drove away. She watched Rudy get farther and farther away until he turned the corner and was gone.

She jerked the thread hard, and it came flying, the loose end taking off into the sky, then losing altitude and landing on the ground. Velma stood with her feet holding fast to the ground, testing the earth. Then she dropped to her knees and crawled as fast as she could to the porch steps, where she climbed up, turned, and sat down, breathless.

The cat looked at her with half-closed eyes and attitude. "Well, it was just a test," she said. She remained on the porch, watching dust and shadow, air and light, move up and down the road, over the house, across the field, and out toward Echo.

The phone rang, and Velma started to pull herself up to get it. But something heavy settled on her, something like a blanket—but not a blanket. Something she could feel but not touch. She reached for the rock in her pocket, wanted to wrap her fingers around it, wanted to will Joe off that upper part of the creek, or wherever he was, to her side. She thought that maybe, just maybe, she was having a heart attack, because the pressing down got heavier, but the symptoms were wrong. Just wrong. She forced her fingers into her pocket and wrapped them around the rock. In the time it took for a fish to rise beyond the surface of the water, to exit one world and enter another, Velma was far away, splitting through curtains of time without effort or sound.

And of all things, she found herself sitting with a young woman. She smiled at Velma like she knew her, and so Velma smiled back like she knew her too. The girl was telling her something, but the words were not coming out as words at all but as music. The girl's voice was all melody and medicine. Velma smiled and nodded even though she didn't understand any of it. All she knew was that somehow the girl belonged to her and she belonged to the girl.

And then she was back on the porch, just as fast as a fish could fall from the air and back into the wet, dark world it belonged to. Her fingers were on the rock, and the weight was trying to push her forward, headfirst down the stairs. But Velma, with a strange melody in her heart, cried out and stood to her feet. She walked down the stairs one solid, sure foot at a time and stepped out into the yard. She passed up the threads flying free from the posts, steps, and plants and walked flatfooted farther away, her teeth clenched, her chin raised in a stubborn streak of pain until she reached the mailbox.

She placed both hands on the door, opened it, and ran her hand inside, jerked it out as if she were escaping a nest of vipers, and then slammed the door shut. She held on to the mailbox, trying to decide how many steps it would take to get her back to the porch. "I won't make it," she said to Tomcat True, who was wrapping around her legs, purring, and head butting her ankles. He stepped in front of her and looked over his shoulder and meowed. "It's no use, Tom," she said. "I can't make it."

Then she heard that music again, that strange music from the girl. She looked up at the space of sky between the pine needles, the blue sheltering the green, and tried to figure out where the melody was coming from. It was the melody of the girl but also the man on the night he came to play on the front porch. It was the music she had heard the night she had danced free in the moonlight.

Velma looked at the dirt between her feet, seeing if it would shift, roll, and try to swallow her like before. But the music lifted her feet, and they began to move of their own accord so that Velma began to dance. Lifting her feet high and then putting them down lightly so that they barely touched the ground, mostly on her toes and on the balls of her feet, her heels never touching. With a circle around the creeping rosebush and two turns around the gardenias, she was at the first porch step, holding on to the banister. She looked out across the yard at the mailbox, at the pattern of her feet dancing across the sand, and doubled over in laughter, unable to stop.

That's the way Sara found her when she drove up to the house in a cloud of hurried, worried dust. She disembarked from the car and approached the laughing Velma.

"Well, have you gone completely crazy, or are you just having a fit?" Sara asked her with her hands high on her hips.

Velma tried to answer, but she couldn't. All she could do was laugh and hold her stomach and say, "Oh me. Oh my."

Sara laid a hand on her shoulder to shake her a little and tell her to straighten up, to get over herself, using her most stern, made-for-business teacher voice. But instead, she fell into a fit of chuckles. Then the chuckles became a stream of laughter. Then she was sitting on the porch steps, laughing just as hard as Velma. She was laughing about the absurdity of her life all the way around. About time and the now and her backwoods, funny friend. And about her new friend and the immediate stupid night, and about her big trip. And still laughing, she spit out, "I'm going to Tangier, Velma. I'm leaving town." Like it was the biggest joke around.

"Tangier?" Velma began to stand a little straighter and to wipe the tears from her face.

"Yes." Sara's face was suddenly very straight and serious. "That's what I've come to tell you, Velma. So you'd better straighten up and get right as rain on this rock business because I won't be here. I'm going to Africa with Mr. Springer."

Velma and Sara looked at each other with all the dignity they could muster. Then they were laughing with the tears rolling again, completely and wonderfully out of control.

Thirty-Four

Mernie sat at the bar, a glass of sweet iced tea in her hand. As usual, she had packed her own thermos of tea, feeling it was going to be a long night. The karaoke machine was hooked up, and already Johnny Pickard had started singing "Stand by Your Man." It was a woman's song as far as Mernie was concerned, and a woman should sing it, but Johnny had already had a few beers. His wife, Jewel, stared out the window. She didn't look like standing by Johnny was what was on her mind. And sure enough, when Johnny got down from the stage with scattered applause from the crowd, Jewel got up and began singing Nancy Sinatra's version of "These Boots Are Made for Walking."

Rose came out of the office. "Are Johnny and Jewel at it again?"

"I guess so." Mernie straightened her wig and sipped her tea.

Rose crossed her arms, leaned them on the bar. "It's the way they solve their marital differences." She smiled at Mernie. "It seems to work things out for them. They're in here about every other month for a sing-off."

Johnny sat, his stare cold as ice as Jewel paced, bent, and

pointed straight at him every time she sang, "One of these days, these boots are gonna walk all over you."

Rose laughed and said, "I'd bet you money that the next song up in this dueling match will be Johnny singing Kenny Rogers's 'Ruby, Don't Take Your Love to Town.'"

"I don't bet," Mernie said, shifting her wig again so that the part felt right sitting on her head.

"Well, that's good, Mernie, 'cause everybody knows there's no such thing as a sure thing." She looked over both shoulders. "Hey, where's Annie?"

"I'm right here." She had brushed her hair and put on her Burt's Bees lip balm. "Time for dinner, right?"

"The man of the hour hasn't shown up."

"Oh, but he will," Annie said.

"What makes you so sure?"

Just then the front door opened, and Rudy walked in. Annie gave Rose a wink and a smile.

Johnny was warming up his Kenny Rogers.

Rose ignored Johnny, keeping her eyes on Rudy. He was showered, clean-shaven, and there was something different about him. She wasn't sure what it was, but she liked it.

"It's all yours, Mernie," Rose said. "Don't let Johnny and Jewel forget to sing a duet before they leave."

Rose and Annie climbed into Rudy's truck. They pulled out of the parking lot, turned left at the red light, and headed out old Highway 41 to the pine-covered backwoods of Echo, where Mullet Creek was running free in the moonlight. Where the old owl was just waking up and getting ready to hunt. Where Velma and Sara were still on the porch steps, fighting off laughing fits and watching the lightning bugs rise higher and higher into the trees.

Thirty-Five

They were winding their way through the late twilight, at the end of a long day but the beginning of a night to remember. As they turned onto Millers Ferry Road, Annie thought the name sounded familiar.

After a few miles they turned down a dirt road and passed a stand of pine trees on their right, and then there was the small white house. They could see the creek running its course one hundred yards or so to the left of the house, offering a good view of the water through the trees growing at the water's edge.

Annie sucked in her breath and then began to cough.

"Annie?"

"Think I swallowed a bug," she said and gripped her guitar. "A big one."

Annie knew this house. This was it. The place she had come to and watched the woman from the woods instead of knocking on the door like she had planned. This was the place her mother had been and where she hoped she might find some answers.

There was no wind, and the threads were lying on the ground where they had last fallen across the front yard. They weren't so obvious when the wind was completely still like it was now, for which Rudy was grateful. He looked up, expecting to see his mother on the porch by now and the porch light coming on, but there was no sign of her. Then he noticed that there wasn't a single light on inside the house. He cocked his head, considering her absence, then took the porch steps two at a time, threw open the front door, and yelled, "Mama?" But there was no answer.

"Looks like something is wrong," Annie said.

Rose stood next to Annie. "This is the place, isn't it? The place in your picture?"

"Yeah. No doubt about it."

The porch light came on, and Rudy came out the front door. He stood in the middle of the porch, his arms folded, staring at the floor. Rose and Annie walked up the porch stairs.

"What is it, Rudy? What's happened?" Rose asked, laying a hand on his arm.

"She has to stay tied to the house," he said, and he looked down at the strings, then waved his hand at them. "That's her thing. She has to stay tied down or something. But she's not here." He looked toward the creek, walked back down the stairs and around the corner of the house, calling "Mama" again.

Annie sat down on a porch step, her guitar resting in her lap. Tomcat True came out from under the house and jumped up beside her. "Well, hey there," she said, putting out her hand and beginning to stroke his fur.

Rudy came around the other side of the house, walked up, and leaned on the railing. "There's no sign of her."

"You worried?" Rose asked him.

"Like I said, she doesn't leave." He looked toward the back of the house. "That is, except to walk to the store that way." He nodded toward the woods that ran along the back of the house. "But she doesn't need anything right now. It wouldn't have been that." He looked down toward the water. "And she doesn't fish anymore since Daddy died." He looked down hard at the ground, thinking. "Y'all stay put. I'm gonna go check the old barn round back." He walked off around the house, leaving Annie and Rose on the porch.

"This is a pretty place," Annie said. She stroked the cat that was purring now and rubbing up against her leg. "Kinda creepy out here but still pretty."

Rose laughed a little, looking around. "Yeah, it is a little creepy, but I bet you get used to it."

They watched the water running off in the short distance. Rose took a step in that direction, stood looking out through the trees for a moment.

"You fish, Annie?"

"Never. I've been a city girl through and through."

"I used to fish," Rose said, "but it's been a long time."

Rudy emerged around the corner. "Nothing. Broken-down old thing and all kind of animals nested up in there. I don't know why Mama don't burn the thing down." He walked over and stood next to Rose. "Think I'll take a walk by the creek. Just see if Mama has gone for a little swim or something."

"Sounds good." Rose put her hands in her pockets. "Mind if we join you?"

"Ahh, not me. I'm good right here." Annie slid her guitar off her lap and made room for the cat.

"We can hear you," Rudy told her as his eyes scanned the edge of the woods. "You don't even have to yell. Your voice'll carry. Just call us."

"All right." Annie bent over and buried her face in the cat's neck.

Rudy and Rose walked toward the trees growing at the edge of the water. Rudy reached down, picked up a flat rock, and slung it out toward the center of the creek, trying to do anything to steady his nerves, to keep those bugs from taking over his skin right now. It skipped three times, sliding just over the water's surface, then it disappeared. Moss hung from the old oaks that stood along the water's edge, mixing in with the palms and cypress trees.

"It's different here," Rose said, and Rudy laughed. "I mean, it's only a few miles from the bar, but it feels like it's a million miles away."

"I know what you mean." Rudy lit a cigarette, looked up and down the creek. "Mama?" he called out and listened for a while, but there was no answer. He bent down to search for another rock. "It was like that growing up. Kids in town lived in another world to me. They might come out on the creek on weekends to fish or swim, but they didn't live out here. It was always different, but it was never weird and crazy. Just boring swamp and bad TV reception." He skipped the second rock but never watched it. His eyes were already searching up and down the banks, looking for a white tennis shoe, for an apron, for anything that might be evidence that his mama had been there.

Rose thought about Rudy as a little boy, about Rudy growing up out here. While other kids rode bikes with their next-door buddies, Rudy would have been doing—what exactly? She didn't know, but she did know that whatever it was, he'd done it alone.

Rudy chose another flat rock, stood up, and started to skip it across the water, but he stopped, turned his head, and listened for something. He looked back at the house, down to the water, up at the thickening clouds, and shook his head. "It's too quiet out here. Way too quiet. I don't like it." There were no sounds of crickets chirping, no night birds calling out in the trees, no owl, not even the sound of the water moving. Then he heard a humming sound winding its way softly down toward him from the house. He turned and looked back up the little hill. Annie was humming again, and he recognized the song. Rudy felt something strange, but instead of bugs, he felt tiny needles pricking his skin. He turned and looked up the creek, squinting into the fading light as the old, familiar refrains of "King of the Road" caught his ear. He started to hum along in unison, but then he saw something

moving, something coming toward him. Then there was nothing there. Then he saw it again.

"What is it?" Rose asked.

Rudy looked at the boat moving slowly down the creek,
coming toward him out of the darkness. "Daddy?" he said,
and before he thought about it, he began to walk out into the
water—shoes, jeans, and all.

"Rudy." Rose stepped into the edge of the water beside
him and grabbed him by the arm, hard. "Rudy, nobody's
there."

"You don't see him?" Rudy asked her, and she followed his
eyes, looked out toward the center of the creek. The cigarette
had dropped from his fingers, was floating forgotten on the
surface of the water. He took another step forward, and Rose
moved with him, her jeans now wet up to the knees. "No,
Rudy, stop." But he was determined, was ready to swim out
to the boat if his father didn't turn toward the bank.

"Go on back now, Rudy," he heard him say. His voice
floated out across the water from the center of the creek.

"Daddy?" Rudy said again. "How'd you get here?"

"Get on back up to the house, Son," Joe said. His voice
was more like an echo, as if Rudy was hearing words spoken
a long time after his father had said them. "Hurry now. Time's
running out."

"But, Daddy…" He wanted to tell him so many things
in that moment that he took another step forward and was
quickly approaching the drop-off that would put him waist

deep, then chest deep, and then over his head. He wanted to tell him that he was sorry for not fishing with him when he had the chance. For getting mad at him when he was just trying to do his best. For getting drunk one time too many and not coming around.

"Son, your mama's coming home," his daddy said, and with that, Rudy turned and looked back at the house. "And you have work to do."

As much as he wanted to climb into that boat and have a long conversation, he turned around and took Rose's hand, and they walked up out of the water onto the bank.

"Rudy." He turned back as his daddy called. He was drifting farther and farther away. "Sometimes you can't fight evil with a shotgun."

Rudy stepped back into the water and said, "What do you…," but no one was there. Just creek and darkening sky.

Annie was sitting in the porch swing with her guitar on one side and Tomcat on the other, looking very much at home. She began to rock, her feet pushing back and forth, back and forth off the porch planks as Rudy and Rose approached with a wet, sloshing sound. "You went in the water?"

Rose and Rudy sat on the steps and began to take off their shoes and socks. Rose rolled up the wet ends of her jeans to her calves.

"Sorry 'bout that," Rudy said, "but I saw him whether

you did or not. It was him; it was my—" But headlights from an approaching car pulled onto the dirt road and interrupted him. Then the car attached to the lights emerged from the edge of the trees—a big blue convertible with the top down. Rudy, Rose, and Annie were caught in its beams, and all stood to their feet before the driver parked the car and shut off the engine. Sara emerged from the car with a great air of satisfaction.

"I've seen that car," said Annie. "I've watched it turning corners."

Sara went around the car and opened the passenger door.

"Hand me a thread," Velma said.

"You don't need a thread," Sara answered.

"Yes I do. I know when I need a thread, and I need one right now."

"Velma, we just rode fifty miles without a thread. I watched you dance all over this yard without a thread. Now get out of the car."

"I was drunk, and now I'm sober. I need my thread."

Rose and Annie looked at each other. They heard a rustle up in the trees somewhere and cut their eyes in unison to a moving shadow above them.

"You were not tipsy, Velma. Now just get out."

"Yes I was. I know tipsy 'cause I've seen it. I may not have touched a drop of nothing, but something got hold of me, and I was loony, downright tipsy—again."

Sara crossed her arms and started pacing, mumbling under her breath. Then she turned. "What did I tell you? I'm going to Africa in four weeks, Velma. Four weeks. And I want to see you well and mobile before I go."

"What's all this about, Mama?" Rudy asked from the darkness behind her.

"Son, would you just hand me a thread?" For the first time Velma remembered that company was coming. "Oh my goodness!" She looked up to see the two people standing side by side on her porch. "Oh my goodness," she said again. "Company came."

"Yes, Mama," Rudy said. "Company came, but somebody wasn't home." He walked to the open car door and leaned in and said again, "Somebody wasn't home!"

And with that he grabbed her and lifted her from the passenger seat, twirled her three times in the dirt of the yard, her legs flying out like a kite, around the gardenia bush, past the climbing roses. And Velma screamed, "Lord, lord, put me down, Rudy! Put me down!" And then added at the top of her lungs, "But not on the ground!"

Rudy laughed and put her down slowly on the first porch step. "You scared me, Mama. Thought that a goblin had carried you away."

Sara stepped forward. "We just took a ride." She looked at Rudy. "And you got her out of the car and to the porch without her having to walk a single step."

"She took a step." He looked at her and smiled. "She actually left the house."

"Rudy," Sara said with a huff of breath, "you should've seen her. She was dancing all over the yard."

"Is that a fact? Dancing, huh?"

"It's a fact, Rudy. I was light as a feather. But I tried to tell Sara, I think I was tipsy again. You know," she leaned toward him and whispered, "like that other night—from the rock and such."

"Well, you high-stepping, gallivanting woman." He turned her around to face Rose and Annie. "I'd like for you to meet a couple of friends of mine. This is my good friend Miss Rose McClarney." He let the last name, brand-new to him, roll off his tongue. "And my new friend, Annie."

"It's good to meet you, and you should know that I don't drink a drop of hard liquor."

"Pleasure to meet you too," said Rose, standing there in her bare feet and wet jeans.

Annie stood, silently watching the woman who had been so close to her that day in the yard, the face of the woman in the photograph. She tried to say something nice, like Rose, but the words didn't come. Instead she stopped and brushed Tomcat again, who was winding his way around her legs and then back across the porch to Velma.

Sara stood at the edge of the porch now, oblivious to the introductions. She was looking up at the early-night stars, thinking about Ahab and Moby Dick and Eddie Springer and Africa.

A shadow flitted through the trees, watching the little gathering in the yard. It dropped a bit lower to get a better look at the group and at what it knew was in Velma's pocket.

Something large, too large for a tree branch, moved suddenly above them in the limbs and leaves. "I don't like the sound of that." Then Rudy said, *"Inside!"* with such force that even Sara moved quickly off the porch.

Rudy looked to the trees. He could see the branches still moving, and for just a second he saw a pale face flash out at him between the limbs. Then it was gone. Rudy jumped back and caught his breath. Then he stepped forward, looking through the treetops again, searching. His skin began to crawl something fierce, but he clenched his jaw—hard. Then he went inside, turned, and locked the door behind him.

Thirty-Six

Eddie Springer was drinking a Heineken, courtesy of Rose's last beer order. He leaned on the bar, checked out the few customers who remained, and then looked back up the bar where Mernie sat with her wig sliding a little too far to the right. He raised his beer and smiled at her. Mernie raised her tea glass, but she didn't smile back at him.

He had called Sara twice with no answer, and he hoped that she hadn't decided to back out. That she hadn't suddenly looked at things a little differently in the light of day and decided that she didn't even know him and was being foolish.

"Don't change your mind, Sara." That was one of the last things he had said to her before going to bed on the sofa. Then she had been gone the next morning before he could repeat it. He had hesitated before picking up the phone, thinking she might be napping. Finally he had dialed her number, which she had written on his pad by the computer, to say, "Don't change your mind, Sara."

If she changed her mind, he didn't know that he wanted to go. Sometimes people weren't meant to travel alone. Maybe that was why he had taken so long to make up his mind. He had been waiting and not knowing that it was Sara Long he had been waiting for to come in and sweep him off his feet. And sweep him she had.

He smiled at the thought of her and turned the Heineken up again. But the smile was short-lived because he remembered she wasn't answering the telephone. He felt like a schoolboy. After trying to reach her by phone, he had gone out to pace on the porch, waiting for Rudy to come home. To tell him what to do or to help him find her. But Rudy never came. Finally, in a fit of desperation, Eddie shaved, put on a clean shirt, called a taxi, and traveled the few miles to Rose's Place, where he thought he'd find Rudy. But all he found was the seriously sober woman on the stool who watched the cash register and the door like a hawk.

Now she was walking toward him. "Don't suppose you care for another one of those?"

Eddie raised the beer, discovered it was empty.

"Maybe just one more, but that's my limit."

"I hear you." Mernie reached under the counter into the beer cooler, took out a cold bottle, opened it, and passed it to him. Then she leaned on the bar and picked up her glass of tea, took a sip, and stared at Eddie. "Want to tell me about it?"

He looked at her and shrugged his shoulders. "I think I'm pretty embarrassed about the whole situation. Do you believe in love at first sight?"

Mernie laughed, but it wasn't a cruel laugh. Before Eddie knew it, he was chuckling along with her. Then she answered

him, "I believe some things sure are meant to be. You know
what I mean?"

"I think I do," Eddie said and spilled the beans. All of
them. Scattered them right there across the bar. He told her
about retiring, about his love of maps, and about how he
would just die if he didn't see some places before, well, before
he died for real. And how he had met this woman, maybe she
knew her, named Sara Long, and how this woman had taken
his breath away from the moment he saw her. He told her
about the picnic in the car and the ride home. About Sara and
him being up to all hours planning their big adventure and
that now his entire world, his very existence, hinged on her
not changing her mind. And how he couldn't find her, and
he'd been trying all day, and that was the reason he had ended
up right here, right now, at this very moment, telling her his
story.

"You don't say." Mernie looked him squarely in the eye.
"Seems to me a person could just not be answering the phone.
Nothing to worry about, you know. Sometimes I get so tired
of those machines calling to sell me something that I don't
answer either. But worried for nothing or not, you've waited
long enough for an adventure. I can understand you being
nervous." She glanced at the clock on the wall as the last customers said good night and walked out the front door.

"C'mon, lover boy. I'll take you home." Mernie closed out
the cash register and put the money in the safe. She reached
up with two hands and twisted her wig as if she were tight-

ening down a hat. She picked up her raincoat, her pocket-book, her car keys. "Sara will turn up tomorrow, you'll see. Before you know it, y'all will be hightailing it to discover the world."

Mernie locked the front door to Rose's Place, and she and Eddie got into her old Ford. They drove in silence down the highway. Both of them noticed that the air felt hot and heavy.

Thirty-Seven

Rudy walked to the window, pulled back the curtain. He wasn't fooled for a second. He knew what he saw. And what he saw wasn't human. Not by any means.

"Hey, Rose, what did you say your visitor looked like?"

Annie came and stood beside him, looking out the window. "Is he here?"

"That ain't no he." Rose stepped up behind Rudy and stood on her tiptoes, trying to see between him and Annie. "That's an *it*."

Velma said, "What're y'all talking about?"

A wind started up outside, a low whistle. Rudy watched the threads on the porch snap up and begin to fly frantically about. Then a pale face emerged from the shadows beyond the porch railing. Annie sucked her breath in, and the three of them jumped away from the window, Rudy dropping the curtain.

"What is it?" Velma took a step forward. "What are you not telling me?"

Rudy walked over and put a hand on her shoulder. "I think we got some serious trouble."

"Yeah," Annie said, "like we need a priest and some holy water or something."

"That might only work in the movies, Annie," Rose said.

"Velma?" Sara said, but Velma didn't answer. "Rudy? What's happening?"

Rudy went back to the window and tried to stay at the edge, but when he pulled back the curtain, the thing was closer, was lifting one of Velma's threads in his hand, was carrying it toward the porch, where it wrapped itself around the porch railing and began to crawl along the banister. Then leering up at the window like he could see right through the curtain into the house and into Velma's pocket, he lifted another thread.

"This thing's been chasing us," Annie said. "Actually, I think it's just been chasing me." She walked over to the couch, picked up her guitar, sat down, and held it against her chest. "I think this is all my fault."

Velma walked over and sat beside her, laid a round hand on her back. "No, honey. I don't know you or what's been after you, but whatever is out there"—Velma pulled the rock from her pocket and turned it over in the lamplight—"has come for this." The rock was plain, dark, nothing but a rock.

"A rock?" Annie peered at it closely. "A rock?" she repeated, not wanting to tell the old woman that it was unlikely what she'd seen would want *that*.

"Trust me, it's not an ordinary rock," Sara said and sat in Velma's chair.

"Then what is it?" Annie asked her. At that moment the rock exploded in so many colors that Velma almost dropped it. "Whoa," Annie said, and even Rose stepped closer. Rudy stayed by the window, watching the man or creature or whatever he was picking up the threads one by one and pointing them toward the house, where they began to grow and circle and change. A thread became a dark, inky vine and crossed in front of his face at the window.

"Um, those threads of yours really have to go."

"Rudy, I don't think this is the time to start fussing with me about my threads."

"Oh yes it is." Rudy looked back at her for just a second, and as he did, the glass cracked where the dark thread pushed against it even harder. "Matter of fact, I might need to take a hatchet to 'em in a hurry."

Velma dropped the rock back into her pocket.

"What is that thing?" Annie said. "Where'd you get it?"

"Storytelling man gave it to me." Velma walked to the corner of the window and looked out past Rudy. Only a slice of the porch light was left; the threads were now all black and almost covered the window. "Those aren't my threads."

"Yeah, they are. I watched that man out there turn 'em on you, Mama." Rudy turned and walked out of the living room, and they all watched him go and then heard a closet door open.

"Rudy?" Velma called after him, but he didn't answer. She looked back at the window. "You mean my own threads have done this?"

"No." Annie put her guitar down and went to stand beside Velma. "This *thing* was after me, I'm telling you. It come after me all the way from Texas and followed me here to Echo, then to Rose's. It was in her car, and now it's followed me all the way out here to your house. This isn't your fault—it's *mine*."

"But, honey, I got a piece of heaven." Velma took the rock out again, shook it slightly in front of Annie. It was full of rolling white light and did indeed look like a piece of heaven. "This here is an original piece of heaven, and hell's looking for it. I know what he wants from me. What have you got that would cause some kind of slinky demon to be chasing after you?"

And for that question, Annie had no answer. Then she said, "My guitar. That's all I have in this world."

Rudy walked back into the room, pumping his daddy's old shotgun as he came. He stood by the door for a moment, then taking a deep breath, put his hand on the door and threw it open. But there was nothing but a solid blackness of threads blocking the way out. Rudy stepped back, fired into the threaded trap. A scattered hole opened up but closed with such quickness that Rudy slammed the door shut. "Reckon that really was Daddy out there on the creek, and he was right." He looked at Rose. "Some evil can't be fought with a shotgun." He looked back at the window, contemplated that if he hurried, he might make it out the back door. "'Course I think if I could get one shot at that pale face through a window, we'd find out how it agrees with him." Rudy took off for the kitchen, looking for a way out.

The front window cracked again, and throughout the house windows began cracking. They were being closed in completely, buried by Velma's threads turned wicked. Rudy yelled, and the shotgun fired, was pumped and fired again.

Sara sat quietly in the chair as if she were supervising a seventh-grade dance. She might not have been talking, but she was thinking. She was thinking that now—when she had finally found somebody and developed one last purpose before she lost her mind completely—she wasn't going to make it to see morning. "Just my luck," she said aloud. But no one, including Velma, was paying her any mind.

Rudy ran back in the living room. "Did you see him? Did you?" The women were still; no one moved. "He was in here. I was firing at him out the back door, and he walked right through it. Walked *right* through it," he said again. "I *hate it* when Daddy is right." He looked at Velma. "Mama, what am I supposed to do if buckshot can't stop something in its tracks?"

Velma didn't answer him directly. She was studying the way that Annie had her lips twisted up to one side, was tugging at a lock of her hair. Velma had seen lips like those before—in the mirror. She recognized her now. She was the girl from her vision, the girl from the future. But she recognized so much more. She saw the cut of that chin, and when

Annie turned and looked at her, she saw the deep dark brown of her eyes. And in the middle of all the madness that had come upon them, Velma smiled. "Oh my," she said. That itch she had felt all night to watch the girl, to watch the way she moved, her facial expressions, that bit of temper, that attitude—all so familiar.

"Mama, whatever that thing is, it's here with us now." Rudy threw open the front door. "If it can't be stopped with a shotgun, I think we need to do our best to get away." But he stopped short, looking at the thing that was now suffocating the house. "Pretty soon there won't be anything left of this place—and that includes us." Rudy tried to close the door, but the black threads had spread over the doorframe and began scaling the inside of the living room walls. They came in through the broken windows, crawled along the floor, began to attach to the furniture.

"Get away from the walls," Rudy said, but it was unnecessary. The women were moving, like him, toward the center of the room, the five of them forming a tiny circle, their shoulders touching one another as they watched the darkness creep toward them. The threads began to weave their way down the hall from the kitchen to climb into the living room from the other direction.

Then suddenly Rudy couldn't breathe. Something unseen had clamped down on his windpipe and was strangling him. The bugs swarmed over him, crawling up his legs, across his back, down his chest. Rudy pointed frantically to his throat.

"Rudy?" Rose yelled. "Rudy?"

Velma brushed her hands frantically across his back and chest, but Rudy shook his head no, pointed to his throat. There was a great splitting sound, like the rupture of an iceberg, and Rudy fell like death to the floor.

Velma took the rock from her pocket, watched the swirling colors it took on for a second, and then slammed it into Rudy's hand. "Take him somewhere!" she screamed and clutched his fingers, forming a fist around the rock. "Get him out of here now!" She held fast to his closed fist, refusing to let Rudy go.

Thirty-Eight

Rudy sat in his daddy's boat, a cane pole in one hand. The red cork bobbed softly on the surface of the water. He lifted it up, checked his worm automatically. Then his daddy said, "It's just the wind, Rudy. Drop it back down." And he did. The sun was baking the top of his head, his shoulders, his back. The cicadas were singing full blast in the trees, dying down when the breeze picked up, then singing again. Stars of light were cast on the water as far as he could see, sunlight in the ripples.

Then it hit him. He looked at his father. Looked over his shoulder for the house, but he knew they were way up the creek, far past the house, even way past the springs and the first bend to the right. He looked at the trees, at the bank. Rudy had the creek memorized, but he didn't recognize this spot. They were farther north than he had ever been. His father began to whistle very softly, his eyes on the corks of the two lines he had thrown out.

"Daddy?"

His father looked up at him.

"Am I dead?"

The whistling stopped. "Well, I don't know, Son." He

cocked his head to one side and smiled a little. "Do you feel dead?" He snatched a pole, began to fight a fish to the surface.

Rudy leaned over and could see the fish swimming fast and furious back and forth, his silver sides shining under the water. Then the fish was free, swimming farther than the line would reach.

"He got away, Rudy. I lost him!" Joe pulled the pole up from the water, looked at the empty hook, and shook his head. "They're not biting at worms today, Rudy. Pass me that cricket bucket, will you?"

Rudy picked up the cricket bucket, put it down between Joe's feet. His father took out a cricket, baited the hook, and wiped his fingers on the leg of his jeans, then dropped the line back into the water. "Now, you were telling me about being dead."

"No, Daddy." Rudy checked his hook. The bait was still there. "I was asking you if I was dead."

"Oh, that's right. And I was asking you if you felt dead." He picked up a thermos, opened the cap, and took a sip. "Well, do you?"

Rudy looked up at the green trees, the tall, tall cypress, the blue, blue sky and said, "Not right now, I don't."

"You want some iced tea?"

"No sir. What I want to know is where am I? I mean, Daddy, you were right to tell me to go back earlier because…" He struggled to try to put some words to everything, to try to describe… "But I think, Daddy, that I was just dying a second ago. So maybe I am dead. I mean, I'm here with you, and you haven't exactly been sitting down to dinner this year."

"Your mama got you out just in the nick of time, I imagine." He smiled without looking up.

"How'd you know?"

"Oh, Velma is such a stubborn woman." He shook his head. "She's lost enough, you know. I don't imagine she's gonna let something snatch you out of the world before your time if she can have anything at all to do with it."

The wind picked up, started blowing hard. The cicada music picked up to a crescendo, becoming so loud it was almost deafening for a moment.

"You might not get to be here, Rudy," he said. "I hear there's some nasty business that has the little house covered up darker than night."

"Something fierce." Rudy lifted his pole up, the bait gone. "I missed him," he said. "I never even knew I had a nibble."

"Minnows got your bait, Son."

"You know, I never could fish worth nothing," Rudy said. "Some things never change."

His father looked at him, and Rudy looked back.

"Some things do, Rudy. They just change a little late."

Rudy nodded.

"But a little late is not the same as too late. Understand?"

"Maybe." Then he shook his head. "No, no I don't understand."

Joe pulled up his pole where the wind had blown the cork too close to the boat, recast it farther out in the water.

Rudy looked up and down the creek. "Daddy, how are you going to hear out here what's going on at the house?"

"Oh, it's easy to hear out here."

The wind died down; the cicadas went silent. A mullet jumped out. Joe pulled up the line, dropped the red cork farther out on the third cast. Satisfied, he let it rest. "Now listen to me. That darkness will eat your mind, Rudy. Yours and everybody else's. And if it gets that, it'll get everything."

Rudy tried to clear his head, felt like he was suddenly three places at once, like times were rolling over him and echoing and changing, melting into one another. There was the voice of his mother crying, and his father saying something about Rudy being born and babies not making it, and then the voice of his mother screaming, "Take him somewhere," and his daddy's voice saying something. But it was getting farther and farther away, becoming muffled. The voices became one voice in his ears, garbled and perplexing.

"Rudy," his father said. "Rudy, look at me."

Rudy looked at his father and saw him, saw the way he was looking at him.

The other voices faded.

"I wasn't a perfect man in my ways. You're not a perfect man in your own ways." He pulled up the pole, checked the empty hook. "Something got my bait too."

They both laughed. Joe started humming his old stand-ard, and Rudy relaxed a little, leaned into the familiar of his daddy and breathed a little easier.

"Bait's all gone. Guess that means I'm done for the day." Still humming, he wrapped the line around the cane pole, spinning it until the line was tight, until the hook was pushed into the bottom of it. Then he stood and looked at the sky. The cicadas began to hum. "But listen. What's in your mind, Rudy, don't give it room. No regrets, Son. Whatever is nag-ging at you, make it better and move on. Because that, and that old nasty scout, feed on regret. Fear, doubt, and regret. You hear me? You tell your mama I said that too. You tell her that scout will pluck those three things out of the back of someone's mind, things they don't even know are there, and it'll get stronger by the second while it's doing it. It feeds on those things. You tell Velma I said so. Now, get up, Rudy."

Rudy just sat, looking at him, still felt like he hadn't set things straight with him.

"Get up, you hear me?"

The wind slammed through the trees. In a matter of sec-onds Rudy watched it go from sunny-day fishing to a violent storm with the boat rocking back and forth.

"Daddy?" Rudy looked at him. "What is this? Where are we?"

"You gotta go home now, Rudy. Stand up!" And with that he stepped over and grabbed Rudy's shirt, powerful as he once was, and jerked him quickly to his feet. He looked over Rudy's shoulder down the creek and said, "Make it all the way home, you hear me? Your mama's waiting on you."

Then Joe did something that he had never done. He grabbed Rudy in a bear hug and pulled him close to his chest, held him tight. And the surprise of it, the long overdue need of it, caused Rudy to choke, and he began to cough to cover up the fact that he was crying.

And then with a strong twist of both his hands, Joe flipped Rudy out of the boat.

The water was colder than anything he remembered. So cold it took his breath away. He was at once motionless and on the bottom and wondering how he could have fallen so deep so fast. He pushed up toward the small bit of light he saw there on the surface, trying desperately to reach the top, to be able to fill his burning lungs. But the light was so very far away.

Thirty-Nine

Velma pursed her lips and looked at the light flashing from Rudy's fist, where she still held the rock secure. "I think he's gonna be all right," she whispered. She looked up at Rose's green eyes and for the first time realized how pretty she was. Not like a young girl but like a woman.

"I think something has got his body, but I got a feeling the rest of him is someplace else," Velma said. She bent down and put her ear next to Rudy's lips. The air was barely moving, but he was breathing. "Of course, if he's going to be on this earth, he needs his body."

Then a wondrous, surprising thing happened. Annie began to sing. Just sing. Her guitar was leaning against the wall. She was standing in the middle of the room, her eyes closed, swaying back and forth and singing like that one small songbird on a frozen winter morning. The one bird that wouldn't be daunted or beaten back, no matter how unsheltered. Annie swayed and sang with a voice that could call souls home. And if the singing wasn't enough on its own, it was the fact that she sang "King of the Road" that amazed Velma. The sound of *that* song, *Joe's* song, coming out of Annie caused Velma to shake her head in wonder.

Velma saw the girl she would become in the days and

years ahead. A life full of light and promise and power that could cast off dark, sick shadows. Velma saw a brief image of the young woman she would one day sit down with. They had a future, she and the girl, she knew. And that day in her future, that part of it, would become a portion of the girl's past and remain there long after Velma had gone on.

Don't we all have our place in this earth? Velma thought. *Aren't we all just swimming upstream in the waters from our birth, trying to do the best we can? To understand it and then float back home again?*

And there was her son, laid out and barely breathing, but still with them. Was he turning into something, becoming something, even in his own way and at this late date? Was he becoming a man?

Like that girl there, and her singing like it was Easter morning on a Saturday night. Even with the light fading, Annie still stood there, humming, swaying, and seeing things that Velma would never know of.

That's when she looked at Annie again. She knew her face so well now. From a night full of love and lights of a different kind. A night full of the smell of pine needles, hot chocolate, and red velvet cake, and she leaned over closer to Rudy and whispered something into his ear. Then she smiled.

Forty

Rudy kicked his legs through the water—once, twice, three times—the light above growing brighter with each kick. Then he broke the surface, took one deep breath and another. Felt hands pulling him out of the water, felt his clothes drying. His body resting warm on the hard...where? He opened his eyes. Saw Rose's face, those green eyes, that dark hair, leaning over him. And his mother on the other side, smiling.

Rudy took a deep breath. He looked down and saw that his fist was tightly closed. He opened it, and there was the rock. Silent. Colorless. His mother plucked it from his hand, placed it back into her pocket, and patted it through her dress.

"Good to have you back, Son," Velma said, slowly pushing herself back into a standing position, her knees cracking as Sara extended her hand and helped her fully to her feet.

Rudy looked back and forth from Annie to his mother. His head was swimming. He felt as though he were still underwater. Rudy could feel the bugs again, but this time it was different. He felt them falling away. Exiting his skin and his life. He looked down, expecting to see them all around him, covering the floor, but there were none. Just the creeping, inky blackness. Rudy grabbed his mother's arm. "Daddy said to tell you, 'No fear,' Mama. 'No fear, no doubt, no re—'"

Before he could finish, Annie shouted, "My guitar!" and jumped forward to grab it from the couch. They rushed to stop her, to keep Annie in the safety of their circle, but they were too late. The watcher from the trees, from the backyard, from the car, stepped out of the walls and wrapped two gray arms around Annie in one fell swoop. Then, leering at Velma, the thing became something else entirely. The sickening, smiling face, the strangely rubbery body flattened out into a smoky, winged thing. It began pulling Annie, who was yelling and kicking with all her might, through those threads and right out the door. Rudy and Rose struggled to get a hold on Annie's legs and arms.

In that moment Velma understood. Hell wanted what she had. And they'd stop at nothing to take it from her. Even if it meant taking everything she'd ever wanted, what she loved most, and everything she had ever hoped for. That was what she had been trying to say, to wish for, sitting on that porch swing on her birthday. She had wished for a way to let it be known that this was life and that it had tasted good. With all the bitter and the sweet, it was still worth the plucking. It was all worth it, and she would do it again.

She had been trying to form those words, and in trying to form them, she had whispered, "Again, please. I'd do it all over again."

The wind had shifted, and she felt the man standing

somewhere out there down the road. That's where he had stepped out of the woods, full of magic, with his boots and wild eyes. And he'd brought her that rock that pulled her out of her skin, cast her under the dusty earth of memory, and then cast her out again onto the shore, back to the *now* to suffer, rejoice, and carry on. *That's what memory is. The taste of a lover's skin. The warm weight of a new baby. The passion of old love. The comfort of warm fires on a cold night. The pain of losing. The pleasure of keeping.*

It would stand to reason that something like that would call out all manner of beasts to try to take it away, but she wasn't afraid anymore. She trusted herself to keep it. It could never be taken from her—not really.

She took the rock, held it in her open palm. "You looking for something?" she said. The thing stopped pulling the yelling Annie. "Yeah, I thought so," she said. "Then maybe you need to put the little girl down and pick on me." Annie fell to the ground, and Rudy and Rose dragged her back through the doorway to the tiny space where they could still see the floor in the living room.

Velma understood now that the scout hadn't wanted Rudy and didn't want Annie. It wanted what she had been carrying in her pocket. But it was afraid of her, afraid of what she could do, which kept it from touching her. So it tried to touch what was closest to her—and to do it using every fear she'd ever carried, every weakness that had walked with those threads.

"You all right?" Rose asked Annie, kneeling down beside her.

"I think so."

Rudy took Annie by her shoulders, stood her up, and turned her around. "Maybe you should sing that song again. We're still not out of this mess."

By the door the pale thing appeared as a man again and was mesmerized by Velma as she moved slowly toward him, her hand held out before him. "That's right. It's just what you been after, just what you been looking for all these many, many years." Velma took another step forward, and the thing the storyteller called Old Slink stepped forward to grab the rock from her palm. But Velma closed her fist. As she did, the threads began to dissolve, to slowly wind their way back through the broken windows. The slink noticed, took a step back, then another.

"I ain't afraid of you no more. I ain't afraid." And as the dark threads fell away, Velma walked that thing back out into the yard, one brave, bold step at the time. With one final shudder, Slink turned to dust.

Forty-One

Velma and Sara sat on the back stoop. The darkness that had covered them was gone. All of it. No sign of the strange, pale face. No creatures trying to carry Annie away. How could they ever explain, any of them, what they'd been through? Who would ever believe them?

"Who would ever believe us, Sara?" Velma asked.

Sara didn't answer. She said what she'd been trying to tell her for weeks now but could never seem to get it said. "Velma, doctors say I'm losing my mind."

Velma didn't reply immediately. She had known for a while that this was coming. "The memory disease?" she asked her, and Sara nodded. "How long have you got?"

"They don't know. A piece here"—she fluttered her hand—"a piece there." Other than this morning, Velma thought Sara always looked so smart, so capable. She seemed stronger than some sneaky thing that might try to steal your mind away like a weasel in the henhouse.

"They say it's early, Velma, but that it doesn't matter what I take," she said, looking at her in all seriousness. "And it doesn't matter what I do, eventually." She looked away. "Eventually I won't be me anymore." Then she cut her eyes back to

Velma's face, and her eyes misted over. "And then I won't know you."

"There, there, Sara," Velma said without moving, just fingering the rock in her pocket, rolling it over and over, offering reassurances as if she were patting her on the back. "You'll always know me, Sara." Velma wrapped her fingers around the rock, grabbed it hard for reassurance. "I'm sure of it."

And something about her simple tone, her simple faith, steadied Sara's shaking hands. She looked in Velma's eyes, at the power that hid behind her soft edges, and Sara took a deep breath because she believed her. Something about Velma made her believe that she would indeed always know her friend. And holding on to one person, just one, full of the knowledge and memory of you, well, that would be enough for her. And Sara tried to memorize every line of Velma's face right there and then. To burn it deeply into the mind's eye of her brain. All the while she kept repeating to herself, *Remember, remember, remember.* Trying to remember had been her hobby, but now the word *remember* would become her mantra. Something she would repeat over and over again until it became the essence of her breathing.

"They could even find a fix, make a shot that cures it," Velma said.

"I thought of that. It's what got me out of the house. That old hope for a cure."

"Old hope's a good thing, Sara. You hang on to that."

Sara smiled at her and put her fingers over her face for a

moment. Then the sound of Annie's guitar strumming came to an end, and they could hear the tones of earnest, muffled voices coming from inside. Sara put her hands in her pockets. "I meant to tell you when we were out driving, but it was just too happy of a time."

Velma wrapped her arms around her. "That ride was wonderful. Just wonderful. I don't think I thanked you." And she squeezed her, hard.

"Now, that part about Africa, well, that was the truth."

"I know it was."

"Am I being foolish? Am I being a foolish old woman?"

"Reckon you'd be foolish not to do it," Velma said.

Sara nodded at her and smiled. "I thought that's what you'd say." She pulled her keys from her pocket and jangled them in her hand. "Then I'm going home and making plans." She didn't bother trying to stifle a big yawn. "Right after I take a four-hour nap."

And she was off, long, tired legs cutting a sharp picture as she walked through the backyard and disappeared around the corner of the house. Velma listened to her car start, could imagine her putting on those dark sunglasses, tying that scarf around her hair and neck, and driving off into the early light.

Morning had risen beyond the edge of the trees, over the open field to where those small, unseen markers rested in the dirt. Velma surveyed it all and thought about planting something new. Sunflowers, she decided. That old garden just lay unturned now. She would fill it full of sunflowers. Short ones and the really large ones.

Fear and doubt and regret. That's what Rudy had told her the threads were made of. And that thing had used 'em, turned 'em on her. On all of them. For two short minutes Rudy had sounded like a tent preacher. "Just lay those things on down," he'd said. "Lay 'em on down, and that dark will roll right out of town."

She fingered the rock in her pocket and thought about the creature that wanted to take what wasn't its to have—a piece of heaven—real life, real memories.

She heard the screen door open, and someone stepped out behind her. Annie stood there, holding a notebook in one hand.

"Hey there," Velma said.

"Hi." Annie came down the steps and sat next to Velma.

"First time I've seen you without that guitar." Velma smiled at her.

"I need to talk to you," Annie began. She looked at Velma and saw an older version of the smile that she'd carried around with her for so many years. She opened the notebook, slid out the photo, and handed it to Velma.

Velma reached for her glasses on top of her head, but they weren't there. She found them inside her apron pocket. She took them out and put them on, looked at the photo in her hand. And there they were—her and Joe and Rudy's last, best chance for young love. They were all smiles, hope, and laughter. Tears came to her eyes in spite of herself, but she blinked them back. Then she looked over at Annie and realized their hopes had come along after all.

"What happened to your mother?" Velma asked.

"How did you know she was gone?"

"I'm an old woman." Velma took the glasses off, looked out over the field at the rosy color of the old wood where the sunlight was hitting the barn. "Old women just know things." Velma put her glasses back on, looked down at the picture again.

"It was a brain aneurysm." Annie leaned over and looked at the picture too. "It was real sudden."

"I'm so sorry." Velma thought about the girl, about the way she had laughed that Christmas, about how full of life she'd been. "She was such a pretty girl. And you are such a pretty girl."

"Not so much."

"Yes, yes, honey. You've just tried to…" Velma searched for the right word. "Mess with it" was the best thing that came to mind. She looked at all the pierced places and the tiny tattoos. "You're going to grow right into your own kind of pretty, just you wait and see."

Annie held her hand out to take the picture. Then she saw the way that Velma was still looking at it, the way she was holding on to that Christmas. "You want to keep it for a while?" she asked her.

Velma smiled at her. "No, you keep it." She handed it

back to her. "I've got it right here," she said, pointing to her heart.

"It looks like it was a good day." Annie stuck a dirty sneaker out in front of her, pointed her toe, and brought it back in again. She was fishing for more story. She wanted to know the things that she suspected.

"It was one of the best days." Velma took her glasses off, folded them, and tucked them back into her pocket. "As a matter of fact, I think in my calendar of days, it goes down as one of my absolute favorites."

Annie smiled but didn't look at her.

"We were so happy about your mama. She was everything we had ever hoped for."

"Who was taking the picture?"

"Oh, now, honey, you don't have to go very far to know who was behind the camera." Velma studied the coloring in her cheeks, the shade of her hair, the shape of her eyebrows. "Maybe only as far as a mirror."

"Does he know who I am?" Annie asked.

"No," Velma told her. "Not yet anyway."

They sat for a little while, silently watching the sky lighten. The reds were turning to roses, to pinks.

"Don't tell him, then, okay?"

"Annie, he needs to know," Velma said. Besides, the fact was, she had already whispered as much in his ear when he was gone. She figured that was the real work that pulled him back.

"But not now. Not yet. Okay?" Annie twisted her lip to one side. Velma twisted her lip to one side too, and they sat there thinking some.

"Okay, for a little while." Velma pushed herself up from the step with a grunt. She stood and stretched those tired, cramped-up legs. "But only for a little while, a month or so…"

"No," Annie said. "Christmas. Give me till Christmas if I'm still here. It's only fitting."

Velma watched her, saw the little miracle that she was. So much the vision of her mother from that Christmas so long ago and also of Rudy. Such a combination. Everything and then some that she and Joe had wished for all those years ago. Funny that it had come around to this. All their disappointment not amounting to much but some missed years. Well, a whole lot of missed years. "No regrets," she said aloud.

"No regrets," Annie said and stood up with her.

"Do you need a place to stay? Wait." Velma tried to stick the odd pieces of her hair back in her bun. "No. What I meant was, do you need a place to live? A home?" She looked at what was left of the house—it looked a little wobbly. "It's not much, but it's what I have to offer."

Annie looked at the house too. She wanted to tell Velma that what she had growing up wasn't any better. Just different. And a whole lot less friendly, that was for sure.

"Oh, I hadn't even thought about…" She looked through the screen door, expecting to see Rose standing there in the kitchen, waiting on her, but it was empty. "That is, I think

I'm okay. I think I have a place." At least she hoped she had a place. She preferred the sound of palm trees to owls. One was kinda calming. One was still kinda creepy.

"Okay, then, for now let's be friends and keep our secret."

"It's a deal."

As they walked up the steps and into the kitchen, Annie rattled a full, bullet-speed report. "Rudy...," she began, but paused when she said his name. "Rudy and Rose walked out the front door to smoke, I guess, even though I tell her every day that it'll kill her and that she's too pretty a lady to smoke."

"Now, that's true." Velma wished she could just lean her tired body up in the corner with the broom and go to sleep. Instead, she turned on the oven and began to get out the things that breakfast was made of. Flour and milk and eggs and butter and sausage. Velma poured herself a cup of coffee, kept listening to Annie with one ear and thinking, *Joe, I just wish you could see this. I wish you could see who we're having for company this morning.* But then she thought about Joe on the creek, about Rudy's words to her that she wasn't crazy, and she thought that maybe Joe could see them. Maybe he'd been watching all along.

Velma listened to Annie prattle on about last night, about music, about singing, and saying, "Who knew that just singing a simple song could be such strong medicine? And you know what? I didn't even know *that* song. I mean, I knew the tune but not all the words until right then. They just came right out of me."

Velma continued saying, "Uh-huh, uh-huh," in all the right places. The wind shifted outside, and she heard her wind chimes. It was only a slight breeze, nothing consequential, nothing a person would notice much. In spite of this, Velma stopped mixing and walked to the back door with Annie at her side. There, sitting on the back stoop, was the man. He had a tiny knife in one hand, a piece of wood in the other, and was whittling something. He turned, lifted that hat a little, nodded to the two of them.

Annie and Velma looked at each other, and when they looked back, he was gone.

"Wow," Annie said.

"You saw him?" Velma asked.

"I saw him."

It was Velma who pushed the door open, and they stepped out onto the stoop. Annie was her shadow, right on her heels, moving every step with her. She leaned over, looked around the edge of the house, out toward the barn, but no man.

"He's gone," Velma said. There was a finality in her tone. A sense that he was truly gone.

"For good?"

"For good, for now," Velma said. She looked into Annie's brown eyes and saw Rudy reflected there. "Gone for good, for now."

Something occurred to her. She reached inside her pocket, fumbled around, shifted the coffee cup she still held in her hand, and then felt inside the other pocket, but came up empty.

"Your rock's gone?" Annie asked.

"Seems that way," Velma said with a mixture of relief and sadness. "Looks like all I've got left now is today."

Annie looked up at the sky, clear and blue beyond belief, then through the trees down to the water. The water caught the light, casting off its diamonds. She could see Rudy and Rose down at the water's edge, could hear the sound of their low voices but not the words they were saying.

She looked at the old woman, shoved her hands inside her pockets, and almost wanted to dance. She felt a laugh coming up from within and put her hand to her mouth to stifle it, but it escaped anyway. "Maybe today's all you need." She did a little quickstep. "Maybe today is more than enough."

Velma looked at her, at this child delivered by such strange grace to her door, this magical, musical child, so young and so full of promise and, oh, Lord help her, so full of energy. Then Velma began to laugh.

The girl took off, dancing around Velma in circles. Raising her legs high, swinging and turning and laughing the whole while.

"Have you lost your mind, Annie?" Velma laughed too, and her question made her laugh even harder. Made her laugh so much that tears were in her eyes, and she had to wipe them away with her hand. She laughed so hard that her coffee spilled everywhere.

The more Annie danced, the harder Velma laughed until she had to set the cup down and bend over, saying, "Woo-shoo, woo-shoo, oh, Annie, woo-shoo," over and over again because her stomach hurt and she couldn't breathe.

And they danced and laughed their way up those few short steps and back into the kitchen, where Velma would cook enough biscuits and grits and sausage and potatoes for a small army. And they would all celebrate finding each other.

❧

When everyone had been delivered back to Echo for naps, showers, work, and thankful prayers, Rudy ushered in the early evening on the porch with Velma.

They didn't say much. Just sat and watched the trees, the water, and listened to cars passing by on the highway in the distance.

The wind was blowing, but it was a normal wind.

Tomcat True came out, purred, and wrapped around Velma's ankle a few times before he settled down next to her chair.

Velma and Rudy looked at each other, and tired as they were, they were both full of smiles. And they were both full of secrets and truths they weren't telling.

"Looks like we made it, Mama," Rudy said, pulling his chair forward and propping his legs on the porch railing. He crossed his arms, closed his eyes, and leaned his head back on the edge of the rocker.

Velma looked over at him, at the cut of the man that he'd become. The man he was becoming still. Then she looked beyond him, down to the water, and in her mind's eye, beyond the first turn in the bend, far up Mullet Creek to where the crystal blue waters bubbled up from beneath that sandy ground.

"There was never no doubt in my mind, Rudy," Velma said, and she too leaned her head back in her rocking chair and closed her eyes. "Never no doubt at all."

Epilogue

I t took a long time for the cold to settle down in the northern neck of Florida, but settle it did. Velma stepped out on the porch, took hold of the rope that ran from the porch to the mailbox. She walked her way out to the box, opened the door. It was almost night, and the metal was cold, and the wind coming up from the creek bit at her enough that she took her hand off the rope, pulled her sweater closer around her neck. Rudy kept telling her that if she could stand by the mailbox with both hands free, then it was proof she didn't need the rope at all. She said, "Hush now." Besides, he was not her mailman anymore, and she was not his mailbox business. Rudy had put in for a full-time, regular route and had been hired. The fact that he'd actually gotten the job had shocked him.

Other than the rope to the mailbox, all the threads were gone, which made the house look a little sad and not nearly as festive, but Velma was determined to plant her feet in the yard, one step at a time. The mailbox was a different story. The rope was her "just in case," as she told Rudy.

There was the circular from the Piggly Wiggly, one from Walgreens, and another postcard from Sara. Velma had gotten a special shoebox to keep the postcards in. She had written

"Sara's Adventure" on the side of the box. She planned to read them all to Sara in the future, should there be days when she needed to remind her of the places she had been. This postcard was from Tangier. And that was what Sara wrote: "This postcard is from Tangier. That's in Morocco, and that's in Africa. It's dirty here, and I'm tired, but all is still exciting. Tomorrow we leave for Spain. Your friend, Ahab."

They had given Sara and Eddie a good-bye wedding party, which was held in high style at Rose's Place—which Velma had to admit had families and pizza. And it wasn't real smoky, and it didn't have dirty pictures on the wall. Not even in the bathrooms.

Rudy had made a toast to Sara and Eddie and to their wedding and to their big adventure. Then he and Eddie had sung karaoke. All of them, including Velma, had a wonderful time. Rudy had sung "My Love Is like a Red, Red Rose," and everyone had known who he was singing it for.

Annie had strapped on her guitar, sat on the stool, turned off the karaoke machine, and proceeded to show them what real music was all about.

Then Rudy had driven Velma home.

But that had been months ago. Velma never thought that Sara could stay gone so long. But her old friend had surprised her.

She placed the postcard on the mantel along with the Christmas cards that were propped up there. Velma didn't know if they had Christmas in Tangier. Maybe Sara would catch up with Christmas in Spain.

Velma had a small fire going. Night was coming, and the temperature would drop lower. Rudy had put up a tree for her in the corner. The lights on it were all lit. With it getting dark earlier now, they shone brighter and brighter.

She sat in Joe's old chair. She sat in it more and more these days, as if she and Joe were becoming one and the same. Annie had claimed Velma's chair on her visits. Curling herself up with every twist and turn while she talked. Velma would watch her, amused and delighted.

Now, a very special present sat waiting against the wall by the tree. Rudy was bringing Rose and Annie out for dinner and then to open presents. Yet here she was—with a red velvet cake to ice—sitting and resting, big as you please, watching the fire with her feet propped up. The guitar shone brighter the later it got. It was hot pink, and it plugged into the wall—Velma knew that meant it would be loud. It was a special present from Rudy. Velma had kept it hidden all this time under Rudy's old bed.

Finally, after some frustrated conversations, Annie's aunt had made Rose the legal guardian for Annie. Velma had wanted to say, "You don't have to worry about all that because I can save you a lot of trouble. One simple blood test will fix that for you. She's not going anywhere." But she had made a promise to Annie. Promised to wait until Christmas. She looked at the tree, at the fire, at the cards on the mantel, and at Tomcat True wandering around in the new red collar with the little bell on it that Annie had brought him—it was Christmas, all right.

When Velma heard Rudy's truck pull up, she opened her eyes and realized she'd been dozing, that her cake wasn't finished and the fire had burned down too low. It took her a minute to get her wits about her, to slowly push herself to her feet, to shuffle toward the door. She had been dreaming about walking in the snow through the woods with Joe. Them old and bundled up, walking under the pines, listening to the snow crunch under their boots.

She looked out the door, half expecting the snow to be there, but there was no snow. Just moonlight on the little yard. And there they were—Rudy, Rose, and Annie getting out of the truck. They were grabbing packages out of the back. Annie jumped up and down, danced around and around, held something in her hands that Velma couldn't see. She twirled and laughed, was so excited and talked so fast that Rudy and Rose laughed with her.

Velma flipped on the porch light and stepped out onto the porch, pulled her sweater tighter against the freezing chill. She needed a jacket on, needed to protect her bones, but she didn't want to miss watching them as they made their way across the little yard, all of them smiling and happy.

She looked up at the winter stars glistening in the dark sky, winking at her when the wind blew through the pine needles. She smelled the oak burning in the fireplace, saw the haze of wood smoke hanging deliciously over the rooftop. She knew Rudy would add more logs to the fire, saying, "Mama, you just about let your fire go out."

Annie would help her ice the cake, licking the icing out of the mixing bowl with her finger, and later, when they had eaten, when the presents were being passed and unwrapped, Rose and Velma would both be full just from watching the people they loved, and then their eyes would meet. And Velma would tell her, without ever uttering the first word, that she trusted her with the hearts of these people. That she would trust her to watch over them long after she was gone. And Rose would hear her, would nod twice to say she understood. And Christmas would roll out around them and within them until they were so full and calm and sleepy that they would sit gazing into the fire, speaking in slow, low tones. And then Annie would tell her story. All of it.

But right now, Velma stood in the biting cold, clutched her sweater, and squinted into the darkness. She slid her glasses down from the top of her head, put them on, and leaned forward. She was watching those smiling faces moving toward her, and she didn't want to miss a thing.

ACKNOWLEDGMENTS

It's never an easy thing to remember all the people who have touched a work in progress, such as *Saints in Limbo,* any more than it is to remember all those who have touched your life. An act of kindness here and there. A key and a quiet room in order to rest, hide away, and work uninterrupted. A dropped-by lunch, a cup of tea, a word of encouragement. Amazingly, those little things seem to come along at just the right time to keep a writer—this writer—on her feet, or in her seat as the case might be, completing the story. And there isn't space to thank everyone for the simple smiles and listening ears that lightened my burden and lighted my way on this journey.

First, I must give special credit to my mother for protecting what our family considers sacred ground—seven swampy acres where Daddy lived as a boy. Where after soldiering and serving his country, he retired so he could fish and whistle with abandon. This is the home ground of *Saints in Limbo,* and truly it is no work of fiction. Thank you, Mother, for protecting the land even when the hordes came after Daddy's passing—folks looking for a place "just like this," developers and spectators of all kinds. You held on to what we loved out of your love for us. I thank you for sister and myself and the boys and for the generations still so young.

A special thank-you to Barbara Thomason for your professional administrative assistance. I don't know how I would have survived the last three years of development, promotion, and publishing without your caring, personal touch.

Todd Champion, I thank you for powering up this remote location. I cannot imagine how the editing and final formation of *Saints* could have moved forward without you.

Eileen Crane, thank you for dropping this title in my lap like manna from heaven. Just look what your simple words created.

Catherine Carminati, your smile alone can heal me when I feel broken down and deadline weary.

And to all my family and friends—husband, sister, cousin, everyone—all thanked before and now thanked again. I can't imagine this writing life without your guiding grace and great patience. Thank you for always believing in me.

And with all due respect to my agent, Greg Daniel, thank you for caring deeply about your writers. You have championed this work exceedingly well.

To Shannon Marchese, her editorial team, and all those at WaterBrook, thank you for helping make this story stronger in every way.

And to you, reader, holding this story close to your heart, thank you for spending time in a place called Echo and remembering that the small moments that make up our lives are something precious and priceless.

My prayerful blessings upon you all.

ABOUT THE AUTHOR

RIVER JORDAN is a southerner with a global perspective. Jordan began her writing career as a playwright and spent over ten years with the Loblolly Theatre group, where her original works were produced, including *Mama Jewels: Tales from Mullet Creek, Soul, Rhythm and Blues,* and *Virga.*

Jordan's first novel, *The Gin Girl* (Livingston Press, 2003), has garnered such high praise as "This author writes with a hard bitten confidence comparable to Ernest Hemingway. And yet, in the Southern tradition of William Faulkner, she can knit together sentences that can take your breath." *Kirkus Reviews* described her second novel, *The Messenger of Magnolia Street,* as "a beautifully written atmospheric tale." It was applauded as "a tale of wonder" by *Southern Living,* who chose the novel as their Selects feature for March 2006, and described by other reviewers as "a riveting, magical mystery" and "a remarkable book."

Jordan teaches and speaks on "The Passion of Story" around the country and produces and hosts *River Jordan on the Radio* on WRFN, Nashville.

She lives with her husband in Nashville, TN. You may visit the author at www.riverjordan.us